The Twelve

Also by Howard and Susan Kaminsky:
Talent

Written as Brooks Stanwood:
The Glow
The Seventh Child

The Twelve

Howard Kaminsky

and

Susan Kaminsky

St. Martin's Press

New York

Library of Congress Cataloging-in-Publication Data

Kaminsky, Howard.
The twelve / Howard and Susan Kaminsky.—1st ed.
          p.   cm.
ISBN 0-312-20601-1
I. Kaminsky, Susan.   II. Title.
PS3569.T3342T88   1999

813'.54—dc21   99-21987
                                                              CIP

First Edition: July 1999

Design: James Sinclair

10   9   8   7   6   5   4   3   2   1

For the incomparable El Bravo and Outerborough gangs:
Forks forever!

And for Jessica, of course.

"The last enemy that shall be destroyed is death."

I Corinthians 15:26

"Perish the universe, so long as I have my revenge."

La Mort d'Agrippine (1653)

The Twelve

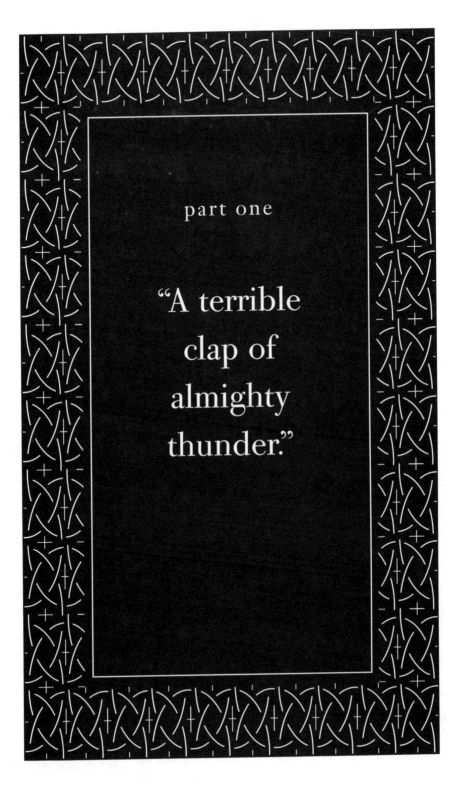

part one

"A terrible
clap of
almighty
thunder."

1994

1 (TRANSCRIPT/MESA BLANCA, AZ/7.9.94/14:26 P.M. M.D.T/ CNN CORRESP. T. MASON)

TODAY MARKS THE THIRTY-SEVENTH DAY OF THE SIEGE OF THE PATRIOTS' REDEEMER CONGREGATION HERE IN MESA BLANCA, ARIZONA. YESTERDAY, TWO MORE CHILDREN WERE ALLOWED TO LEAVE THE COMPOUND BY THE GROUP'S LEADER, JOSIAH HUMMOCK. THE CHILDREN, A BOY AND A GIRL, WERE THE NINTH AND TENTH TO BE SENT OUT OF THE MILITANT EVANGELICAL GROUP'S HEAVILY FORTI-FIED REDOUBT HERE IN THE REMOTE HIGH-DESERT CANYON COUNTRY NEAR THE NEVADA BORDER. A SOURCE INSIDE THE FBI COMMAND POST TELLS US THEY EXPECT HUMMOCK TO SEND TWO MORE CHIL-DREN OUT SOMETIME THIS AFTERNOON. AS IN THE PAST, THEY WILL BE PICKED UP BY THE FBI SPECIAL AGENT NICHOLAS BARROWS, WHO'S IN CHARGE OF THE OPERATION, AND CHILD PSYCHOLOGIST DR. SAN-DRA PRICE OF GEORGETOWN UNIVERSITY. AGENT BARROWS, ONE OF THE FBI'S SPECIALISTS ON CULTS AND PARAMILITARY GROUPS, HEADS UP THE FORTY-ONE AGENTS WHO ARE DEPLOYED HERE. THE DIRECTOR OF THE FBI, EDWARD TRAINOR, IS FLYING IN TODAY TO CONFER ON THE SITUATION. HE IS EXPECTED TO HOLD A PRESS CONFERENCE AFTER HIS MEETINGS ARE CONCLUDED.

THE TENSION HERE HAS RATCHETED UP DAY BY DAY, AS JOSIAH HUMMOCK, THE CHARISMATIC LEADER OF PATRIOTS' REDEEMER, RE-

FUSES TO ALLOW AUTHORITIES TO INSPECT THE COMPOUND. THE BU-
REAU AND LOCAL LAW ENFORCEMENT MAINTAIN THAT HUMMOCK HAS
BEEN GIVING PARAMILITARY TRAINING IN THE USE OF AUTOMATIC
WEAPONS AND EXPLOSIVES TO THE GROUP'S CHILDREN. WHEN THEY
TRIED TO INSPECT THE COMPOUND OVER A MONTH AGO, SHOTS WERE
FIRED AND TWO AGENTS WERE WOUNDED. IT IS THOUGHT THAT SEV-
ERAL MEMBERS IN THE CONGREGATION, INCLUDING A CHILD, WERE
ALSO SHOT. HUMMOCK HAS CONSTANTLY REFERRED TO THE CHIL-
DREN AS "GOD'S LITTLE ARMY." THE CHILDREN NUMBER HALF OF THE
CONGREGATION'S SEVENTY MEMBERS.

THE ADMINISTRATION IN WASHINGTON IS CLOSELY MONITORING
THE SIEGE. SINCE NATIONAL ELECTIONS ARE FIVE MONTHS AWAY, THEY
DO NOT WANT A REPEAT OF THE LOSS OF LIFE THAT OCCURRED AT THE
BRANCH DAVIDIAN COMPOUND OUTSIDE OF WACO. THEY WANT TO
DEMONSTRATE THAT THEY CAN HANDLE THIS SITUATION IN A FIRM
BUT TEMPERATE MANNER. CONGRESSIONAL LEADERS HAVE IMPLORED
THE WHITE HOUSE TO BACK OFF FOR A WHILE SINCE JOSIAH HUM-
MOCK HAS INTIMATED THAT IF THE SIEGE ISN'T LIFTED AT ONCE, "A
TERRIBLE CLAP OF ALMIGHTY THUNDER" WILL LAUNCH HIM AND HIS
FOLLOWERS INTO HEAVEN. MUNITIONS EXPERTS BELIEVE THAT HE HAS
THE MATERIALS NECESSARY TO CONSTRUCT A BOMB THAT MIGHT CON-
TAIN MORE THAN A TON OF DYNAMITE.

THIS IS TOM MASON REPORTING FROM MESA BLANCA, ARIZONA.
AND NOW BACK TO OUR MAIN STUDIO IN ATLANTA.

2 "Good morning, Josiah."

"And a good morning to you, Agent Barrows. Have you prayed today?"

The daily morning phone call to Josiah Hummock always started this way.

"I'm afraid not, Josiah."

"There's still time, Agent Barrows. I've always felt that you're basically a good man. But those above you are wicked. Wickedness proceedeth from the wicked. When you follow the serpent you have to slither in the dirt. It is too late for them, but not for you. The government in Washington is Mammon's creation. One day we will bring it down and crush all who believe they can run our lives for us."

"We've been through this before, Josiah. You know I have a job to do."

"You call it a job, I call it the devil's work. All we ask is to be left alone."

Nick Barrows watched the tape recorder on the table spin from one spool to the other, recording yet another of his conversations with Josiah Hummock. The agent in charge of communications, earphones on, sat next to the machine, occasionally adjusting the levels. How many words he had spoken, and how little they had moved this man. Hummock's beliefs, strong as the rocks that made up the mesa that his congregation sat on, were beyond his reach. Beyond anyone's. He had been telling this to his boss, Ed Trainor, for weeks, and to anyone else he knew who had any power in Washington. They had lost the battle of reason with Hummock. Nothing was going to make him give in and let Barrows and his team enter his stronghold. And the longer the siege continued, the more Barrows saw Hummock becoming irrational and truly dangerous. The man was going to do something terrible to himself and all his followers. It was just a matter of time.

"Josiah, I plan to come up at three today with Dr. Price to pick up—"

"I had a vision last night, Agent Barrows."

"Dr. Price and I—"

"It was a terrible vision. Exodus says, 'The Lord is a man of war.' The destruction of this group of patriots will be the first thunderous crash of this war. Flesh will be ripped from bones, muscle cleaved from tendons. We will return to dust in a mighty roar, but our army will still prevail. The vision was as clear as a pool of water formed by a cloudburst."

"Josiah, what about the two children you said we could pick up today?"

"Be at the gate at three. The children will be ready." Hummock's voice suddenly seemed to be coming from far off, his tone flat as the desert floor.

"As I said before, Dr. Price will be coming with me again."

"These will be the last, Agent Barrows."

"What do you mean 'the last,' Josiah?"

"I have many things to tend to. I will see you and Dr. Price at the appointed time."

"Josiah, you promised that you would send out more—"

"Save it, Nick, he's hung up," said the communications chief as he switched off the tape recorder.

"Damn!" Nick shouted, as he slammed down the receiver.

"He's sounding nuttier every day," said the young assistant to the attorney general, who had joined them the week before.

"Can it, will you? You've been here less than a week and now you're an authority."

"I'm sorry, Nick."

"It's okay. But I think you're right. If we don't pull back and give him some breathing room, there's no saying what Hummock will do. The main thing is we've got to get as many kids out of there as we can. As fast as possible."

The trailer that served as the command center was little bigger than the type that cars towed on highways. It was packed with communications gear, and the six agents that manned it at all times barely had enough room to move about, let alone when other agents were present.

"What time is the director coming in?" Nick asked the communications chief.

"ETA is five-twenty. Cheney and Wallach are picking him up. Do you think you can convince him to scrap this op for a while?"

"If I don't, CNN will get quite a ratings boost. Hummock has the potential to make Koresh look like a school crossing-guard."

3 The jeep slowed to a stop at the fence encircling the base of the mesa. The two highway patrolmen at the gate leaned down to look at the man and woman inside, then waved them on. After a mile, the paved road gave way to a dirt track that was little more than a dusty, rock-filled depression in the desert scrub. As it moved upward, the jeep labored slowly through the long switchbacks that led to the top of the mesa. Nick Barrows and Dr. Sandy Price were silent. Below was the black ribbon of the two-lane highway they had driven on from the command center, ten miles to the south. Sandy Price, watching a lone pickup truck barreling along, stared down at the highway as if it were of utmost importance to her to measure the time it took for the truck to appear at one end of the road, then disappear into the haze at the other end. As the jeep climbed, the dark piñon pines and yellow grasses gave way to stunted bushes and a phantasmagoria of sandstone rock formations.

Nick, who was tall and muscular with dark hair and darker eyes, was in his mid-thirties, but looked older. "How are the kids?" he asked.

"The same. No changes."

"I keep hoping you'll answer that question differently."

"I wish I could, but you know what they're like. The small ones seem calm, unconcerned, as if they just walked out of a playground, not a siege. I can't get anywhere with them. They pay attention to me when I ask a question, but the only answers I get from them are, 'Mary will tell you,' or 'Ask Jebediah.' If they want something I can't give them, they don't argue. They just sneer and walk away."

"What sort of things do they want?"

"To talk to Josiah, for instance."

"That's it?"

"Mostly. But that shouldn't surprise you. It seems like Josiah was their life. All their life."

"Yeah, and a horrific life."

"I'm worried about them, Nick, I really am. They're so disciplined, like a marching band, and as cold as can be. Every day they do an hour and a half of calisthenics, sometimes twice a day, whether it's raining or a hundred degrees. They have prayers in the morning and evening. Everyone participates, even the little ones. And with only a nod from the older two they all get down on their knees facing in the direction of the compound. Mary and Jebediah are the absolute leaders. There's never any doubt about that. They have total control over the children, but it's Hummock who pulls their strings. Whenever Mary or Jebediah strike up a conversation, it's just a ploy to pry information out of me."

"About what?"

"Oh, what our plans are for them. How long they are going to stay with us. That sort of thing."

Sandy unconsciously licked her lips, trying to offset the enveloping heat that made everything dry as a matchhead. She was a generously proportioned woman who you knew would never turn soft. Her hair was the color of fine sand and she wore it to her shoulders, framing a long and graceful neck.

"Hold tight," said Nick, pulling sharply on the wheel to maneuver around a rock the size of a hassock. Sandy braced herself against the dashboard. Nick straightened out the jeep and turned to her.

"You haven't overheard anything useful?"

"No. I've told you that."

"Well, you see them. I don't."

"They're infuriating. When they're together, and that's practically all the time, they hardly talk. They even have—I guess you'd call it an exercise—where they stand in two lines facing each other."

"And?"

"That's it. Nothing. They just stare at each other. Sometimes for up to an hour. I asked Jebediah why they do it and he said, 'It helps us think of Josiah.' But I don't believe that. It's just another technique that Hummock used to control them. They never watch TV or listen to the radio, and the only thing they read is the Bible. And then it's only the passages that must have been marked for them by Josiah. Mainly Revelations."

"Josiah must have sent those two out first to take care of the younger kids. And all we have is a total of ten," said Nick.

"Right. Too few."

"And today, hopefully, eleven and twelve. That means there may be as many as twenty kids still in the compound."

"It's going too slowly, isn't it? Do you think there's a chance of the Bureau lifting the operation?"

"I doubt it. The White House is scared shitless of what happened at Waco. Their answer to that is to just plod along, not rocking the boat, hoping it will all work out. Like in a TV movie."

"But it won't."

The compound came into view and they stopped talking. It was made up of half a dozen low cinderblock buildings, connected by enclosed walkways and surrounded by a high chain-link fence topped with coils of barbed wire. If it wasn't for the wooden cross rising above one of the buildings, it could pass for a military base in a third-world country. A scrim of majestic snowcapped mountains in the distance highlighted the drabness of the buildings. Nick drew the jeep up to the gate and pressed the horn twice.

"The director is flying in today. I'm seeing him after this," he continued. "I tell him every day that Hummock is getting weirder and weirder, but I'm afraid that might make him think now's the time to put the screws to him. They've got to understand: We have to back off. This whole thing started because the state was worried about how the children were being treated. Well, we got a lot more to worry about now."

Sandy nodded, pushing her hair away from her forehead. She and Nick climbed out of the jeep. Almost at once, a door in the building opened. There, framed in the doorway, dressed in fatigues, was Josiah Hummock. He was a big man, at least six-two and weighing close to two hundred and fifty pounds, with gray eyes that burned with a feverish brightness. Around his neck was an immense cross. It was as wide as the span of a man's hand and studded with precious stones. Though Josiah was only in his thirties, his hair, pure black and worn long, almost to his waist, coupled with a dense beard laced with white streaks like lightning bolts, thrust him into the timeless role of patriarch. If Hollywood wanted to remake *The Ten Commandments*, he would be perfectly cast as Moses.

"I'm glad to see you, Josiah," said Nick.

"You know I honor my promises, Agent Barrows."

"I'm seeing the director later today. I'm going to try to persuade him to lift the siege and give us all some time to cool off."

"You know that won't work. The money changers would still be plying their trade if the Lord hadn't chased them out of the temple. Your chief is in the employ of Satan, as are the others."

"The others?" Nick pulled out a handkerchief and wiped his forehead. The only relief from the sun was in the shadow of the building Hummock had stepped out from.

"You know who they are," he said, as his voice rose. "There's the attorney general, a loyal worker in Satan's vineyard. He will reap the vengeance the Lord has instructed me to mete out. And don't forget the media, particularly those two black-tongued reporters who spread falsehood to the unknowing. And, of course, there's the archfiend of all."

Hummock reached down and cupped the cross that hung down on his chest, and kneaded it in his hand as if it were made of clay.

It was a movement he repeated frequently, a gesture he seemed to use to calm himself.

"Who is the archfiend, Josiah?"

"Don't play the innocent, Agent Barrows. It's a role that doesn't become you. You know who I'm talking about. The man you call president. Benjamin Wesley Harpswell—a godless man who will be punished severely. Life will be taken from him."

"A threat to the president, Josiah, is a federal offense. A serious one. But I'll pretend I didn't hear you say it. And I'm sure Dr. Price will maintain her silence, too. I'll do it if you release the rest of the children. That's all I want. That will satisfy everybody. People all around the country are concerned about them."

"No, Agent Barrows. I will handle this the way the Lord, my Father, has instructed me to. We know our enemies and we know how to deal with them. The accounts will one day be tallied. We have God and we have time."

Hummock looked up and stared at a hawk riding an updraft over the top of the mesa. "The Lord is like that red-tailed hawk. He watches us quietly from above, and when he has to, he strikes furiously and suddenly without warning or apparent reason."

"Josiah—" Nick started to say.

"How are my children, Miss Price?"

"They're fine. Very well behaved and friendly."

"I expect that. They embody both the goodness of the Lord and his righteous rage. They are the seeds from which my crusade and empire will grow."

"Can we expect two more children tomorrow?" asked Nick.

"No, Agent Barrows. I don't think there will be any more children for you to collect. All of us, the children and the rest of the congregation, are preparing for a new beginning."

Hummock turned his back on Nick and motioned toward the compound. The door opened and out came two men, each holding the hand of a young boy.

"These are two of my closest and most trusted disciples. Enoch and Gabriel." The two men nodded gravely. Hummock looked down at the two boys. They were both about nine. "This is Caleb and Seth. Two beautiful and fierce young warriors for God." The two boys, as if on cue, walked over to Nick and Sandy and shook their hands.

"I will call you tomorrow morning at our regular time," said Nick.

"Good-bye, my children," Hummock said to the two boys. They ran to him as he opened his arms and then bent down to embrace them. "Remember my teachings, boys. You have the knowledge. Follow it and it will protect you. And remember, I am always with you."

Hummock smiled to himself, then abruptly turned and walked back to the compound with the two men. None looked back. Sandy helped the two boys into the back of the jeep. As they began their slow descent to the highway below, Nick whispered to Sandy, "He's right, you know, about the president and the rest of them. In a way, they are his enemies. They won't give an inch to him. Not with the election just ahead. They need to appear in control."

"He really got to me this time," said Sandy. "That line about 'a new beginning' . . . I was worried driving up here. Now, I have to admit, I'm terrified."

4 The *Gulf Stream II* banked gently over Page, Arizona. The plane was at twenty-nine thousand feet and the Colorado River below looked like a snarled green cord set against the red stone floor of the immense plateau that straddled it. They would be starting their descent within a few minutes and Ed Trainor, the director of the FBI, was almost finished going through his briefing book on the Hummock siege.

The Bureau, like most federal agencies, had a number of business jets at their disposal. Ed Trainor preferred this one for long trips because of its size and the fact that a small office was set up for him in the back. There was a partition in front of it so he also had some privacy. He was traveling with his secretary, two public-affairs people, Laurie Abbott—an official from the ATF who was a friend of Nick Barrows—and Phil LaChance, his head of investigations. He hadn't planned on taking LaChance, but Clayton Bosworth, the attorney general, called at the last minute and asked to include him. LaChance had been briefing the attorney general on the siege so the request was not out of bounds. He knew that LaChance was in Bosworth's pocket, the same relationship he had with a dozen other important senators and congressmen. He was about to close the briefing book when Laurie Abbott came to the back of the plane.

"Ed, do you have a minute?"

"Sure. Come on in."

Laurie Abbott was a short, slender woman with a turned-up nose and lively green eyes. She looked as if she worked out daily, and moved with the ease and economy of an athlete.

"I don't know if anyone mentioned it, but Nick Barrows and I have known each other for a long time. A very long time."

"I never heard that."

"Law school. We were best friends from first year on."

Ed smiled. "You have something on your mind, don't you, Laurie?"

"I guess I do. It's not easy to reach Nick these days but I finally got through to him last week and he sounded . . . well, I'd say pretty stressed out. We used to talk to each other all the time, maybe every other week. I know he's got a lot on his hands but he didn't seem like the Nick I know."

"You *are* a good friend. But rest easy. I'm keeping a close watch on the situation—and on Nick. Maybe I haven't known him quite as long as you have. But I know him pretty well. And I care for him a lot—like you. Believe me, everything is going to work out fine."

"Ed, it's important," said Phil LaChance, sticking his head in the office doorway. "It's the president," he said, with a self-important look. "He wants to talk to you. He's on the yellow phone."

Laurie Abbott got up from her chair and started to leave but LaChance was blocking the way. He seemed ready to stand there while Ed took the call, but Ed would have no part of that. "Thanks, Phil. I'll see you when I'm finished."

"Sure, Ed," he said reluctantly.

"Hello, this is Ed Trainor," the director said, when he picked up the phone.

"One moment, Mr. Director," answered one of the operators who handled the White House switchboard. A moment later the voice that even a schoolkid could identify came on the line.

"Hi there, Ed. How you doing today?"

"Fine, Mr. President. What can I do for you?"

"I want to share something with you," said Benjamin Wesley Harpswell, President of the United States. "I'm sitting here with the vice president and Murray Saltzman—you know, my head of polling. I'm looking at the numbers on our handling of the Hummock business. What do you think they look like, Ed?"

"I have no idea."

"Well, Ed, these numbers are as good as they get. They're just about bouncing off the damn page. Only a beautiful virgin with a rich daddy could look better."

Ed Trainor could hear the laughter of the other two men in the background.

"The country feels we're dealing with this fruitcake Hummock exactly the right way—firm and responsible; nothing rash, but just strong and sensible action. That's what the American people want, and that's what we've been giving them. And that's the way we have to continue to handle this thing. Do you understand?"

"Yes, sir. But my man in charge, Nick Barrows, believes that Hummock is becoming more irrational and we should back off—"

"I'm sure Barrows is a good man, Ed, but these numbers are gold. They smell like a lot of votes and the election is right around the corner. You just tell your agent in charge to just keep the operation going the way it is. Our fellow countrymen believe we're doing the right thing. We don't back off but we also don't provoke. You're on the same page as I am on this, right Ed?"

"Yes, Mr. President. I understand."

"One last thing, Ed. Next month we're having a little dinner in the White House for the prime minister of England and his wife. I sure hope you and Marge can attend."

"We'd be honored, of course, sir."

"That's great. Now you have a great day, Mr. Director, and keep up the terrific work."

 "Jesus, this coffee tastes like mud," said Ed Trainor, his large mouth pursed like a carp's. "No. It's worse than that." He placed his cup on the table, pushed it away, and lighted a cigar.

"You should get a taste of what they make it from. The water here is as hard as a backboard. In fact, aside from the sunsets, I don't think there's a thing I like here."

Nick Barrows got up from behind his desk and walked to the window. The small trailer, stationed a hundred feet from the other trailers, served as his private office. Anytime he needed to be alone, he came here. It was away from all the agents and state and local police, the press, the constantly ringing phones, and best of all, from Hummock. An hour earlier, Ed Trainor, director of the FBI for the last two years, his boss, mentor, and, yes, friend, had flown in to Wiggins Air Force Base, sixty miles away. It was only his second visit since the standoff began and Nick could sense he wanted nothing better to do than to leave as soon as possible. This was a trip to buck up and pacify the troops, Nick in particular, and both of them knew that Trainor didn't have his heart in it.

"Nick, I just want to tell you that everyone, and I mean everyone, including the guy in the Oval Office himself, thinks you're doing a great job with a lousy situation."

"Ed, let's cut the crap." In front of anyone else it was always "Mr. Director," but they had known each other long enough and well enough to allow Nick to speak this way. (Trainor had been best man at Barrows's wedding ten years earlier, when Barrows was working for him in the New York office.) "Things suck and they're going to get worse. A lot worse."

"Why are you so sure?"

"Because I'm the guy who talks to Hummock every day. And I've met with him personally half a dozen times when I've picked up the kids. I've gotten to know him, as well as anyone can know a man who thinks he's the Messiah and who has a group of people around him who believe he is."

"What do you think he's going to do?"

"I don't know, but it'll be terrible. Will he take the Jim Jones route and lead all of them out of this world with poisoned communion wafers? Will it be some other form of mass suicide? It doesn't matter how he does it. What does matter is that he's going to do it."

"What do you want?" Trainor stretched his legs out and dug his hands into his pockets. He was a tall man, and rail-thin. If he wasn't as fit as when he joined the agency twenty-six years earlier, he was close to it. Every morning he rowed his scull on the Potomac. Like Nick, he was career FBI, both having entered the agency a dozen years apart right out of law school.

"I want to stop this operation. Shut it down. Period. Tow your trailers away. Take down the perimeter fencing at the compound. Leave. Let this situation cool off."

"I've spoken to the attorney general and the vice president. And they've talked with the president. There are absolutely no plans to have you stage a dynamic entry. No flash-bang grenades. No assault vehicles. No tear gas. Nothing like that. We learned something from Waco. But they feel we can't look weak, either."

"What's wrong with looking 'weak' for Christ's sake?"

"Come on, Nick. There's a fucking election in a few months. They don't want a Waco, but they can't be seen backing down to Hummock. That just won't play."

"They're wrong. And I guarantee you when this thing comes down it's going to be my ass. And yours, too."

"Don't worry about that. You're covered. And so am I. I'm retired in three years and you're moving up. How does Associate Deputy Director of Investigations sound to you? That's a direct line report to the Deputy Director. You'll be on track to getting my job someday. And I have no doubt that you will."

"Where've you been living, Ed? Nepal? The Vatican? If this turns to shit, as it surely will, I don't know how many heads will be offered up but yours and mine will be there. Right in the center of the platter. Your retirement will be sooner than you think and your reputation will look like a pair of boots in mud season."

"There's no way you could be wrong on this?"

"Of course I could be wrong. But what if I'm right?"

There were two sharp raps on the door and before Nick could say, "Come in," Phil LaChance walked in. "Attorney General Bosworth is calling on the secure line," he said to Ed Trainor. "Over in communications."

LaChance was a big man just beginning to turn to fat. He always wore a dark navy suit. He parted his short gray hair with a draftsman's precision. His small pale blue eyes looked even smaller behind rimless glasses. He looked like a priest you wouldn't want to give your confession to. As head of the Investigations Division he reported directly to Ed Trainor. He was the consummate bureaucrat who had more contacts on the Hill than he had friends in the agency. His career had been advanced by a few powerful senators and congressional committee chairmen, and Ed had privately told Nick that he would do everything in his power to see that LaChance never got the top spot. "The guy is as trustworthy as a hungry dog," he had once said to Nick.

"Thanks, Phil. Tell him I'll be with him in a minute."

LaChance nodded and left the trailer.

"Marge and I saw Linda at a cocktail party at the Smithsonian last week. She looked great." Trainor mashed the cigar he had been smoking into the ashtray with more force than it needed and stood up. "Are things okay between the two of you?"

"Who knows? We speak once or twice a week and when we do she's always on her portable phone going somewhere and it breaks up before we get a chance to really say anything. It's not easy being married to a lobbyist and almost impossible when the lobbyist is successful like Linda. Her T and E is more than I make."

"This is a little out of bounds, Nick, but you two thought about having kids?"

"Yeah. A long time ago. Now, Linda's as much interested in having a family as Hummock is in going to Stallone's latest movie." Nick looked at his watch. The press conference should have started ten minutes ago.

"Is there anything else I can do for you?" Trainor asked as he opened the door of the trailer.

"Yeah." Barrows put on his jacket and started for the door. "Pray."

6 The town of Soda Flats (population 531) was no more than a crossroads: an aging general store and U.S. post office, an adobe church with a black, hand-painted cross above its entrance, the schoolhouse where the children released by

Josiah Hummock were living, a small drab motel, and, oddly, an old movie house. The movie house looked as if it had been out of the business for at least a dozen years (a poster in the interior, which someone with a sense of local history had preserved as a relic of the past, announced the opening the following week of *E.T.*) but it had been given a new life as an all-purpose auditorium for the county. Since all the trailers that made up the command post were too small to accommodate a group of reporters, this—the "uniplex" as they dubbed it—was the site of the twice-weekly press briefings given by Nick Barrows.

Barrows dreaded them. Unlike Ed Trainor, whose confidence in the government's view of Hummock made him impervious to press sniping, Nick, who knew too much firsthand, was vulnerable. He knew in his gut that time was running out and he was afraid it showed in his face.

Trainor's press conference a few days before had been a valentine to the official Washington position, a reiteration of worn-out thinking, a joke. No, the FBI wouldn't pull a Waco. No assault, no tear gas, nothing. But neither would they back off. They would not show weakness. They would stand firm for as long as it took.

The public might buy this reasoning, but Hummock, never. Ed Trainor might be Barrows's best friend and a man with sharp intelligence and instincts, but the higher Ed rose and the more powerful he became, the more the system was shaping him. He was fast becoming as much a stock figure as the G-man in the 1940s movies that celebrated J. Edgar Hoover's FBI, part of a polished law enforcement package, strong and predictable, with no surprises. Nick had hoped Trainor's visit would have enabled him to cancel his own upcoming date with the reporters, give him a breather from the press grilling, but he had not been let off the hook.

Each press conference lasted fifteen minutes. Nick was adept at sensing the approaching end of the period, like a person in an exercise session who knows that release from his physical duress is almost at hand. So far, this session had been an easy one. Lots of softballs. He'd avoided a pair of high-visibility reporters who were his nemeses by not calling on them, and had compensated by paying more attention to other reporters from the networks and major publications. Several of these, including *Newsweek*, wanted to concentrate on Ed Trainor's statements. These Barrows confirmed and elaborated on. A reporter for *U.S. News and World Report* asked how the children were doing. This he could answer in his sleep. After another few minutes, he announced that there was time for one more question. Immediately two hands shot up, frantically pummeling the air. His two chief antagonists: Bernie Willis of *Time* and Fran Marcum of the *Washington Post*.

The two of them had been making big names for themselves with their aggressive handling of the story, aided by an inside source Nick had not been able to identify so far. They were the leading talking heads on almost every news show that had a segment on Hummock. And they were intense rivals. They always sat near each other in order to keep tabs on one another and to make sure the other did not have an advantage.

"Ms. Marcum?" Nick asked finally.

"I have information that Hummock has control of twenty-four million dollars given to him by his followers. Twenty million of it came from Brenda Rawlins of the Rawlins Brake and Engine family. Her family contends that the money was transferred to an offshore account controlled by Hummock. Have you been able to confirm that yet?"

"No, we have not," said Nick, trying mightily to keep his patience in check. The figure was accurate and it was true that they had not found out where Hummock stashed the money. Who the hell was leaking? "Ms. Marcum, hasn't it become apparent to you yet that we are more interested in people than money? This is not an operation to uncover fraud." He looked up at the other reporters. "The press conference is over."

Before Nick could duck out of the auditorium, the two reporters cornered him.

"Nice dancing out there, Nick," said Bernie Willis.

"What other unsubstantiated rumors do you two want to float today?"

"Have you picked up anything from the microphones you secreted into the compound in their groceries? My source says that Hummock discovered them immediately and all you've gotten so far are his sermons."

"Where'd you get that one? *Hard Copy?*" said Nick, putting on his best stone face. They'd hit another top secret on the head.

"Don't you wish," answered Bernie. "My sources are ten times better than theirs."

"Listen, you two," Nick said angrily, "you've been reporting hearsay and innuendo all along and this is more of it. Your editors must love it."

"No, our readers do," said Fran, smirking.

"Even when your so-called information is patently false? You know we're dealing with a volatile situation and an extremely unstable man."

"Can I quote you?" asked Fran.

"No, damn it, you can't."

"You don't think Hummock tunes in every night to CNN, do you?"

"For all I know, Fran, he does. He has the technology to watch anything he wants. I don't want to provoke him."

Nick tried to reach the door to the parking lot, but the reporters were still at his heels.

"One last question," shouted Bernie. "Is the administration refusing to back down because their poll numbers look so good by taking this stance?"

Nick stopped and wheeled around. "There you go again. I understand that for some people a Pulitzer Prize and big lecture fees are more important than ending a terrible situation like this without anyone dying, but that doesn't wash with me. Or with any other decent person. And if I can prove that you have been obtaining FBI information illegally, I personally will see to it that you are prosecuted to the full extent of the law."

He reached the door and slammed it in their faces.

Late that night the phone rang in Fran Marcum's motel room.

"Go to the usual place," a man's voice said. "Five minutes."

She jumped out of bed and hastily put on her clothes. It took her three minutes to drive to the 7-Eleven near the interstate.

Fran Marcum was ten feet away from the booth next to the convenience store when the phone rang. She dashed to the booth and picked up the receiver.

"Yes?"

"Good evening, Miss Marcum. I have something for you."

"I'm ready," she answered, as she placed her notepad on the shelf beneath the phone.

"I think you should ask Mr. Barrows about the bunker that Josiah Hummock built beneath the compound one year ago. It cost over eighty-thousand dollars in materials alone. It can hold his entire congregation. What's its significance, you might be thinking. As protection from the threat of nuclear annihilation that the Soviet bear might toss his way? I don't think so. I wonder what Mr. Barrows thinks it's for."

"How big is the—" Fran started to ask, but the line was dead.

He put the receiver down and smiled. He used a different phone each time to make these calls. This one was in a cocktail lounge in Bethesda, Maryland. FBI training was useful in everyday life.

Phil LaChance went back to his stool at the bar. He was feeling expansive so he ordered another Heineken and pulled the pretzel bowl closer. *Sometimes*, he mused, *the race isn't won by the swiftest but by the one who watches his step.* Nick Barrows was Ed Trainor's fair-haired boy, and though everyone regarded Nick as Ed's eventual successor, it wouldn't hurt Phil to take out a little insurance against that. If Nick Barrows, and by extension, Ed Trainor, got bruised up by the Hummock siege, it would add a little polish to his own portfolio. In the world of government, a report card of solid B's always beat marks of perfect A's marred by one fatal F. He sipped his beer and smiled again. Life wasn't so bad at all.

7

"I think I just lost you."

"Nick . . . Nick . . . are you there?"

"Yes, Linda. I hear you now. Where are you?"

"In a town car. We just went through a tunnel. I think it's okay now."

"How're things going?"

"The usual. Busy, busy, busy. Right now I'm heading to the Hill. There's a committee vote on cable rates that I have to catch. Then it's a meeting with the chairman of the Subcommittee on—"

"I miss you, Linda."

"Me too, dear. When do you think that nut Hummock will listen to reason?"

"This is an open line, Linda. You know I can't—"

"You're becoming famous, Nicky. There's hardly a day I don't see you on CNN. Why, they even mentioned you on the *McLaughlin Group* the other night."

"Do you think you can come here for a few days? It's been so long since I last saw you."

"I'd love nothing better, sweetheart. But you know how it is. There's a ton of bills coming up that I have to track, and I'm close to getting a new client. A real big one. If I land it, we'll be able to build that tennis court we've always talked about. And not an asphalt one, either. Har-Tru. Like the one Ed and Marge have."

"Sounds great."

"Keep your fingers crossed, Nicky."

"Just to have you down here for one night would be great."

"We're pulling into the garage now, hon—have to say good-bye. I'm sending you lots of kisses and tons of—"

8   Like all of the public rooms in the compound, the communal kitchen was large and unadorned. It looked like a facility one would find in a suburban high school. There was a permanent crew of six women and two men assigned to cook, serve, and clean up. Enoch (born Lawrence Taylor Mueller), one of the disciples closest to Josiah Hummock and one of his two chief aides, was in charge of running it.

Everyone in the Patriots' Redeemer Congregation had a job to do. For the small children it might be as simple as turning off lights or passing out bed linen, but all the members worked. Every day after the midday meal was served, Enoch reviewed with the kitchen staff the tasks and menus for the following day. Since the siege had begun, food supplies had to be watched carefully.

Enoch had met Josiah Hummock five years before, in Flagstaff, Arizona, where Hummock had run a small storefront church. Josiah's congregation totaled less than a dozen. Enoch knew later it had been the hand of God directing him into the dimly lighted "church," wedged between a laundromat and a liquor store, that hot September afternoon. He had been teaching biology at the University of Northern Arizona for three years. He was on a tenure track, had just bought a new Jeep Wagoneer, exercised every day, and belonged to an amateur theater group. He seemed content and successful to everyone who knew him, but there had been an emptiness deep inside him that was suddenly and miraculously filled when he met Josiah Hummock.

Enoch had resigned from the faculty the next day and turned

over his savings and belongings to the Patriots' Redeemer Church. From that moment on, his family were his fellow church members and his new father, Josiah Hummock. Two years ago Hummock had chosen a fellow believer, Ruth, to be Enoch's wife. Enoch knew he would follow Josiah anywhere, confident that in the end he would sit beside Josiah in Paradise.

"Josiah wants to change the midday meal to just soup and bread, except for children under the age of twelve," Enoch told his crew. "Our food supplies are being stretched, and though Josiah's agreed to continue to accept milk from the outside for the babies, he's concerned that other food offered us might be tainted in order to cause illnesses among us that would render us defenseless. The young children will continue to get their normal rations. Is that clear?"

"Might we be able to prepare some rice and gravy every other day? Everyone likes it so, and it's very filling," asked Miriam, a large black woman who had joined the congregation the year before.

"Perhaps later, Miriam. Right now Josiah wants us to—"

The door to the kitchen opened with a crash and Josiah Hummock entered, followed by Gabriel, his other key aide.

"Enoch, I have to see you now," Hummock said from the doorway.

"I'm almost finished, Josiah. I'll be with you in a moment."

"I said *now*, Enoch. This is important."

Hummock turned and left the room, Gabriel and Enoch trailing behind. He walked briskly down the hallway, past the children's classrooms, to an unmarked door leading to a steep flight of stairs going downward to a heavy steel door. Hummock, even with his size and strength, could only pull it open slowly.

The fortified bunker on the other side of the door was large enough to hold the entire congregation. The walls were lined with concrete backed with half-inch-thick iron plates. They were ringed with tiers of shelves that contained several months' worth of food and water. When Hummock had ordered the bunker built the year before, he had named it "the Armageddon Shelter."

Josiah Hummock sat down in an oversized armchair in the middle of a small stage where he addressed the congregation and gave his sermons. Enoch and Gabriel pulled folding chairs from a pile in the corner and sat before him.

Hummock looked at the two a long time before he spoke. Actually, he wasn't thinking about either of the two men, but about the bunker. He thought again, as he looked around it, that the FBI knew all about this room. They probably had all the bills for the concrete, the iron plates, the air-conditioning units that he had bought from a lumber-and-supply store twenty-six miles away. The false name he had used in making the purchase wouldn't have fooled them. *Yes, Agent Barrows,* he thought, *I'm sure you've had the FBI's engineering department back in Washington, D.C., work out exactly what could be built from those materials. Thickness of walls, ceiling height, how many people it might contain, right down to the color of the matting on the floor. You know it all. What you don't know, Agent Barrows, is that I let you find out. I wanted you to know about this room. That might surprise you but it's true. It's always been part of my plan. But there's more. Other important work was done that you don't know have a clue about. You know a lot of what I want you to know, but what you don't know could fill a book. You keep forgetting that I'm the Lord's son.*

"Do you believe in the Almighty with all your being?" Hummock asked, with a suddenness that made the two men before him jump, almost as if an electric charge had run through them.

"Of course," they answered in unison.

"And do you, Enoch, believe that I am His son and Chosen One on Earth?"

"Yes, Josiah," said Enoch, his voice wavering.

"Do you believe that only I can lead you and all the others to Paradise?"

The two men nodded vigorously.

"Do you believe that all of our family feels the same way?" asked Hummock, his voice rising.

"Yes, Josiah," Enoch answered.

"Then how do you explain this?" Hummock demanded, slamming a small portable radio against the arm of his chair. The batteries from the radio tumbled to the floor like thrown dice.

The two men stared at Hummock, their raspy breathing the only sound in the cavernous room.

"Do you know where I found this?" he asked, holding the radio between his fingers like a dead animal until he dropped it to the floor. "In your room, Enoch!" Hummock thundered.

"That can't be."

"Your wife, Ruth, was listening to it. And what was it tuned to? The news, that's all. The news! The devil's words they want us to listen to so that we lose our belief. If the serpent in the Garden of Eden had bitten Eve, they would not have been cast out. It's the words that contained the poison. A poison that expels belief, a belief you must have in the Almighty and in his Chosen One. Me! Enoch, I want you to get Ruth and bring her here to me immediately."

"What will you do with her, Josiah?"

"That is for God to decide and for me to act upon."

"She's a good woman, Josiah."

Hummock held up his hand.

"Bring her. And tomorrow after breakfast, I want the whole flock to assemble down here. That means everyone—those in the infirmary, even small ones who would normally be napping. Now, send Ruth to me."

Though his back was turned to her, Josiah knew Ruth was standing at the door. Her breathing was shallow and he could smell the fear that rolled off her like the steaming, misty sweat of a horse after a morning workout.

"You can come in, Ruth," Hummock said, still turned away from her.

Ruth was in her early thirties, tall, with pale skin and large brown eyes. Her hair was dark, almost black, and like all the women in the congregation, she covered it with a small white scarf.

"Please forgive me, Josiah. I was wrong but I can explain—"

"No explanation can excuse what you did, Ruth."

"It's not that I don't completely believe and trust you, Josiah, it's just that—"

"I don't want to hear the devil's words, Ruth. That's what you heard and that's what has infected you."

"I'm sorry, Josiah," Ruth whispered, her head bowed.

"You've betrayed me, Ruth. Which means you've turned your back on God, my Father. You must be punished."

The woman's sobs were soft like a child's.

"Remove your clothes and lie facedown over there," Hummock said, indicating a cot by the wall.

She took off her clothes and started for the cot.

"Your undergarments, too, Ruth."

When she was lying facedown, Hummock approached her. He removed his thick leather belt and quickly brought it down upon her back. The woman shuddered and groaned as the belt met her flesh again and again.

"From pain and blood," Hummock chanted, "comes repentance and understanding." The slashing leather moved down to her buttocks, then to her legs.

He thought back to when he had brought her into his fold. It wasn't a matter of luck that she had found him. It was a sign from the Almighty. She had been named Brenda then. Brenda Rawlins. A rich, spoiled girl from a fancy college. She had wanted someone to believe in, and she found Josiah Hummock. Himself! When he had no longer needed her, he had given her to Enoch.

Finally Josiah Hummock dropped his belt. He bent over Ruth

and ran his hand over her crimson back. He brought his blood-wet hand to his mouth and tasted it. "Roll over," he said.

The woman whimpered and remained still.

"I said, roll over. Now!"

When the woman slowly turned onto her back, trembling with the difficulty of it, he straddled her. As he bent over her, his enormous, heavy cross hit her hard in the face. She winced, and he let the cross swing again, this time deliberately and with more force. He could see she wanted to cry out, but she didn't. Her cheek was beginning to swell. He observed her new pain with satisfaction, then spoke again.

"Now that you have been excoriated, you will receive the renewing seed of the Lord. Are you ready, Ruth?"

The woman mumbled something into the mattress.

"I didn't hear you."

"Yes, Josiah," she answered.

"That's not my true name, is it, Ruth?"

"No."

"Call me by what I am."

"Yes, Father."

"That's better. And are you ready?"

"Yes, Father. I'm ready."

9 The motel in Soda Flats was Nick Barrows's one luxury. Mostly he slept on a cot in the trailer he used as an office at the command center, but two nights a week, on Tuesdays and Saturdays, he checked in to the motel to catch up on his sleep and distance himself from the pressures of the command center. The owners of the motel saved him the same room each week and never asked questions about the siege. The town was a jumping-off point for people headed to Chaco Canyon to see the Anasazi rock carvings and kivas, and their talking and laughter as they milled around the motel were a tonic for Nick. Josiah Hummock was never absent from his mind, but the backpackers jolted him back to reality. After a quick meal of badly prepared Tex-Mex, he would hole up in his room and turn on the TV, distracting himself for a while from the Messiah on the mesa; his stressed-out team of agents, alternately bored and squabbling; and his own, deepening frustrations.

On this Sunday morning, as he was preparing to return to the command center, Nick took a long shower, wrestling again with the question of who was leaking details of their operation. He had not been able to pin it on anyone, despite questioning the entire staff and making a raft of telephone calls to headquarters in Washington.

As he let his thoughts drift away from this mystery, he caught a phrase from *This Week* on the TV, which he had left on. It was something about the siege. He jumped out of the shower, grabbed a towel, and turned up the sound. The vice president, "Big Jim" Avery, former governor of Oklahoma and a politician to his bones, was being questioned by Sam Donaldson.

"Would you care to comment on that, Mr. Vice President, as you are the administration's point man on the Mesa Blanca siege?" Donaldson was saying.

"'Point man'! Sure—and Sharon Stone is running our space program," said Nick, addressing the TV.

Vice President Avery answered Donaldson. "We are taking every precaution necessary to avoid a tragedy like Waco. I spoke to FBI director Trainor this morning and he assured me that that our policy of firmness in the face of this messianic threat is working. We have a seasoned team of FBI agents on the scene at Mesa Blanca, and we believe the situation is totally under control. We continue to maintain communications with the Reverend Hummock, who shows signs of coming around to—"

"Shows signs of leading his congregation of lemmings right off the cliff," snorted Nick.

"—our point of view. We are confident that the standoff can be brought to a peaceful conclusion, with all weaponry surrendered and congregants free to leave. 'Patience' is our byword."

"Let me ask you about something I've been hearing," said Donaldson. "That the cult's leader, Josiah Hummock, is giving indications of increased irrationality. People on the scene are questioning the length of this siege. Might this be the time to pull back and let things settle down?"

"Way to go, Sam!" cheered Nick, like a fan at a football game. "I've changed my opinion of you. You're terrific. I'm going to buy you a new rug for Christmas."

"We can't let down our vigilance, Sam, when innocents—I'm talking particularly about the children now—are concerned," the vice president intoned. "If the Reverend Hummock releases all the remaining children, a relaxation of tension would certainly occur. But these children are citizens, too, who need the protection of their government. We will not stand down until we are assured of their safety."

"Sources have told me that our people at the site, the FBI team in charge, are truly worried about what Hummock might do," said George Will. "Does the upcoming election have anything to do with your policy on this matter, Mr. Vice President?"

"Only a hundred and seventeen percent, Georgie boy! Keep it up," shouted Nick.

The vice president's face flushed. "This has nothing whatsoever to do with politics. Nothing at all. It is about innocent children. Exclusively. Children whom this administration is dedicated to protecting, whatever the consequences. As the president stressed in his last speech, the children of today are the leaders of tomorrow."

"Mr. Vice President, gentlemen, we have to break for a commercial," said Donaldson above the fray. "Cokie Roberts will join us when we return. In a moment."

Nick laughed, turned up the volume, and climbed back into the shower.

"He's got the whole world in his hands. / He's got the whole world in his hands. / He's got the whole wide world in his hands. . . ."

It took him a half a minute to realize he was singing.

10 They stared up at him with the pinched, anxious look of fledglings waiting for a parent to return to the nest. All of them had given up everything—family, friends, money, career—to follow him and be part of his flock. They had cut themselves off from the world to enter another life which he assured them, and they believed, would lead to Paradise.

Josiah Hummock sat in his armchair on the small stage in the bunker. He slowly rose and stood a long time before speaking. He closed his eyes and tilted his head heavenward. He knew they were staring at him the way survivors at sea scan the horizon for a ship. They were frightened—not the fear one has in the instant before a collision, but a slow and consuming dread that pulled like a riptide. Since the beginning of the siege, Hummock had fed that fear, artfully tossing dark images at them like a stoker feeding a fire. The more they were afraid and uncertain, the more they looked to him to lead them to a safe harbor. A few were beginning to doubt him. The radio he found in Ruth's room proved that. Before too long the doubters would infect the rest, like algae slowly but inexorably turning a clear pond green. He still had them, but for how much more time could be control their minds and souls like a skilled magician? Conjure up visions of damnation as real as the sandy hills surrounding them?

"Close your eyes and bow your heads, my children," he intoned in his deepest voice, "that you may better see the God that is in you."

With their heads down and eyes shut, the group stood silently, the only sound in the room the mechanical whisper coming from the air-conditioning unit.

"Unto you is Paradise opened," he suddenly shouted, causing an involuntary movement in the crowd like a banner riffling in the wind. "I talked to my Father last night. I told him I was worried about some of you losing faith. Faith in him. Faith in me. He told me that I was wrong. 'Your faith,' he said, 'is as strong as the mesa this congregation sits upon.'" Josiah continued, in a soft voice now, that was almost inaudible. "He told me that we were close, very close, to feeling his embrace. First, our trials here will be lifted. Our greatest dreams made true. And then we will enter his home. All of us."

Though none showed any outward sign, Hummock could feel the tension and fear begin to leave the group.

"Our enemies, and we have many, will pay many times over for the torment we have received. That, too, he told me. The strong will be made weak, the mighty will be brought to their knees, and all will meet a death that will be fearsome and unexpected. All will know that Josiah Hummock, the Lord's son, reigns supreme."

Hummock slipped off the long white robe that he always wore over his other clothes when he spoke, and let it fall to the stage. He then removed the huge cross from around his neck and placed it on the chair.

"I am going to speak with him again right now. He's waiting for me. I want all of you to stay the way you are until you hear my voice again."

Hummock turned and stepped off the stage. He didn't have to look back to see if his congregants were following his commands. He almost smiled as he thought, *The time has finally come.*

11

Nick Barrows gave a thumb's-up to the communications chief poised to start the recorders, and put the phone on speaker. It was almost three hours earlier than his usual morning call to Josiah Hummock, and the sun had not yet risen. In the last week the Bureau had varied their calling times in an effort to break the impasse they had reached. He knew they were running out of time. He and the other agents in the trailer leaned forward in anticipation.

"*. . . preparing for a new beginning.*" Hummock's words the last time he had seen him had kept Nick awake every night, like the verse of a song, a dirge really, that he couldn't drive from his mind. "*These will be the last.*" The words kept spinning in his head, like a caged mouse racing around a wheel.

"Good morning, Josiah," said Nick into the phone, hoping Hummock would answer. For almost a week, there had been no response. No response, no children.

"And a good morning to you, Agent Barrows. Have you prayed today?"

"Pray? I have done nothing but pray," said Nick, giddy with relief at hearing Hummock's voice. "That you will release the children. All the children. That you will give them to us to care for until we work this thing out. It would be best for everyone. Especially the children."

Nick paused for Hummock's answer, but it was the dirge that rushed into his consciousness again. He tried to fight it off, but he couldn't. "*These will be the last.*"

"*. . . My flock and I are ready for the divine and patriotic task to which we have been appointed,*" he heard Hummock say, above the roar in his head. "Our might will live on to cleanse this wicked land of the forces of evil . . ."

Hummock's voice sounded strange, almost unfamiliar, and he hadn't said a word about the children. Then Nick's heart fell. He suddenly understood what was happening.

"Stop!" he shouted to the chief of communications. "Hummock isn't there. It's a tape."

"What's happening?" the young man from the attorney general's office asked no one in particular. "I don't get it."

Nick threw open the door to the trailer. "Call the troopers and tell them we're on our way," he said to one of the agents. "You"—he gestured back to the others—"follow me, and move it. Fast!"

Booming out of the trailer, Hummock's voice followed Barrows: "We will live on. . . . The seeds of retribution have been planted. . . ."

Nick ran to his jeep and pulled open the door. As he started to hoist himself in, he suddenly felt a wave of heat and a blast of air, then, seconds later, heard the sound of an immense explosion. He looked up toward the mesa, where all he could see was a towering cloud of smoke, skewered by ragged bands of fire hanging above what had been the compound. He knew at once that Hummock and all his followers were gone.

Nick slumped against the jeep, frozen to the spot, unable to move. He had been right about Hummock, but there was no satisfaction in it. He started to cry bitterly in a way that he hadn't done since he was a kid. He couldn't stop. Not even when the others were grouped around him, waiting to be told what to do.

12 As soon as Sandy Price stepped into the classroom where the children were praying, a cooler of sodas in her hand, she spotted the small girl alone in a corner of the room, her back to the others: Sarah, the girl with ash-blond hair, almost three, the youngest. The girl's shoulders were shaking and, above the sound of the prayers, Sandy heard snuffles, strangled sobs, hiccups. She would stop for a few moments, then begin again. Sandy looked at Mary, who ignored the girl, her attention on the others, all on their knees. Sandy recognized the cadences of this particular prayer, one of a handful they repeated twice a day, but with voices so low, almost whispering, it was impossible to decipher what they were saying. The only word she heard was "Josiah," again and again.

As she waited for the prayers to end, Sandy watched the little girl, now openly crying. She kept glancing over her shoulder at Mary—beseechingly, her face red, her large eyes streaming with tears—but Mary did not once look her way. As miserable as the girl was, her tears, in a strange way, were a relief to Sandy, for in the weeks she had lived with them in the schoolhouse, this was the first time she had seen any of the younger children express any emotion.

After the explosion the day before, Nick Barrows had called the children together to express the government's regret for the tragedy at Mesa Blanca. They would launch an immediate investigation into the circumstances. "And for you," he had said quietly, "it is time to go home, to family and friends." The children had remained silent. Perhaps the only sound they heard, ringing in their ears still, drowning out Nick's words, was the sound of the explosion itself as it had reverberated across the empty plain between the compound on the mesa and the schoolhouse, as resonant as if it had occurred in an amphitheater.

Sandy had come to them this morning, hoping she could help them talk out their feelings about what had happened. She ran her eyes over the group. Mary and Jebediah Hummock—Hummock had given all of them his surname as well as new first names—faced the others, who echoed their gestures, heads bowed or eyes raised upward. Mary and Jebediah, the oldest and the first of the children Hummock had released, always led the prayers.

Mary's straight hair, parted in the middle, fell over her face, obscuring her features which would have been pretty if they weren't always so pinched. One of the younger children, a girl named Hannah, who was six, resembled Mary so much that Sandy thought she must be her sister. It was guesswork, though, since they still had almost no background information on the kids. When Sandy asked Mary about Hannah, her only answer was, "We are all brothers and sisters, and Josiah is our Father." Jebediah, tall, powerfully built, but with the awkwardness of a teenager, as if his sense of himself had not yet caught up with the maturity of his body, was always at Mary's side. The two conferred constantly.

When the children prayed, they always lined up in the same way, as if they were following stage directions. Hannah and Sarah were in the front row. In the next were three boys and two girls—Job, Solomon, Mark, Rachel, and Rebecca—fifth or sixth graders, she guessed, whose dark hair and coloring suggested they might be cousins or even siblings, followed by Caleb and Seth, the latest arrivals. The last of the group was Matthew, a year or two younger than Mary and Jebediah. Every now and then Sandy saw a hint of resentfulness pushing through his blandness: he wanted to be on a par with the oldest two.

When the prayers ended, Mary strode across the room to Sarah. She grabbed her by her arm and lifted her to her feet. "I told you before, stop sniveling."

"I can't. I'm sad," said the little girl, trying to put her arms around Mary.

"You have no reason to be sad," Mary said, brushing the girl's hands away from her as if they were insects. This triggered a fresh outburst of crying.

"Stop crying right now. If you don't, I'll put you in the closet. And lock it."

"No!"

Mary took the girl's hand and slapped it, hard. "I said, stop."

Stop? thought Sandy, watching the two of them helplessly. Stop feeling, stop needing, stop being a child three years old? What was going to happen to these children when they went out in the world? Had the seeds of trouble been irrevocably sown? She felt a terrible sense of dread for all of them. Maybe the younger ones like

Sarah could escape without serious harm. Maybe she, Sandy, could bring Sarah home with her, give her back her life—become her mother. Sandy knew something about children. And about the effects of trauma. It was her profession after all. But the idea of bringing Sarah home was a fantasy, Sandy knew. She had no reason to believe the little girl would not have family members waiting for her.

Sarah finally stopped crying, whether from the habit of obedience or from Mary's threat and slap, Sandy couldn't say. As they began to turn to the others, Sandy remembered the drinks in her cooler and caught up with them. "I brought some cold sodas with me, Mary," she said. "What about going out to the playground before it gets too hot?"

Mary nodded, and she and Jebediah herded the children out. Sandy passed out the sodas, and then a soccer ball and a Frisbee. The younger children went to the swings. Jebediah and Mary sat with Sandy under an old bent pine, watching them.

"What was bothering Sarah?" asked Sandy.

"That is none of your business, Dr. Price," Mary said angrily.

"You may not realize it, but I'm your friend. I want to do anything I can," said Sandy.

"Friend?" asked Mary. "What do you mean?"

"Exactly what I said."

"Well, I'm not *your* friend, and don't use that term with me or Jebediah."

"Don't you see, all we're trying to do is get you settled, get you home—"

"Home! A disgusting thought. I wouldn't go to my father's 'home' if you paid me. He's as godless as a sewer rat and just as filthy."

"You're not serious, are you?"

"I certainly am!"

"You don't get it, do you?" said Jebediah.

"We already *are* home," said Mary, speaking slowly to Sandy, as if to a half-wit. "We're together, Jebediah and I and the young ones. And Josiah's spirit is watching over us."

"Josiah. . . . I have to tell you something—" said Sandy.

"We know," Jebediah broke in.

"The explosion was not the work of the Bureau. And it wasn't an accident. We believe Josiah chose to die that way."

"We just told you, we know already," said Mary.

"How?"

"Josiah told us what would happen," said the girl. She and Jebediah stared coldly at Sandy.

"There's only one thing we want," Jebediah continued. "You have to make them let us stay together. The younger children would be lost without us. We're their family. We can care for them and each other as well as anyone."

"I realize that."

"Then give us your word on it," said Mary.

"I can't do that. Most of you have lost a parent; some, both parents. . . ." There was no reaction. "But you have other family members who will want you with them. You are also still minors. So you see, there's nothing I can do."

"We knew you'd say that," said Mary, her tone bitter.

"I'll do everything in my power to make sure you regularly see each other."

"Regularly see each other! That's a joke. We're a family. Not friends who drop by to see each other," Jebediah said angrily. "In the beginning we thought you would be different. You're a woman and would understand. But we were wrong. You're just like the rest."

Sandy stared at them and then realized she no longer heard the sounds of the other children. She stood up and hurried around to the side of the schoolhouse that faced the mesa and there, by the fence, were the children, faces as empty as nests in winter, looking toward the place where the compound had been and where now only tendrils of black smoke spiraled into the air.

13 A half hour after bedtime, Sandy went to the small room at the back of the schoolhouse that they used as a dormitory for the young children to see if they had fallen asleep. Mary, Jebediah, and Matthew had their own rooms, and the older preteens a room off to the side, but the little ones stayed here. The room was quiet. She stood in the doorway peering into the darkness, listening to a strong wind blowing out of the west.

Sandy reached down to the first bed to see if the young occupant's blanket was pulled all the way up, canting the beam from her flashlight to the floor to cut back on the amount of light. She found nothing but rumpled bedclothing. The bed was empty. She frantically ran her hand the length of the bed, though she did not need to do this to confirm that no one was in it. She hurried to the next bed. Again, no one.

Switching the flashlight on high, she wheeled the beam the length of the room. She knew already there was not another soul present. She fought down her anxiety and strode to the back door in a corner of the room, which led to the yard. There, bunched together on the steps descending to the yard and holding each other's hands tightly, were the little children. At the sound of the door opening, in unison they raised their heads from what they had been looking at, and turned toward Sandy. The full force of the wind blew straight at them, but they weren't shivering.

"What's going on? Why are you out here?" Sandy asked. They watched her unblinkingly, but no one answered. "Tell me why, please," she repeated more forcefully. No one moved, no one spoke.

As she waited for a response, which she didn't expect, not even from Sarah whom she'd seen in tears only hours ago in the schoolroom, Sandy heard another sound over the wind. It was a soft but insistent, almost rhythmic banging.

"What's that?" she asked, listening for a few moments, puzzled.

As she ran her eyes over the children, she caught sight of something peculiar: a dog's leash was wound tightly around the base of one of the railings. Uneasily she walked quickly to the edge of the landing and leaned over. Now she could see what the children were staring at through the openings in the boards. There, hanging below, was Crackers, a puppy given to them by a local policeman, its neck twisted at a hideous angle, its small plump body banging against the building. Suddenly the sound of Mary's voice cut sharply into her consciousness.

"Anything wrong, Dr. Price?" she asked, smiling.

"Get back to bed, children," Sandy said. The children looked past her to Mary and immediately rose and without a word scurried back inside, not a tear among them.

Sandy walked down the steps to the puppy. As she tried to undo the leash from around Crackers' neck, she looked up at Mary still standing in the doorway.

"How did this happen?"

"I have no idea," Mary said, an odd look of amusement on her face. "Accident, I guess." Her voice was devoid of emotion.

Finally Sandy had the puppy in her arms. Cradling its lifeless form, she walked back to her room, knowing that its death was a message from the older children, a message she wasn't ready to confront yet.

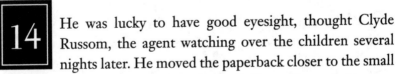 He was lucky to have good eyesight, thought Clyde Russom, the agent watching over the children several nights later. He moved the paperback closer to the small light he had balanced on a crate in the hallway. Russom, just two years out of the FBI academy, pulled the "dead" shift at the schoolhouse, midnight to six A.M., twice a week. He was able to get through it by reading, drinking a thermos of coffee, and stretching every thirty minutes. He was positioned outside the door to the

classroom that had been turned into a dormitory. Except for an occasional request for a drink of water, the children never gave him any trouble. They all went beyond the phrase "well-behaved." He was a bachelor, but he'd been around enough children—his two sisters had five between them—to know that these kids were different. They were more polite than any kids he had ever met and showed none of the fidgeting and mood swings he associated with their ages. And after all that had happened to them. Amazing.

Clyde stood up, then exhaled deeply as he bent at the waist and touched his toes—just. Jesus, he was stiff. He vowed, not for the first time, that once this operation was over and he got back home, he would join a gym and get back in shape. He sat down again and opened the book. Damn, Elmore Leonard was good. Great dialogue, and all the police stuff was right on the money. He turned the page and once again edged closer to the light. And then he heard a scream. It came from one of the rooms near the dorm. He was barely out of his chair when Mary came running out.

"Agent Russom! Come quick. It's Matthew. He's hurt!"

Clyde Russom followed Mary into the room. There in a corner, sitting on the floor, was Matthew, a bloody towel wrapped around his foot.

"What happened?" asked Sandy Price, who'd been awakened by Jebediah. She kneeled down next to Matthew. He was a little younger than Jebediah, but about the same size. His face was pale and he was biting down on his lower lip, obviously in pain.

"He got up to go to the bathroom and stepped on this," answered Jebediah, holding up a long, red-streaked nail.

"Let me take a look at this," Sandy said, as she undid the towel from Matthew's foot. The nail had ripped through the soft tissue between two of his toes. Clear through. The wound was still bleeding and would certainly need stitches.

"We've got to take him to the hospital," she said to Russom. He nodded and reached for his two-way radio to call the command center.

It took Sandy awhile to get the younger children calmed down and back to sleep. It was almost two hours later before Agent Russom was able to return to his post and pick up Elmore Leonard again. During that confused time nobody had noticed Jebediah enter Sandy Price's office. He spent over forty minutes there, carefully taking down information from FBI files that Nick Barrows had given Dr. Price. Jebediah had been instructed before he left the compound to get them. They included transcripts of conversations with the director and the attorney general, names and addresses of all personnel involved in the siege, and a lot more.

Josiah had been right, as he always was. These FBI people weren't dumb, but they didn't have the Lord's light—Josiah Hummock's effulgence—to guide them. None of them had noticed that Jebediah had driven the nail into Matthew's foot from above. And he was sure the doctors hadn't noticed, either.

 (Excerpt from "The Doctor Who's Caring for the Hummock Children," *The Washington Post*, Style Section, C1, 7/24/94, reported by Cyndi Margolies)

The first thing you notice is the quiet. Oh, there are some sounds: the page of a book being turned; chalk squeaking against a blackboard; the click of blocks carefully placed one atop the other. But that's about it. These children are very quiet. The twelve who were sent out by Josiah Hummock from his mesa redoubt, the only ones of some seventy people to survive the massive explosion, now live together in a small school in the nearby town of Soda Flats. The school served this town and the nearby area until two years ago when the county built a large, modern regional school in Puma Valley, thirty-seven miles away. Now it's just the twelve Hummock children, ages three to seventeen, plus child psychologist Dr. Sandra Price, her assistant, and two FBI agents.

"... Yes, Mrs. Prentice, Rachel's fine. Her appetite? It's excellent. You're leaving for here tomorrow? Flying? I look forward to seeing you. Have a good trip."

That's Dr. Price on the phone. She's talking to the grandmother of one of the children. She spends a lot of time every day with the relatives of the children, reassuring them of their well-being. All of them—grandparents, aunts and uncles, surviving parents who were not part of the Hummock group—will be arriving in the next few days to take the children home with them. Most of her time is spent with the children themselves, comforting them, and—what a professional like Dr. Price can never stop doing—trying to understand them.

"How are the children coping?" I ask after Dr. Price has taken a sip of coffee from a cup that she seems to refill constantly. She's an attractive woman, in her early thirties, tall with pale hair thick as a brush, who looks like she competed in athletics when she was in school, and whose movement is still fluid and graceful.

"Very well—considering, I'd say. They've all suffered terrible losses."

"Have they talked to you about Josiah Hummock?" I ask.

She hesitates, fiddling for a moment with the spoon in her coffee cup.

"Not too much. He was probably the strongest figure in their lives." She pauses to take a sip of coffee. "I believe he remains so."

"Hummock has been quoted as saying he was a messiah. Do you think the children believe he was?"

This time Dr. Price picks up her cup, takes a swallow, then another before carefully placing it down and answering.

"That's hard to say. Some do."

"You're an expert in abnormal psychological trauma in children. What effect will this—the time spent on the mesa, Hummock, the explosion—have on them?"

"Only time will tell. I intend to continue to help and to monitor these children for a long while. My work has shown that children are amazingly resilient to this kind of event. I believe that they can eventually lead normal, productive lives. That's my hope, anyway."

The phone rings. It's an uncle of one of the children. He's taking a bus here from El Paso. He's en route. He'll be here tomorrow afternoon. As Dr. Price answers his questions, I decide to walk outside.

The children are now seated in a circle on the raw, red earth. The two oldest, a boy and girl both in their late teens, stand in the center. I edge closer to hear what they're saying. The younger ones are listening with an intensity that belies their age. As I near, they all turn toward me. The older two smile first, then all of them smile. But they stop talking.

16 There were three more to go, and that would be it.

In the last twenty-four hours, Sandy Price had parceled out nine of the Hummock children to their old lives, or to lives that bore some resemblance to their past: an uncle standing in for a father, grandparents in the role of parents, and, in a couple of instances, real fathers or mothers who had not followed their enraptured spouses into the holy clan on the mesa. The only child who did not possess a parent or relative to take care of her was Sarah, both of whose parents had been killed on the mesa. Though she had told no one, Sandy had decided to take care of

Sarah. And, she hoped, in not too long a time, to adopt her. She knew she could love and nurture the little girl. Sandy strongly believed the girl's extreme youth would cause her to forget most, if not all of the horror.

In the long, grueling weeks before the explosion, Nick Barrows and Sandy were unable to discover much about the backgrounds of these children, but after the explosion, the situation had been reversed. Once the country focused on the fact that the FBI was holding twelve young survivors of the devastation, the command center was overwhelmed with information and queries.

But it was the media, led by Fran Marcum and Bernie Willis, that infuriated the agents the most. Ugly and voracious, made hungry by the absence for a number of months of this kind of nationwide, sensational story, they pumped it up for all it was worth. There were endless profiles of Josiah Hummock and sketches of the children who had been released, all incorporating each new detail as it emerged, no matter how trivial. Worst of all, were the invidious comparisons between the explosion and the earlier tragedy at Waco. The FBI was now portrayed as being as inept and insensitive as the ATF. Could U.S. law enforcement agencies do anything right?

Nick, despondent and needing distraction, spent increasing amounts of time with Sandy Price in those final days. Whenever he could get away from the excavation of the ruins, he drove to the schoolhouse. Together they witnessed the children's departures, some with relatives who were well off, others with those who were visibly not. As for the children, they had been as thoroughly drilled in saying good-bye as in everything else: they shook hands with Sandy, her assistant, and the agents, formally thanking them, and then climbed obediently into the vehicles transporting them back to the normal world.

Jebediah, Mary, and Hannah, who was indeed Mary's five-year-old sister, were the next-to-last group to leave. Though Jebediah and Mary must have cared for each other, they showed no tears or emotion as they hugged each other and then went their separate ways: Jebediah into a polished Lincoln, driven by a middle-aged, well-tailored woman who was his aunt; Mary and her young sister, into a battered truck. The truck had seen better days. It was a mass of dents and dings, with a large spidery crack in the front window and a mounted rifle gracing the back one. The driver of the truck, who had the kind of face in which sourness and anger had stamped deep lines, slammed the door shut after the girls, said not a word to them, and sped down the road. The driver was their father.

To avoid the knots of reporters, many of who were still gathered at the schoolhouse, Nick and Sandy skirted around to the back of the building.

"Do you have much more to do?" asked Sandy.

"No, the engineers and the forensic people are almost finished. What was left of the bodies has been taken over to the Puma Valley school. There's a makeshift morgue there. They don't think they'll be able to positively ID very many. Maybe ten percent at best."

"That's awful."

"The blast was a monster. Its concussive force was like that air crash on the West Coast a few years ago, when the plane went down at a ninety-degree angle. What made it so devastating was the thickness of the walls in the bunker. It multiplied the concussive force by a lot. The carnage was incredible. The bodies of the people were reduced to a pulp of bone and flesh and their teeth were fragmented. We've got our best people working on it, but there's not much they can do. Hummock had no tattoos or scars that we know of, so our chances of identifying his body seem remote. Knowing him, he was probably sitting on the bomb when it went off," said Nick. "Got him to heaven a little quicker. It's strange, but the only positive ID we've made so far is on that huge iron cross Hummock wore. It looks like it went through one of those machines that crushes cars, but it was still easily identifiable."

"What will happen when you finish here?"

"You know the answer as well as I do. There'll be further agency investigations and then hearings. In both houses. Everyone will jump in with his two cents' worth. They'll look for someone to blame. And you can bet they'll find someone. They always do. And I have a sneaking suspicion who that's going to be."

"You? Even though you warned them what might happen?"

"People hear only what they want to hear. I love the FBI, and I can't think of doing anything else." He stopped for a moment, looking out toward the mesa, then added, "It'll be okay. I'll survive. . . . What about you?"

"I have another year on my grant. After that, maybe I'll teach. I've had some interest from schools in the area. William and Mary has made an overture about teaching a graduate course or two. And I have a good contact at the University of Maryland."

"Would you like to teach?"

"I think so, but I don't have to make up my mind for a while." Sandy smiled. "There is one more thing I've been thinking about."

"What?"

"I'm thinking of adopting Sarah."

"The real little one with the very blond hair?"

"That's her."

"I'm a little surprised."

"Why?"

"Well, I guess just because it's such a big step."

"I think I'm ready for it. I've been considering adopting for a long time. And Sarah needs a family. Both her parents died in the explosion and she hasn't any relatives to go to. She's all alone."

"What does your boyfriend think? The good congressman from one of the Dakotas."

"You got the first letter right. He's from Delaware." Sandy smiled and studied him for a moment. "I'm sure I told you, Peter was the person who recommended me for this."

"Well, I'm glad he did. You've been great."

"I haven't told him about Sarah yet, but I'm sure he'll feel the same way I do."

"It's nice that one kid's getting some good out of this tragedy."

"I also made up my mind about something else. I'm going to keep track of the other children: do follow-up visits and interviews; see how they develop after an experience like this; how they deal with it. It should help me understand Sarah better."

"I really meant it when I said you've been terrific."

"It's my first time at something like this. I don't know if I ever want to go through it again, but I've certainly learned some things you can't get out of books or by controlled observation. You know, Peter's a very busy guy, but he always has some time here and there. Maybe we could all have dinner when we get back."

"Terrific idea," said Nick, laughing. "Maybe my wife will have a break in her schedule in a couple of years." He looked at his watch. "I've got to get back to the compound. We still have a lot more to examine, though I don't expect any surprises. Our investigation has quite a way to go. So if I don't see you tomorrow, good-bye—and thanks."

"'Bye," said Sandy.

"Sure thing."

They looked at each other and reached out in an awkward but real hug. Then Nick walked back to his Jeep. As he started the motor, he looked toward Sandy. She was walking away from him, but as she felt his eyes on her, she turned and waved.

And then he was gone.

part two

"Now
we're
together."

1999

1   The young man had driven down and back on Route 25 every night for the past week. It was dusk when he started, the mountains off to the west backlit by the setting sun into an enormous wine-colored ink blot. By the time he reached Albuquerque, darkness blanketed the rocky peaks, leaving only the icy points of stars visible. He drove at a steady sixty-five, always in the right-hand lane. He was looking for a hitchhiker. He tapped the brake pedal when he saw a figure standing at the side of the road perhaps a half mile ahead. The car slowed and he saw that it was a woman. She was young. And quite good-looking. She smiled as he approached. And then he slammed his foot down on the accelerator in frustration. He could see the look of surprise on her face in the rearview mirror as the car sped away. The highway was lightly traveled at this hour and it was twenty minutes before he saw someone else. This time it was a man. He touched the brake again as he drew near. No. No good at all. Now he knew he would have to do what he had been avoiding since he'd started this search. He would have to go to one of those bars. Time was running out. *Just trust in Josiah*, he thought, as he turned off the highway and headed back to the lights of the city.

"First time here?"

The young man nodded.

"I saw you looking at me. You look good. Work out?"

"A little."

"I'll bet it's a lot more than a little. My name's Alan."

"I'm Jerry."

They shook hands.

"Nice to meet you, Jerry. How about a drink at my place? Drinks cost too much at this joint. I don't live too far away."

"Sure."

"You have a car?"

"In the lot out back."

"Great. Mine's in the shop."

"I told you to take a left."

"I need some gas."

"You should have told me. The Chevron's the other way. Near the interstate."

"There's one down this way. I saw it on my way over."

"You're wrong. There's no gas station over this way. I do live here, after all."

The car moved slowly down a rutted road that skirted a deserted industrial park. And then it stopped.

"What's wrong?"

"I think I have a flat."

"Fuck."

"Don't use that word."

"You're a real Boy Scout, aren't you, Jerry? I like that. It makes me think you're really hot." Alan reached across the seat and ran his hand across Jerry's thigh. "I think this is—"

And then Jerry's arm was around Alan's neck. Though the two men were the same height and weight, there was no comparison in strength. He was careful not to break Alan's neck. That wouldn't do. He watched the dashboard clock and kept Alan in his suffocating grip six minutes after Alan stopped thrashing about.

On the drive back north, he drove at precisely the speed limit and paid no attention at all to the hitchhikers that stood by the side of the highway.

 "What time's the show?"

"Seven and nine."

"Seven's too tight."

"You're right. Let's grab a burger and some beers, take it easy, and then catch the nine."

"I hope this one is better than his last."

"Suddenly you're a fucking film critic."

"His last one truly sucked."

"All Van Damme's movies are good. The more he kicks the shit out of guys, the better the flick."

The six-thirty shift at the Penny Saver Supermarket had just ended and the three young men who did the clerking and bagging were changing in a small utility space off the loading dock that served as a locker room.

"Hey, Jerry. Why don't you come with us?" asked Billy Wells.

"Yeah, Jerry. I know you have some very fine pussy stashed out at your place in the boonies, but give it a rest tonight. You never come out with us. Is it my deodorant?"

"Sorry, but I got something to do tonight. And there's no reason to use that language, Wayne."

"Oh, go fuck yourself, Jerry. Save the choirboy shit for Sunday."

"Knock it off, Wayne. Leave the guy alone," said Billy.

Jerry Howland, born John Phillip Harris, baptized and renamed Jebediah Hummock by Josiah Hummock on March 9, 1992, quickly finished dressing and left.

"I don't know what you see in that guy," said Wayne Fullmer a few minutes later as they got into Billy Wells's pickup.

"Why don't you lay off him? Jerry's okay. He's just quiet."

"Quiet? He's a fucking mummy. How long has he worked here? Almost two years? Has he ever invited you or anyone else to his place? Has he ever even had a beer with you? He's a weirdo."

"So what? How many holiday shifts has he taken for you without asking for a favor back? If he wants to keep to himself, that's his business."

"I still think the guy's strange."

Jebediah lived in an old farmhouse almost twelve miles outside the town of Chimayo, New Mexico, north of Santa Fe. His nearest neighbors were an old Spanish couple who grew chilies on a small ranch a mile farther down a narrow, rutted road that hooked in and out of the rock outcroppings like a piece of string that a kitten had played with.

The sun was setting behind a ridge of gray cliffs as Jebediah entered the house. He slowly walked through the rooms making sure that everything was in place. He took a paper out of his pocket, containing a list he had made that morning.

He went first to the hall closet off the kitchen and pulled out the body of the man he had met at the bar in Albuquerque two nights earlier. He had dressed him in clothes identical to those he was wearing. Same Swatch on his wrist. Same Nikes. Same Ray-Bans in the shirt pocket. He dragged the body into the living room, lifted it up and let it drop so that the man's head hit the corner of a coffee table made from the base of an old cast-iron stove. The sound of tissue ripping and bone cracking caused Jebediah to jump back involuntarily. He stood there looking down at the body for a long time before he pulled out the list again. He went to the bedroom and brought out a space heater. Back in the living room he placed it under the man's feet, as if he had tripped over it. He plugged it into the outlet so that it was halfway out. He had frayed the cord around the plug so that if he turned on the heater it would spark. He then took down a kerosene lamp from the mantel and dropped it next to the body. The kerosene spilled out and soaked into the fake Persian rug as if it were blotting paper.

After he took a knapsack down from a shelf and strapped it on, he went back into the living room. He stood over the body and examined the scene. When he was sure that everything was as it should be, he took out a matchbook, struck a match, and held it against the rug, then walked quickly to the door. The rug burst into flames almost instantly. He stayed there, watching the fire cover the body and then spread over the pine floor.

He walked a few hundred feet up a rise behind the house to where he had hidden a Honda motorcycle he had bought in Gallup the week before, using a driver's license he had stolen, and paying in cash. By the time he had driven down to the road, flames were lashing out from the windows. As he rode away he didn't look back. And for the first time in years, he smiled.

3 It wasn't easy to skateboard in Crandall, Massachusetts. The small hilltown on the edge of the Berkshires didn't have smooth macadam streets like those in the city. In fact, it had only one street to speak of. Its main street (named Main Street) was barely two hundred yards long and was cratered by potholes and wavy with frost heaves from the long, hard winters. All the roads that led away from the street pitched steeply up to the hills that framed the village. The school's playground—grade K through 8—was about the only place you could do any decent skateboarding and that was where Caleb Warden was headed this bright summer afternoon.

About to start his sophomore year at Pioneer Valley Regional

High School, Caleb, a tall boy, had a disarmingly direct expression, made even more so by large gray eyes the color of the sea during a storm. He lived with his mother and stepfather on a small farm above the town. He pedaled his bike down the driveway, his skateboard under one arm. At the dirt road, he stopped by the mailbox attached to a post that leaned precariously to the side and which Paul, his stepfather, regularly said he was about to fix. Caleb carefully looked through the mail as he did every day. It was a running joke in the family that for someone who received so little mail—a couple of magazines a month, some junk mail—he was obsessed with being the first to go through it.

This time, however, there was a letter for him. He had been waiting for it for a long time. It was in a large, thick envelope, bill-boarded with stamps to ensure sufficient postage, with his name neatly printed in capital letters. The postmark was blurred but he knew where it came from. He ripped it open. There was no letter inside. He didn't expect one. Wrapped in a piece of lined notepaper were five brand-new fifty-dollar bills and ten twenties. There was also an open ticket to Boston for the bus that stopped twice a day in front of the post office in town. Clipped to that was a one-way Delta ticket from Boston to Las Vegas.

Caleb looked at his watch. The bus would be stopping in less than forty minutes. He leaned the bike against the mailbox and tossed his skateboard into the trees. He ran back to the house and took the stairs two at a time. His backpack, which he kept buried in his closet, had been ready to go for over a year. As the front door slammed behind him, he heard his mother call out to him.

"Caleb. Where you going?"

He wanted to stop. To rush back to his mother and hug her real hard. She was the only one who loved him. All the kids in town and in school thought he was strange. Weird. A freak. They could not understand the power of Josiah. *You don't need friends when you have him.* But there was still a part of Caleb that loved and needed his mother. If he could only just see her one more time. But he knew he couldn't. The word had finally come and he had to go. To start his new life. To serve Josiah Hummock. To do his work.

"Just to town," he shouted. "Be back soon."

4 The First National Bank of Twin River Falls, Minnesota, was located on the corner of Hazel and Rosewood in a granite-faced building that had been its home since 1923, the year it was founded. There were only two teller windows in the bank, and this morning, gray and threatening with clouds that seemed to hang within a baseball throw of the ground, one of the windows was empty. Benson Hubbard, the bank's manager, couldn't understand it. Mary Forbes, was an excellent employee, perhaps the best he'd ever had, and here it was almost ten and she still hadn't shown up. He dialed her number again. Still busy. Benson Hubbard was beginning to worry. It was very unlike Mary to be late. Actually, she had never been late before. And if she was sick or something was wrong, she certainly would call. He was worried enough to say to himself that if Mary didn't show up in a half hour, he'd go out to the trailer park on the edge of town where she lived and see what the problem was.

If Benson Hubbard had looked out the window at that moment, he would have been able to stop worrying about Mary Forbes. For, just then she drove past the bank, a trailer hitched behind her Bronco. She had planned to be out of town before nine, for the only road out of town passed directly in front of the bank. But one of the tires on the Bronco was flat and then the battery went dead. Luckily, the old man who lived with two dogs and seven cats in the next trailer had jumper cables.

She drove east for a couple of hours, farm country turning to forest. Houses became fewer as the forest grew denser. She was now on state land in an area with many lakes—lakes that were remote and, most importantly, deep.

Mary finally arrived at her destination: Crossbow Lake. She parked near a high ledge that had a view of the entire lake. The ledge was at least fifty feet above the surface. She got out of the car and looked around. She saw neither boats nor campsites. She had come here many times and didn't expect to see anyone. Though the lake was beautiful, there were few places to launch a boat and, the cardinal sin to the outdoor-minded citizens of the state, it wasn't stocked and therefore fishing was poor. She sat down on the ground and continued to look out over the lake. Mary waited a half hour before she rose and went into the trailer.

The interior had that scrubbed, neat look that one sees when something is for sale. The only jarring note was the body of a woman lying on the bed. The woman was dressed exactly like Mary, down to the gold heart pendant she always wore. She was the same height and weight, her hair the identical color and cut. Mary picked up the body and carried it out of the trailer. She had been working out with weights for the past year and had no trouble getting the body to the car and into the driver's seat. She then went back in and brought out a small suitcase. Mary walked to the edge and sat down again. She scanned the lake. She was absolutely alone. It was only then that she reached into the Bronco and started the motor. She reached across the dead woman and put the gear lever into drive. She tugged on the brake release and the car and trailer lurched forward. Mary was just able to slam the door shut. Within seconds the car and trailer were over the edge and dropping into the cold, dark water. It took longer than she thought—almost two minutes—for it to sink. A state map had shown the water to be over a hundred feet deep at this end of the lake. She peered down for a long time and could see no trace of it. Finally satisfied, she lifted the suitcase and walked a half mile up the road. There, just out of sight, was the Jeep she had left the week before. Mary Forbes, born Martha Fricker, rebaptized Mary Hummock, started the car and drove slowly out of the underbrush. She had a lot of driving to do because she had someone she had to pick up. She felt good. Soon the family would be back together. And then they would take up God's work. Josiah's work.

 She had told her father that it was a wrong number. He gave her a funny look. They didn't get many phone calls. Most days the phone didn't ring at all.

"You sure about that, Hannah?" he asked.

"Yes, Daddy. They wanted someone named Mitchell."

"Mitchell," he rolled the name around in his mouth like a gumball. "No Mitchell 'round here."

"That's what I told him."

"It was a man who called?"

"Yes, Daddy."

"You seemed to be talking a lot for a wrong number."

"No, I wasn't."

"When you get a wrong number you just say, 'No one here by that name,' and hang up. That's all. Nothing else. Understand?"

She nodded and stood very still.

He gave her that look again. Then he remembered something he had to do, and turned and walked out of the house. Hannah watched him as he walked toward the barn. She had wanted to kill him for a long time. She knew how she would do it. After supper when he was asleep in his chair. She would empty a can of lighter fluid on him. Then drop a match in his lap. Simple as that. He was an evil man who deserved killing. But she knew that wasn't part of the plan. She waited a few minutes after he entered the barn before she left the house. She ran down to the dirt road as fast as she could. She kept running until she reached the county road almost a mile away. She was afraid to look back. Most of the roads in this part of Nebraska were straight as rake handles, and lightly traveled. Where the dirt road met the paved, she edged back into a field of wheat and crouched down. And then she saw it. The Jeep was black and moving fast. Hannah stood up and the Jeep stopped next to her. A door was thrown open and she jumped in.

Mary released the clutch and the car leaped away.

"You're the last to be picked up. We have a lot of driving to do. In two days we'll be with the others." *All of us. Except for one*, she thought to herself.

"I can't wait," said Hannah.

"Neither can God," Mary answered.

part three

"The children
have
vanished."

1 The two young men drove at a steady pace through the leafy streets. The car was a dusty, dark blue Honda, the kind nobody would notice or remember. The passenger appeared somewhat younger than the driver and held in his hand a map of Georgetown, which he didn't need to consult. They already had made several dry runs and knew exactly how to get to the school, without hesitations or wrong turns.

When they saw the single-story brick building, its two wings of classrooms wrapped around a playground swarming with children, they stopped a short distance away. Without a word, the young man on the passenger side got out of the car. He had long blond hair that was neatly groomed, and that, combined with his well-pressed chino jacket and plaid shirt, allowed him to blend in easily with the teachers and babysitters near the school. It was the end of the day, and the children, who had just been released, pushed and pulled, teased and giggled among themselves as they waited to be picked up. He was pretty certain that he spotted the little girl he was looking for in one of the groups.

Just inside the front door was the Office of Administration. The young man knocked on the door, then approached the middle-aged woman at the desk who raised her head inquiringly.

"Hi . . . Miss Wolfe," he said, glancing at the placard on her desk and smiling. "I'm Tom Carter. I'm here to pick up Sarah Price. Her babysitter couldn't make it today."

"Oh?"

"Here's a note from her mother."

The woman took the note, written on Dr. Sandy Price's stationery, and scanned it. "Fine," she said, standing up. "But excuse me a moment. I always follow the rules."

The young man watched the woman disappear into an adjoining room, pulling the door behind her. The door did not entirely close and through the opening he saw her pick up the phone and begin to dial. She had to be calling Sandy Price.

He hurriedly left the building and strode out to the playground, looking for the little girl he had seen earlier. When he was standing next to her, he called out softly, "Sarah?" The girl turned and looked up at him.

He reached out and grabbed her hand. "Sarah, you have to come with me."

"Who are you?" said Sarah, yanking her hand from his grip.

"Come on," said the young man, taking her hand again.

"Where's Gina?"

"She's got a bad headache. As soon as we get home, you'll see her." This time he held Sarah's hand tightly and started to quick march her toward the street.

Suddenly he was conscious of a woman's voice shouting from the school building. "You . . . young man . . . You, stop where you are!" cried the woman from the office. "Let go of that girl."

"Leave me alone!" screamed Sarah, trying to pull her hand from his. "Let me go!"

Everybody had turned to stare, frozen for a moment by the scene they were witnessing, like watching a stunt plane plummet toward the ground. Then in a split second, everyone was in motion. A tall woman reached the young man first and took hold of his shoulder. He pushed her away with a vicious shove, still hanging on to Sarah. From the other side a male teacher charged at him. The young man punched him in the face, then with a karate chop dropped him to the ground.

Realizing he had let go of Sarah, he spun around, looking for her. There she was, bunched together with the other frightened children in the corner of the playground that was farthest from him. He thought maybe he could dive into this knot and pull her out, but seeing from the corner of his eye two men in workclothes running toward him, he knew it would never work.

He raced out of the schoolyard to the waiting Honda, which had edged closer. As soon as he jumped in, he and the other young man took off in a squeal of burning rubber.

2 As the sun started to edge behind the office building across the street, Nick Barrows pushed his chair away from his desk, stretched his legs, and yawned. The day had been a zero, a tedious flow of routine matters—a minor-league car-theft ring, a penny-ante mail-fraud con—to the point of boredom, and then to exhaustion.

The phone on his desk rang. He rolled his chair back until he could see Maria Lozano, his secretary, and pointed his finger at her. *You pick up*, he signaled. Ordinarily he took his own calls, but he had a hunch who was calling.

"Dr. Sandra Price," Maria said, after she put the call on hold. "Or should I say, Dr. Persistence."

God, she was determined, and what could she want? To rehash the good old times at Mesa Blanca? They had not seen or talked to each other in four years. Over the last several weeks she had bombarded him with letters and faxes. He glanced over to an unread stack of them at the corner of his desk. Then the calls started. At least two or three a day. It was as if she were stalking him.

"Tell her anything you want, but get rid of her. Tell her I'm away for a week. West Coast. It'll give me some breathing space." He remembered liking her, but he had had enough of the Hummock affair to last him several lifetimes, and why else would she be calling?

When his secretary hung up, he walked over to her desk. "It's almost five, right?"

Maria nodded.

"That's respectable enough for me. I'm going to call it a day. Hold the fort for another half hour, then you take off, too. And if Dr. Price calls again, tell her you made a mistake. I'm not away for a week, I'm away for a month—make that a year."

Maria giggled, briefly lifting Nick's spirits. It wasn't a particularly funny line, but it was good to get a laugh. The door to the hallway read Federal Bureau of Investigation, Tulsa Division, and reading it again drove the laugh down his throat, almost making him gag. A secretary and four agents under his command—one rookie and three a year away from retirement. This two-bit operation was where his career at the Bureau had taken him. Shutting the door behind him, he whispered to himself his mantra, "Hang in there."

At Healey's Bar and Grill, a block from the office, the proprietor and bartender, Frank Healey, had Nick's favorite drink in front of him before he could say hello. A double Scotch Mist. None of that trendy Chardonnay crap, thank you.

"Your day been good?" asked Nick, after he drained half the glass.

"I'm not complaining."

"The sign of a good man, Frank."

Looking up as he spoke to the bartender, Nick caught his image in the mirror: circles under his eyes, suit rumpled, tie hanging limp on his chest like the drooping sail of a becalmed boat. He bent down and took another swallow of his drink. He sensed someone slipping onto the bar stool next to him, and turned his head slightly to see who it was. It had been four years but he had no trouble rec-ognizing the woman next to him. Sandy Price. She still looked ter-rific—and yes, he *had* liked her.

"I'll have a white wine," she told the bartender. "Chardonnay." She turned to Nick. "You're a hard man to reach."

"You're even harder to avoid. No 'avoid' is not fair. It's just I knew that seeing you would bring it all back."

Sandy held up her hand. "I understand. I wasn't sure I should get in touch with you, but I really need to talk to you."

"I see things aren't going too well for you, either, or you wouldn't be here in Tulsa."

"I'm visiting someone here." After a pause, Sandy answered the question Nick didn't ask. "You."

"That's an excuse, at least, though I don't know how good it is. Tulsa's not Washington. There's nothing new and exciting about it, which makes it a nice place to raise a family—so they say. But I wouldn't know, since I happen to be single." He gestured around Healey's. "Obviously I haven't gone up in the Bureau. Matter of fact, Frank's establishment is one of the few places I'm appreciated. Haven't gone up or down in my marriage, either. Just out. What about you? Did you marry the congressman?"

"No, I didn't."

"And the teaching?"

"It worked out fine. William and Mary really came through."

Nick smiled at her. His first smile of the day? Maybe. "I'm glad, but I don't think you're here to talk about careers or marriages. And I'm sorry I didn't return your calls."

A large man in a windbreaker came into the bar and sat down on the stool next to Sandy. He signaled the bartender for a vodka and tonic.

"Excuse me, buddy," said Nick to the man. "This lady and I are having a private conversation. Could you please move down a bit?"

"I don't see a Reserved sign. I'll sit where I want."

Nick got up and went over to the man.

"I said, move."

"Hold on, Nick," said the bartender, coming around the bar. He had witnessed a number of these scenes with Nick over the past few years. They generally ended in a fight. Frank liked Nick and tried to watch out for him. "I haven't seen you in here before," he said to the large man, "but I don't like what I see. Now get the hell out."

The bartender and Nick stood side by side, staring down at the man.

"Okay," he finally said, turning toward the door. "I don't forget shit like this," he muttered as he left the bar.

"Sorry about that," said Nick, when he sat down again. "Now, where were we before that asshole—excuse my French—sat down?"

"This may sound strange, but when I couldn't reach you, I figured there was only one way to get to you. Come out here."

"I'm flattered you thought I was worth the trouble."

"Don't be. I need your help."

He had been in a funk for so long it was difficult for him to climb out of the hole he'd dug himself into. "All right," he said finally, "what's on your mind?"

"I'm very worried. Something odd is going on with the children."

"You mean who I think you do?"

"The Hummock children—exactly," she said. "I'm sorry to drag you through this again, but I have to. You were right when you said they would blame you for what happened. It was so unjust."

"Well, that's the way the Bureau crumbles. But go on," said Nick.

"Okay. What's happened is that last month two of the kids supposedly died and the others disappeared from their homes. You remember Jebediah and Mary, the two oldest? They're dead. Both in accidents. One in a fire, the other by drowning. But I don't believe it."

"What do the police say?"

"To me? Nothing. I'm not family and I'm not police. They're not interested in talking to me."

"But you said a month has gone by since this happened. And you're respected in your field. They should want to talk to you."

"But they don't. Now do you see why I'm so frustrated? My assistant at the university and I are the only ones tracking this. It's pathetic."

"What happened to the younger ones?" asked Nick. His cheeks were flushed and he felt a tug in his gut that he thought he had lost forever. He was beginning to care.

"They're gone. Ran away. All of them. And it isn't a coincidence."

"But this happens all the time with kids," said Nick.

"Not with these. Ever since the explosion I've kept in touch with them. They haven't been particularly cooperative, but people close to them have been. I'm learning an amazing amount about the effects of trauma." She couldn't have kept the passion out of her voice if she tried. "How brainwashing, deep, mind-altering experiences, extreme violence—the whole bundle—continue to shape the lives of people caught up in it. The Hummock children seem to be coping beautifully. They seem to be entirely normal, but I suspect they're just keeping up appearances. What matters to them is kept secret. I can't quit on them now. I hoped you would help me find out what happened to Mary and Jebediah, and help find the others."

"If only it were that simple," said Nick, in a voice that for a moment had a tinge of sorrow before turning professional. "Unless these kids were forcibly taken across state lines or coerced into participating in a federal crime, the FBI isn't interested."

Sandy stared hard at him before speaking. "Are you trying to tell me that you're *not* interested?"

"No, I'm very interested."

"Then show it, damn it. I'm trying to save a life here!"

"What do you mean?"

"Remember Sarah? The youngest child released? Barely three? I told you I was thinking of adopting her, and I did."

"Well, congratulations."

Sandy took a long swallow of her drink. "They know I have her—and they want her back."

Nick looked at Sandy, the feeling of hopelessness he had felt during the siege rushing back at him.

"They've already tried to take her from me. Kidnap her. Unless they're caught, I know they'll try again."

"What happened?

"A week after the children disappeared, I got a call from Sarah's school. A woman in the office told me a young man was there to pick up Sarah. He had a note, supposedly from me. I hadn't authorized anything of the kind! The man saw the woman was checking on his story, so he grabbed Sarah and tried to run off with her. Luckily a couple of workmen scared him off."

"Jesus."

They lapsed into silence. After what seemed like an hour rather than a minute, Sandy stood up. "I've got to get some sleep, Nick. I'm worn out from traveling. I'll see you in the morning. We'll talk some more then."

Nick watched Sandy leave the bar before signaling Healey for another drink. Later, when he reached home (as usual, he had no idea how much later), he found Sandy standing by his front door. There was blood on his shirt and a bruise on his cheekbone. His ribs ached from being kicked. The large man had been waiting for him outside the bar, and had quickly and efficiently administered a nasty beating. It would have been worse if Frank the bartender hadn't rushed outside with a baseball bat and driven the man off. Now he gratefully leaned on Sandy, and as soon as he managed to unlock the door and stumble into his bedroom, he fell on the bed and passed out.

3 Nick Barrows raised his head from the pillow and looked around the room. The window shades were up, which they seldom were, and light flooded the room. He sat up and surveyed himself, fully dressed except for his shoes. Sinking back onto the pillow, easing the headache that raged behind his eyes like a gang of rioters, he tried to think about the night before. He remembered talking with Sandy Price at the bar and a little about the fight later. His whole body ached and the blood in his mouth tasted like dirt.

At that moment, Sandy appeared in the doorway, holding a cup.

"What's that?" was all he could spit out.

"We call it coffee," she said, as she walked into the room. "It'll help."

"I don't want to wake up. I want to be left alone. I can't stand people smiling at me at the crack of dawn."

Sandy laughed. "It's almost noon."

"So?"

"That won't do. Stop being a crank and get out of bed."

Something in her voice persuaded Nick to swing his legs to the floor and sit on the edge of the bed. He felt like shit. His life was shit. He didn't give a shit. What the hell was this woman doing in his apartment?

His head pounded, but his vision was now steady enough for him to take in the room. "There's something strange about this place."

"Perhaps because it's clean."

"So you're my new housekeeper, who just spent the night with me."

"The couch isn't bad, but stop stalling. I need you to come to Chimayo with me. It's in New Mexico, near Santa Fe."

"Can't do it. I have to go to work."

"You really are in bad shape. It's Saturday."

"Where'd you say you wanted to go?"

"Chimayo. Where Jebediah lived. And supposedly died. Don't look at me so blankly, Nick. I know you know who I'm talking about."

"I guess so, but you didn't tell me much about it."

"That's why I want to go to Chimayo. To find out what happened. I've got two tickets on American to Albuquerque. We'll rent a car from there. The plane leaves at two-fifty, so you have to get moving."

"Why have I been selected for the honor of accompanying you?"

Sandy looked at Nick with exasperation. "Isn't that sort of obvious? You've been in on this from the beginning," she said, biting off her words. The trace of a Southern accent she must have picked up in Washington evaporated. "And I need a man with me. A man with training in law enforcement. I've had enough of macho cops, and I suspect that New Mexico sheriffs are especially nasty to single women."

"This sounds like a wild-goose chase."

"Please. Do it for me. It's important."

When he didn't say no, she handed him a ticket. "Believe it or not, I have an old friend who teaches here. I promised I'd meet her for lunch. It's now nearly noon. Meet me at the gate at two-thirty, okay?"

It was two forty-five and the final boarding call for flight 53 to Albuquerque had just been announced. She had given up thinking Nick would show up. She watched one more person rush to the gate. Then the attendants shut the door and headed off toward the main terminal, gossiping and laughing together. Sandy trailed behind them, looking for the American ticket counter, thinking it had been a long way to come to have lunch with the classics major who had lived down the hall from her their junior year at college.

And what was she going to do about the kids, now that Nick had handed her a dead end?

She spotted the ticket counter soon enough. "When's the next flight to Washington, D.C.?" she asked.

4 The first slant of light from the sun hitting the silver waters of the Gulf woke Ed Trainor. He had read once that Hemingway always said he was born with thin eyelids that caused him to rise early. *Well*, Ed thought, *maybe I have thin eyelids, too.* The mornings were the best time of day anyway, and waking up early was never a problem for him. He slipped out of bed in order not to wake Marge, and went into his study to dress. He always laid out his clothes the night before, and now that he had been retired by the FBI, the suit had been replaced by a pair of shorts, a T-shirt, and sneakers. The marina where he kept his scull was only a mile away and this morning, like most, he biked over.

The marina was deserted except for one of the dockmen, who waved to Ed as he lifted the slender boat off the rack and put it into the water. It took him awhile to get into his rhythm, and it wasn't until he was three hundred yards from shore that Ed felt his arms and legs moving smoothly and efficiently, the racing shell slicing through the water like the fin of a fish. He had rowed at Williams, and from the time he left school he had never stopped. All through law school and the FBI he rowed every morning except when he was traveling or the weather was foul. He believed it was the perfect exercise, both for the heart and the tone and suppleness of the body. It was also an ideal way to think. Unlike running, with the distractions of other runners, cars, dogs, and general noise, rowing, particularly at this hour, left one alone, truly alone.

For the first year of his retirement, after he and Marge had moved down to Sanibel Island, the time he spent rowing was not a good time. It just gave him a chance to go over again and again, like a dog gnawing at a favorite bone, the events that had led to his leaving the agency. Oh, they called it a retirement, and if you added the modifier "forced," it was true enough. But the press wanted someone to pay for the Hummock disaster, which, of course, made Congress bloody-minded, and who better to be offered up than the director of the FBI. Simple as that. Although that wasn't the worst part. He had been slated to retire in a couple of years anyway.

It was Nick Barrows who had borne the real brunt of it. From having a great shot at becoming the director in several years, he had been moved down, way down, into a nowhere post in Tulsa where his career now had the flight path of a fighter plane hit by a missile. Ed had tried to get him transferred to another agency, like the ATF. No such luck. Whatever juice Ed Trainor once had, was now dry as dust. And even if he had been able to pull a few strings, Nick's name in the government was as good as Howard Stern's at the FCC. And now even their friendship had turned sour. The only time they spoke was when Ed called him. Ed had tried repeatedly to get Nick down for a visit, once even sending him a round-trip ticket. "Too busy," was the response. Yeah, too busy knocking the booze back. He could hear it in Nick's voice. *If only I had listened to him*, Ed told himself for the hundredth time. But that was in the past and Nick's future was in the grim present, and he, Ed Trainor, was in part—a large part—responsible.

And, to top it off, who had got the director's job but LaChance! All his ass-kissing of congressmen and senators finally had paid off. And just as bad was LaChance's pushing Nick as far down as he could, even though Ed had pleaded with him to give Nick something decent, not a desk in a backwater office. There are demotions and there are demotions.

Come on, he told himself, *you've played this tune too many times already. Get on to something else.*

He picked up his stroke, concentrating on his entry and recovery, using the mechanics of rowing to clear his head. He stayed with it for a few minutes until suddenly he heard something that made his head jerk up. It was one of those awful racing boats. Long and powerful, with an engine sounding like something you'd expect to find on an aircraft carrier's deck. Ed had never seen one out this early.

It was a half mile away, and headed right for him. He dropped the oars and started to wave. The damn wake of the thing could swamp him. His hands flailed in the air but the boat didn't move off its line. It was ripping along, a dancing rooster spray hanging in its wake. Ed pulled one of the oars out of its lock and swung it wildly from side to side like a huge metronome.

The boat's bow moved a few degrees away. *Great*, he thought, *they see me.* By now he could make out the occupants: a young man at the wheel, another next to him, and two children. The boat was only a couple of hundred yards away when it moved its bow again. Right toward him. The four in the boat were waving at him. And laughing. He started to scream but all he could hear was the hellish roar of the boat. And then it was upon him. And Ed Trainor went, just like that, from daylight to darkness.

5 "Well, Mr. Stagg, I'd say things were pretty shitty. What's your story?"

Nick's feet were up on his desk and his chair tilted even farther back than normal. He held the phone in one hand while he doodled a picture of an airplane with the other. He had had lunch at Healey's (a mistake) and after half a sandwich and two double Scotch Mists he felt loquacious. Who better to call than his old buddy back at FBI headquarters, Nelson Stagg? Stagg, whose family name had been Hirsch (the German word for stag) when they emigrated from Bavaria, had gone through training with Nick at the FBI academy. Now holding the position of Deputy Director for Policy, he was both a good friend and Nick's only source of inside information at headquarters.

"Things are just smashing here, Mr. Barrows. Mr. LaChance, our beloved director, is as uptight and mean as ever. I once thought he had a ruler up his ass. Now I'm convinced it's a yardstick. You been behaving?"

"Hard not to, here in the heartland. 'Temptation' is a word used only in Scrabble in these parts. How's Claudia and the kids?"

"Expensive and noisy. In that order."

Maria, Nick's secretary, pushed open the door and stood in the doorway. She signaled to Nick that he had a call on the other line. He started to wave her away but she shook her head firmly. This call was important.

"Nelson, something's come up. I'll call you back later."

He punched the flashing button.

"Yes?"

"Nick, it's Marge." And then Ed Trainor's wife lost it. Great, wracking sobs, almost like a choking fit, poured out.

"What's wrong, Marge? What is it?"

And then he heard a man's voice. "It's Bryce, Nick."

Bryce Trainor was Ed's oldest son.

"What's happening, Bryce?"

"It's Dad. He's dead."

"Oh, no. What happened?"

"There was an accident. Mom wants you to speak at the service. It'll be down here in three days. Can you make it?"

"Of course, Bryce. I'll be there."

6 Six people spoke at Ed Trainor's funeral service. First was his youngest son, Randall, a senior at Yale. Then Ben Summers, an old college friend. Jenny, Ed's daughter, and Bryce, his oldest son, went next. The man who had succeeded Ed—Phil LaChance, the current director of the FBI—spoke just before Nick did. His eulogy was pure LaChance: correct, devoid of emotion, long-winded. Nick glanced at the closed coffin and thought, *I guess this proves you're dead, old buddy. Because if there was any life in you, you'd be out of there right now, throttling this smug, uptight prick.*

And then it was Nick's turn. He walked past the family in the front pew, the children on either side of Marge, hands clasped together. He placed what he had written the night before on the podium before the altar. Sunlight streamed in from a clerestory window below the roof's peak. Nick squinted as he looked out at the packed church. He spotted a score of old friends from the agency, including Nelson Stagg and the team that had worked with him at Mesa Blanca. In the row behind the family sat the former attorney general, Clayton Bosworth. His nickname in the press was "Marathon Man"; he had been the first person in a long time to hold the cabinet post through two administrations. Secret Service men flanked the aisles, earpieces and sunglasses in place, since Big Jim Avery, the vice president, was in attendance, seated next to Bosworth.

Nick smoothed out the paper and then, just like that, folded it and put it back in his pocket. What he had to say about Ed Trainor was in his heart, not on a piece of paper.

"I met Ed Trainor on May twelfth, 1981, at the FBI academy. He was my teacher. He bawled me out that day—I mean, really read me the riot act, for doing something so incredibly stupid that I have trouble talking about it today. But when he finished, he put his arm around my shoulder and took me out for a drink. That was Ed. Tough but compassionate. He cared about what he did because he cared about this country. He cared about people, each and every one of us. There was nothing theoretical about his commitment. It was real."

Nick stepped out of the church into the intense glare of a sun that shone from a pale blue, cloudless sky. The light stung his eyes. A number of the men from headquarters waved to him, but he had no interest in talking to them. He embraced Ed's family and quickly walked down the street looking for a taxi to take him to his hotel. As he neared the corner he saw a woman across the street who was waving at an approaching taxi. It was Sandy Price.

What was she doing here? He ran across the street as the taxi pulled up.

"Room for a hitchhiker?" he asked.

"I didn't want you to see me here," Sandy said, as she got into the cab.

"Does that mean no?"

"I'm still angry with you."

"Would a drink and an apology from me help a little?"

"I have a plane to catch in two hours," Sandy said coldly.

"That's enough time for a drink. The apology might take longer."

"Well, do you forgive me?"

"Will it make you feel better if I say I do?"

"Yes," Nick answered, as he signaled the bartender for another Manhattan.

"Then, no. I don't forgive you."

"You're a hard woman, Dr. Price," said Nick, smiling.

"Not hard, Mr. Barrows, just frightened."

"How can you be so sure that these children are dangerous?"

"Because I've observed them for over four years and they don't show any of the typical signs of early trauma. Chronic rage, impulsiveness, nightmares, hyperactivity—the characteristics we look for are totally missing. The coping skills of children exposed to stress generally show up in a test developed at the University of Minnesota. The Hummock children showed skills that are absolutely normal. There's an ongoing project called the Epidemiological Catchment Area—"

"That's some mouthful," said Nick.

"Sorry about that. We refer to it as ECA, actually. Anyway, the post-traumatic symptoms I would expect to find in them are just not there."

"Meaning?"

"It's inescapable. These children have been so brainwashed, so molded by Hummock, that even though he's no longer alive he still controls them. The word 'dangerous' doesn't begin to describe their potential."

"What term would you use?"

"How about 'murderous'?"

"You must be joking."

"Not at all. I believe these children killed Ed Trainor."

"That's crazy. It was an accident. I've talked with the local cops. They're sure it was a bunch of teenagers. They've seen lots of cases like it before. And I feel in my gut they're right."

"I thought FBI agents look for proof, not stomach rumblings."

"Sandy, you're wrong about this. The cops think they'll catch the ones who did it in a few days. Teenagers, but not the Hummock kids. They found three empty six-packs in the boat that hit Ed. I'm positive they'll find out the kids were drunk and just out to have some fun. The boat was big and powerful. Too powerful. Probably, they lost control of it. Ed had the misfortune of being in the wrong place at the wrong time."

Sandy finished her drink and stood up.

"I better get going. I'm cutting it close. Thanks for the drink, Nick."

"Let me drop you off."

"That's not necessary. I told the taxi to wait. It's only a short drive to the airport."

"Will I see you again?"

"I doubt it, Nick. Two foolish trips are enough, even for me. I thought you might understand and help . . . but I guess I was wrong."

On his way to the Fort Myers airport the next morning, Nick had the taxi driver stop at the marina where Ed had kept his scull. Nick had gone there when he arrived two days before, with the local detective handling the investigation. There wasn't much to see. The plastic shell had cracked like an egg that had fallen off a table. Several pieces were missing and the remaining shards of blue plastic looked like an exotic puzzle. But something made Nick want to see it again. It was still covered by a canvas tarp. He pulled it away and looked down at the sorry remains. The detective had drawn an outline of the boat on the planks of the dock. He had then tried to fit the pieces between the chalk lines. With imagination one could see that it once might have been a boat. The largest part missing was in the center where Ed had sat. It looked as if he had been hit almost exactly midships. Nick walked slowly around the wreckage. No one had seen it happen. The racing boat, a high-speed Donzi, was found the next day, beached ten miles down the coast. It had been reported stolen the night before.

"Kids," the detective had told Nick. "In Newark they steal cars and joyride. Here, it's high-performance boats. Most of the time no one gets hurt. Fucking kids."

Nick looked at his watch. He'd better get going. He pulled the canvas back over the bits and pieces. *Kids . . . kids . . . kids . . .* The word kept ringing in Nick's head. The detective was probably right. It must have been kids who did it. Nick turned and walked back to the taxi.

7 On the flight home from Ed Trainor's service, Nick could think of little else than Ed, and Sandy Price's idea of how he died. Nick's eyes glazed as he tried to distract himself with the papers and magazines he'd bought, until he gave up and dozed fitfully for the rest of the trip.

First thing the next morning, Saturday, he telephoned Nelson Stagg at his house. Stagg's voice on the other end sounded groggy. "I hope this is important," he said.

"It might be. Did I wake you up?"

"Of course not. I always wake up an hour before the alarm clock goes off. Saves the batteries."

"Sorry."

"No, you're not. But that's okay. I was going to call you later on anyway, to tell you your eulogy was terrific. You really caught what made Ed different."

"Thanks," Nick replied. "I need a favor, Nelson."

"I don't like the sound of that. I hope it's a lawn mower you want to borrow."

"No. I need the Hummock file, particularly all the stuff on the kids."

"What for?"

"I'll tell you later—after I've looked at it."

"Well . . ." answered Stagg, drawing out the word, buying a little time to think. "I don't know. That piece of business is like Chernobyl. Nobody wants to go near it."

"Come on, Nel, I wouldn't ask you if it didn't really matter."

"It's just too tough, Nick. I don't think I can do it."

"I can't believe you're saying this to me."

"If I get caught, my ass will be shipped farther west than yours," Stagg groaned after a moment of silence. His voice was resigned.

"That's my man."

"I'll copy it Monday and FedEx it. You'll have it Tuesday morning."

On Tuesday, Nick called Maria to say he had the flu, made himself some coffee, and sat watching *Regis and Kathie Lee*, then C-SPAN, waiting for the front doorbell to ring. The FedEx package arrived shortly after eleven. Inside was a scribbled note from Stagg:

> *This was a bitch to get. I Xeroxed it myself last night after everyone else had left. As I said, it's still dynamite. Don't forget that LaChance got to be director because of this and he doesn't want the subject to pop up ever again. He considers it a dead issue and wants to keep it that way. Whatever you do, don't let anyone else from the Bureau know that I was the one who got it to you. Okay?* No one.
>
> *Nelson*

Nick put the file on his desk and started leafing through it. His own reports were in it as well as his failed time line for the release of all the children from the Hummock compound. The other agents present at the siege had all been debriefed, but since their contact with Hummock had been less than his, there were no surprises. A daily summary of the media coverage also had been dutifully assembled, prominently featuring Fran Marcum and Bernie Willis, but neither their coverage nor the sensational stories in the tabloids and the plodding profiles prepared by the serious press told him anything he did not know.

Far and away the most compelling material in the file were the notes Sandy Price and her assistant had made. Sure, at the time of the siege she had kept him informed, but subtle details he had forgotten, or maybe even missed, now leaped from the pages. Why hadn't she shown him these notes when she came to Tulsa? He wouldn't have been so slow to understand, to help her find out what had happened to Jebediah in Chimayo. The children had seemed so quiet and docile, but the further he read and thought about them, the more he felt there was something vital he had missed. Sandy's point of view was beginning to make sense. He had accepted the local cops' explanation of Ed Trainor's death at face value, but why?

My God, if he could only get to the truth of his old friend's death. Feeling almost buoyant, he stood up and headed for the bottle of Johnny Walker in his kitchen, for a jolt of something strong to fortify his resolve. He started to twist off the cap, then put down the bottle. It was much too early for this.

Nick had read through the file twice by the afternoon, and had made twelve pages of notes. He picked up the phone and dialed Kevin Hornsby, his superior, the Special Agent in Charge of the Southwest District, in Oklahoma City, to explain that he needed to take a few days off because of a family problem.

"Of course, Nick. Feel free," said Hornsby. "I can't remember the last time you took a vacation."

"Thanks. I'll be back in a couple of days."

Later that afternoon, Nick went to his office, forestalling Maria's solicitude with a quick word to her that he was feeling one hundred percent better. He returned the calls he had received, and met for fifteen minutes with a young, gung-ho agent, about a bank job in Stillwater. ("Sounds like you've got one of the perps. Sit on him hard and he'll spill the others.")

As he ducked out soon afterward, even though it wasn't five yet, he stopped at Maria's desk. "I'm off now."

"To Healey's?" she asked with a wink. "I mean, in case something important comes up."

"No. To Albuquerque."

8 Nick rented a car at the Albuquerque airport. Since he had time to spare, he skipped the interstate to Santa Fe and instead chose the Turquoise Trail, a two-lane road that twisted in and out of arroyos and high-desert mesas and past a few small towns that had the look of places that had been bypassed long ago by the highway. His appointment with Detective Lamar T. Hitchins in Chimayo was still an hour away, so he parked a block from the police station and walked down the street to a bar for a bowl of chili. As he ate, he looked again through his folder on the children, particularly the material on Jebediah. He had studied it several times the day before, but something was still bothering him. Sandy had given the children a battery of psychological tests, including several he had never heard of. None of them suggested that Jebediah had a depressed or suicidal nature. Granted, that was four years ago and the boy could have gone through a lot of changes, running the gamut from drugs to bungee-jumping. He glanced at the clock above the counter and saw that he was about to be late. He closed the folder, looking at Jebediah's picture once more, seeing his large dark, sad eyes that brought to mind the vacant stare survivors of combat often have, and left.

"Just seems kind of odd, Mr. Barrows, that you'd be coming to see me a month after the boy's death." Detective Hitchins wore boots made of snakeskin that shone like a new car. He slouched in his chair, the boots stretched before him until they almost touched Nick's chair.

"I was out of the country. Belgium. I was told when I got back. The details were . . . I guess I'd say, skimpy."

"And you're Jerry's uncle?"

"Jebediah's. That's correct," Nick lied.

"He used the name Jerry in Chimayo. I investigated the fire with the local sheriff there."

"And what did you find?"

"Electric-heater fire. Boy must have hit his head tripping over the thing. Knocked over a kerosene lamp. The house was old and made of wood. Dry as a butt in the pocket of an old suit. Place was totally engaged when the fire department got out there."

"Nothing suspicious at all?"

Hitchins saw something that displeased him on the tip of his boot and carefully wiped it with a handkerchief. "I told you it was an accident, Mr. Barrows. Sad when someone that young dies. But an accident nonetheless."

"Where was my nephew buried?"

"I guess folks in your family aren't too close. The boy's body was claimed two days later by"—he paused to look down at an open file on his desk—"Marian Ransome, a cousin. I suspect you know her."

Nick nodded and waited for the detective to continue.

"She had the body, or what was left of it, cremated at Maitland's, a funeral chapel in Chimayo, the next day." Hitchins bent over his desk and wrote something on a piece of paper. He folded it and slid it across the desk.

"Since you been in Belgium so long," Hitchins said, with the kind of smile a man has when he knows his opponent's hole card, "I wrote out your niece's address and phone number. Below that are directions on how to get out to where your nephew lived. Have a good day."

He was back tending to his boot as Nick walked out of the office.

9   All that was left of the house Jebediah had died in was a chimney made of rough gray stones that stood against the hillside like a broken finger. If anything else had survived the fire, it wasn't visible. A bed of ashes, like the kind in a

fireplace grate, made up the contents of the house. Nick picked up a stick and started to scratch around in it. It was as fine as talc. He moved around the outline of the building, probing here and there. By the time he had circled the site, all he had raised was a cloud of dust that hung in the still air like cigarette smoke in a crowded room.

He was walking back to his car when he noticed what looked like a deer trail leading uphill behind the house. The grass was pushed down in a distinct line. He followed the mark a few hundred feet to where it suddenly stopped. There, a small patch of weeds was flattened. He stared at the ground. He noticed a dark, shiny spot. Nick knelt down and touched it. He sniffed his fingers. Oil. Someone had kept something up here. A motorcycle, most likely, he thought. He continued to search the area, and then, under a clump of weeds, he spotted a matchbook. He reached down and picked it up. The sun and rain had faded the writing on the cover but Nick could still make it out: The Cauldron—the "Hot" Bar in Town. The address was in Albuquerque. He put the matchbook in his pocket and walked back to his car, knowing that he had another stop to make before returning to Tulsa.

10

It wasn't four o'clock yet, but the bar already had a dozen patrons, all male. Above the entrance was the outline, in brilliant red neon, of a large cauldron, blinking bubbles of steam. The front window was made of dark-tinted glass, almost black, so that those inside could look out, but the viewer from the sidewalk could not see in, except to catch an occasional disembodied arm or head, illuminated, ghostlike, by overhead spotlights. Nick Barrows knew exactly what he was stepping into before he'd pushed open the door. Not that he cared one way or the other.

After his eyes adjusted, he pulled up a stool at the bar and ordered a double Scotch Mist, then a moment later, watching the bartender reach for the Black Label, canceled it and asked for a ginger ale. The tepid sweetness of the drink, as cloying as the aroma of pressed flowers, almost made him shudder, but he persevered. He had to start somewhere, pulling himself together. In the last four years the only habit from his earlier life that had flourished was his drinking, and it had become the center of his existence. Though the demands of the Tulsa job were minimal, he was only hanging on, and unless he forced himself to change, he would never leave this post—or he might even lose it. Either way, it would be an ignominious end.

He took another swallow, then asked the bartender how he could reach the owner. Did he have an office here? Would he be in later?

"You're in luck, my man. He's right over there," the bartender answered, motioning to an older man sitting alone at a table in the back. Nick got off the stool and walked over to him.

The owner looked up at Nick with curiosity, then, when Nick flashed his ID, with alarm. "Is anything wrong?" he asked.

"No, not at all," said Nick. "I have no problem with your operation." He looked around. "What I need is information." He extracted a snapshot of Jebediah and slid it across the table. "Do you recognize this fellow? The photo's a few years old."

The man twisted in his seat, holding the photo up and turning it to catch more light. Before he handed it back, he already was shaking his head. "Never seen him." Raising his voice, he called to the bartender and handed the snapshot to him. "Stan, do you know this fellow?"

"No. I see so many—but no, I've never seen him."

Nick studied the two men for a moment. "Any regulars stopped showing up in the last month or so?"

"No, I don't believe so," said the owner.

"Hold it," said the bartender. "There is a guy, Alan something, either Stone or Storm, who hasn't been around for quite a while.

Used to come in almost every night. Told me he wanted to sell his car. I had a friend who was interested. Tried to reach him a couple of times on the phone, but he never returned my calls."

"Hello. This is Sandy. I am not in at the moment, but leave a message at the sound of the beep, and I'll get back to you as soon as possible. If this is a client and you need to reach me, please call 347-8713."

"Sandy, this is Nick. I'm calling from the Denver airport. Just flew in from Albuquerque. Been nosing around a bit on Jebediah and have some info I think will interest you. I've got an early flight from here to Minneapolis tomorrow morning. Want to check up on Mary. I'll be at the Radisson and will try to reach you again from there. Talk to you soon."

Nick glanced at his watch while he waited for the reservation clerk at the Radisson Hotel. It wasn't yet ten A.M. Twin Falls, the town where Mary had lived, was almost at the Canadian border and Minnesota was a big state. It would probably take him most of the morning to drive there. If everything went smoothly, he thought he would be able to get back to Minneapolis by evening.

"Yes?" said the clerk.

"Barrows. First name, Nicholas. I reserved a single."

The clerk tapped at his computer terminal, then looked up. "Barrows, Nicholas. I see your name, but there's a little problem, sir. Your room reservation was canceled. About an hour ago. Unfortunately, we have a software convention in town and we're—"

"Canceled? There must be some mistake. I just made the reservation last night. Why would I have canceled it?"

Nick felt a tap on his shoulder, and turned around to face a woman with a shock of pale hair. "Sandy!" he said.

"I got your message—obviously," Sandy Price said, with a quick smile. "I was the one who canceled the room. I thought it would be better if we drove directly to Twin Falls and spent the night there, so I made reservations there for both of us. It's one hell of a long drive. Also, the roads near the town apparently are none too hot. It's nine hours up and back. At least."

"But how did you get here so—"

"You were traveling east and losing time. I was heading west and gaining on you. Plus, I got an early direct flight from D.C. Come on, we'll talk in the car."

Thompson's Funeral Home on Hazel Street in the center of Twin Falls looked exactly like its neighbors—white shingles, neat lawn, picket fence—except for a discreetly lettered sign halfway between the fence and the front door. The owner was cordial and readily agreed to look up his records on Mary Forbes.

"You asked if the body was cremated," he said to his two visitors, as he returned carrying a file folder. "The answer is yes, it was."

"How many days after it was found?" asked Nick.

"Three days later."

"Let me guess who claimed the ashes," said Nick. "It was her cousin."

The owner smiled broadly. "You're wrong, Mr. Barrows. It was her brother."

"Does this look like the fellow?" said Nick, showing him the snapshot of Jebediah.

The owner took the photograph and walked to the window behind his desk. He studied it for a few moments. "He's a bit older now, but I'd say that's him. Definitely."

12 Former attorney general Clayton Bosworth hated it when his schedule was thrown off. In the summer he reserved Wednesday mornings for mowing the lawn that wrapped around three sides of his Georgian home in Leesburg, Virginia, and for tending his flower beds. Though he employed a full-time household staff that included a cook, handyman, and housekeeper, he refused to hire a gardener because he insisted that nobody else could do the work the way it was supposed to be done.

But on this Wednesday he had had to attend a Board of Directors meeting of the Comtron Corporation, one of the six he sat on. As a former attorney general, he was a hot commodity in the world of corporate board rooms. His life as a board member produced a comfortable living without his working too hard, leaving him time for his memoirs and his passion for gardening. Comtron always sent a limousine to take him to and from the meetings (this was a special meeting of the board to vote on an acquisition), but the meeting hadn't ended until two and it was almost three-thirty when the car dropped him off.

Once he reached his bedroom, Clayton Bosworth quickly changed, dropping his clothes to the floor, as was his custom, and putting on the workclothes he used when he gardened. He had been a widower for almost eight years, and aside from dining alone most nights, his life had hardly changed. He was seventy-one and except for an extra fifteen pounds put on because his cook was a little too able with *tarte tatins* and peach cobblers, he was still strong, stood up straight, and had a ruddy complexion that made him look ten years younger than his age.

As he walked to the gardening shed at the back of the property, Bosworth inspected his lawn closely. He was ever vigilant for signs of moles. Their meandering burrows just under the lawn's surface left ridges like the raised scar tissue above a boxer's eyes. And then he spied something. He stopped, bent down, and carefully pulled out a solitary plantain weed.

The shed was the size of a small living room, the outside clapboarded and painted white to match the house. The walls were arrayed with tools, each in its assigned place, from spades to hoes, trowels to rakes. Each implement gleamed, since Clayton Bosworth insisted that his handyman clean every one of them immediately after he used it. Some of the tools he had bought when he was in law school and they still looked almost new. He despised throwing things away, ascribing it to his Scottish heritage. He couldn't stand this modern, "disposable" culture. "Buy something that's well-made, take good care of it, and you'll find that you'll fall apart first," he would always tell his children. And then a frown crossed his face. He was looking at his lawn mower.

He had owned it for over twenty years and it was in perfect shape. It was a traditional model. Bosworth couldn't stand the sight of men riding atop the newfangled ones, looking like so many self-satisfied children. His handyman oiled and sharpened the blade every other week. But the fool had left it turned the wrong way. Instead of being able to push it easily out of the shed, Bosworth had to awkwardly pull it backward. "Damn idiot," he muttered under his breath, as he struggled to move the mower out. He clanked it against the potting bench before he got it through the door and onto the lawn. He leaned down to inspect the damage. There was a small scratch near the front left wheel. A little paint would fix it up fine. He would still tell the handyman a thing or two about doing a chore the proper way. He would make sure to speak to him when he was finished. Now it was time to get to work. He grabbed the pull cord in his right hand, bracing himself against the mower with his left, and pulled. The explosion that resulted from the two pounds of Semtex that was packed under the machine broke windows five hundred feet away and dug a crater large enough to bury a full-size sedan. Clayton Bosworth's left hand, wedding band intact, was found the next day in a yew hedge that fronted a large brick house two blocks away.

13 Nick and Sandy sat side by side on two worn leatherette stools in the Stratosphere Lounge at the Minneapolis–St. Paul airport. The lounge had made a serious descent over the years and was now a rather shabby bar, filled with tired, bored travelers waiting for their flights. A television set with the sound off and a problem with its vertical control hung above the bar, showing a soap opera that no one was watching. Behind the bar several hot dogs that looked as if their shelf life had ended sometime during the Reagan years circled endlessly in a warming oven. A half-empty glass of ginger ale sat in front of Nick. It was almost flat. Nick stared at it, watching the occasional listless bubble coil up from the bottom. Sandy sat next to him, slowly twisting the stem of her glass of white wine as if she were winding a watch.

"I'll be back in a minute," Sandy said over her shoulder, as she got off the bar stool.

"Sure," answered Nick, without looking up.

He was trying to sort out his thoughts. Actually, he had been struggling to do that since they had left Twin Falls. What the hell was going on? If Jebediah and Mary did fake their deaths, why had they done it? What did the disappearance of all the other children mean? Were they all together somewhere? Could they really be behind Ed Trainor's death? The more he churned over these and other questions, the more uncertain and confused he felt. The "Hummock thing," as Nick always referred to it, had derailed him once already. Why should he have anything to do with it now? It had been poison four years ago, and poison doesn't lose much of its potency over time.

Nick started to signal the bartender for another ginger ale, when he saw the face of Tom Brokaw on the screen with a superimposed SPECIAL BULLETIN banner below.

"Excuse me," Nick called out to the bartender. "Could you please turn the sound on? I think something's happened."

The bartender aimed his remote at the set in time for Nick to hear Brokaw say, "... and our preliminary report has been confirmed that only former United States Attorney General Clayton Bosworth was killed in the explosion."

Some footage of Bosworth taken when he had testified before a Senate committee appeared on the screen.

"There was extensive damage to his home and others in the surrounding area. The explosion was apparently a very powerful one and the police have not given out, as of yet, any information on what caused it. Bosworth was an influential and prominent figure in two administrations. A tough, no-nonsense enforcer of the nation's laws, he had both admirers and detractors. He ..."

Sandy slid back onto her seat.

"What's going—"

"In a second," Nick muttered, holding up his hand.

"... The explosion apparently occurred just before four o'clock Eastern daylight time. Now, to recap: Clayton Bosworth, the former attorney general, was killed in a tremendous explosion at his home in Leesburg, Virginia. We will interrupt regular programming as more details become available.

"From New York, this has been Tom Brokaw for NBC News."

"Jesus," Sandy said finally, as the soap opera came back on the screen.

"I can't believe it."

"How did it happen? Who did it?" Sandy asked.

"They don't know."

They sat there for a few moments looking up at the rolling image of the soap opera, not really seeing it.

"That was your flight," Sandy finally said.

"What?"

"They just announced your flight. Gate twenty-seven. They're boarding now."

"I'm not taking it," Nick said, turning toward Sandy.

"I don't understand."

"I don't know if I do, either, but I'm coming with you to Washington. I have to see Phil LaChance."

 Riding into Washington from the airport with Sandy Price, Nick thought back to the last time he had been there, two years earlier. The occasion was to sign his divorce decree.

When he was banished to Tulsa, the only hold the city had had on him was his wife, Linda. Linda the lobbyist, first and foremost. Clever, attractive, persistent, and ever more successful, she'd built her client list to include cable, tobacco, mining, and logging interests. With close connections to some of the most powerful members of Congress, she performed wonders for all her clients. When she had landed the logging industry and began making frequent trips to the Northwest, they had talked about her stopping en route to Tulsa, but somehow, like most things in their marriage, it never happened.

Apart from the wedding itself, the day of purest satisfaction he had got from their relationship was the day he walked out on her. Linda, who hated to lose at anything, even to the point of holding on to a husband she neither loved nor needed, was shocked. When she had realized Nick had no intention of asking for money or a share of her property, her shock had given way to smiles. He could still hear her now: "You always were a gentleman, Nicholas. We were like a pair of beautiful trains pulling out of the station at the same time, but you headed in one direction, and I went in the other."

"Yeah," he had answered (and he still regretted his bitterness at the time), "that's true, but it was more like planes than trains. You went up and I headed down, and I haven't landed yet."

When he broke out of his reverie, Nick saw they were entering Georgetown. He looked at Sandy in surprise. "This isn't the way to the Hay Adams."

"You're right, it isn't, but you're the only one who believes me about the children. And I happen to know your salary won't pay for a room bigger than a linen closet at the Hay Adams, if that, so I thought you should stay with me instead. Okay?"

Before Nick could answer, Sandy pulled up in front of a small, handsome brick townhouse, framed by the driveway on one side and a low boxwood hedge on the other. "Pretty terrific, isn't it?" she said, seeing Nick's admiring look. "And I'll answer the question you're wondering about. How did I, a mere academic, swing it? I got lucky, is how. I could never have afforded it if it hadn't been a total wreck—not quite as bad as *Animal House*, but close, and it had been on the market for over a year. We—that's Peter and me—worked our tails off restoring it. I paid for the house, but when we split up I got his sweat equity, also. For keeps."

"It's beautiful."

"Thank you. You have the top-floor bedroom. I'll show you up. You'll meet Sarah and her nanny, Gina, tomorrow. Gina's part of the family. They've been staying at Gina's sister's in Bethesda while I've been out of town."

"Who's the gardener?" asked Nick, as he looked out a large window in the living room that faced the backyard.

"Another one of my secrets. I guess I'm a shrink with a green thumb instead of a green couch."

"What's that little shack for?" He gestured toward a small structure that was painted a bright red.

"Don't ever call it a shack around Sarah. That's her playhouse. It's her pride and joy. She practically lives in the place. Now, are you ready to climb some stairs?"

The next morning when Nick came downstairs, Sandy had already left. His first move after brewing a cup of strong coffee was to place a call to Phil LaChance's office. LaChance's appointments secretary told him the director could not possibly see him. He was tied up in emergency meetings all day. "Tomorrow?" Nick had asked. "No, I'm afraid not. No time at all." Nick could hear the pleasure at turning him down in her prissy tone of voice, and it took all the control he could muster—like refusing an ice-cold double Scotch Mist—not to slam down the phone.

After a moment of thought he telephoned Nelson Stagg. Stagg, too, was in a meeting, but Nelson called back within an hour.

"Nel," Nick said, "I need another favor."

"What now, Nick?"

"I have to see LaChance, and his tight-ass secretary won't give me an appointment. I'm on to something that may affect the Bosworth investigation. It's urgent. Can you get me in to see him?"

"Oh, man, not another urgent problem."

"Did you read the stuff you FedExed me?"

"No! I barely had time to copy it," answered Stagg, his voice rising. "What the fuck are you thinking? That I curled up with it like a good novel? Dickens, say? Or Thackeray?"

"If you had, you'd understand why I need to see LaChance."

"Look, this whole place is in an uproar over Bosworth's death. Particularly LaChance. Unless you have a very, very good reason—*ironclad*—to see him—"

"I do. I promise you, man."

"Okay," he said, with resignation. "I'll do what I can."

Later that day Stagg called to say that LaChance would see Nick for ten minutes at six-thirty the following day. He sounded weary. "Don't think it was easy getting that appointment. LaChance is under a tremendous amount of pressure over the Bosworth killing. I just hope you know what you're doing."

It was after eight P.M. the next day when LaChance's secretary, looking as if she smelled a dead rodent, finally led him into the director's office.

Phil LaChance stood up behind his desk and shook Nick's hand. "I looked for you after Ed Trainor's funeral, but you'd disappeared," he said.

"I'm sorry we missed each other," said Nick, playing the pleasantry game right back.

"Take a chair, Nick," said LaChance, gesturing expansively at the one nearest to him.

As he sat down, Nick glanced around the office. Next to LaChance's huge desk was a large, upright American flag, and on the wall above him, an inscribed, gold-plated golf club, but it was obviously the photographs, covering all table surfaces and most of the wall space, that mattered most to its occupant: LaChance with the president; playing golf with the veep; salmon-fishing with the director of the CIA; shaking hands with a dozen senators; receiving an award. On the corner of his desk was a photograph of his family—his wife, three kids, and the requisite yellow lab. Nick looked for a photograph of Ed Trainor, but he found none.

"I don't know if you're heard, but I've been in close touch with the local police in Florida about Ed's death," said LaChance. "They're confident they've got the kids who plowed into him. No confessions yet, but they'll be forthcoming. They both have records for stealing boats and one of them came within a hairsbreadth of a head-on collision last year. Be great to see their asses in jail. So . . . what's on your mind?"

"It has to do with the children released by Josiah Hummock before the explosion."

LaChance looked disgusted. "Haven't you had enough trouble from that Hummock business?"

"I guess I have, yes—but I've come upon something that might make a difference to you. I don't think anyone here has been tracking the children who were released, but I have, and some pretty strange things have happened."

Nick then laid out the story: How Sandy Price had discovered that all the kids who got out of Mesa Blanca before it blew up had disappeared in the last month, two apparently faking their deaths. How he thought the many threats Hummock had made toward government officials were now being systematically carried out by the kids. How Ed Trainor had been threatened and then had been the first to go. "And now Bosworth, whom I also heard Hummock vilify. The kids have taken care of him. With a nice bit of flair, I'd say," Nick couldn't resist adding. Bosworth had never been one of his favorites.

"This is bizarre," said LaChance. "What gives you this cock-eyed idea?"

"Because of what I just told you. I've checked it out. It may sound crazy but it makes sense."

"Well, it doesn't make sense to me. I think you've been in Oklahoma too long. It's hard for me to believe, but maybe even that backwater's too much pressure for you. You've had an excellent career, Nick, but I think you've plateaued."

"I'm not interested in talking about my career," said Nick, inwardly furious. "I want to talk about Trainor and Bosworth and who killed them. And who'll be next in line, unless we find a way to stop it."

"You'll probably resent me for having a lot more information on this than you, but I know who killed Bosworth."

"Well, who?"

"You'll hear this on the news tonight, probably while you're pouring your third or fourth drink, but we just received a communiqué this afternoon from a terrorist group called the Fertile Crescent—you know who they are, don't you?—taking credit for Bosworth's death. They used the same explosive material when they tried to assassinate our ambassador in Cairo last year. I don't see a clear connection to Bosworth yet, but we'll get to the bottom of it. Possibly it was his bureau's involvement in the prosecution of two of the Fertile Crescent terrorists during his last year as attorney general."

"I see," said Nick, feeling momentarily confused. LaChance was all wrong. He had to be.

"Nick," said LaChance, who had been watching him. "May I make a suggestion?" He paused, but Nick gave no answer. "You've had a good career, a fine career, but maybe it's time to step away, get your life in order. Maybe dust off your law degree and start something new." He paused again, then continued, his voice rising, "Nick, this whole Hummock episode has been your tar baby. It got you dirty once and you're begging to let it get you again. But I won't allow it to foul this agency! Do you understand? And if you don't, you'd better learn it real fast!"

part four

"He's
a danger
to our
mission."

1 "I sure hope you two have a big boat," said the fat clerk behind the counter. Her laugh sounded like the bark of a small dog.

"Oh, we do," said the young woman standing in front of her. "It's a houseboat. It has a huge deck and an awning so you don't get scorched. It belongs to my parents."

"It's fabulous," said the young man beside her.

"My, my," said the clerk, as she began punching the cash register to total the groceries the couple kept piling up at the checkout. Her round red face creased like a handkerchief as she smiled. Most of her customers stopped in for cigarettes or beer. A big purchase usually yielded change from a twenty-dollar bill. She couldn't remember when anyone had bought this much.

The Beatty Mini-Mart in the Nevada town of the same name sat halfway between Scotty's Junction and Stovepipe Wells on Route 95. To the east stretched hundreds of miles of high desert studded with mountain peaks that stood out like jacks tossed on a floor. The town, which was cradled in the Amargosa River Valley, looked west to Death Valley and the line of mountain ranges, the Grapevine and the Funeral, that marked its entrance.

"I think that's it," said the young woman, smiling.

"I should say," the clerk answered as she added the last item.

"Two hundred and eighty-one dollars even. You sure'll be able to stay out on the lake for a while."

"Some friends are coming along with us," the young man added.

"Hope they have good appetites."

"They have—and other things, too," said the young woman. She poked the man next to her in the ribs. "Right, Jerry?"

"Absolutely," said Jebediah, with a short nasty laugh, as if they were sharing a joke.

The clerk looked at them sharply. What a strange way to refer to friends.

As they were leaving with the last of over a dozen bags of groceries, the clerk called out to them, "Hope you have a fine time."

"I'm sure we will," said the man, holding the door open for Mary as the searing desert heat pushed in past them.

Must be just married, the clerk thought. *Certainly don't have a clue about how to shop. Imagine buying fourteen loaves of bread! They'll be stale before they're out on the lake two days.*

She watched them finish loading a Land Rover and then get in. The car had a fine coat of dust that puffed off as they drove away. "That's funny," she murmured aloud, as she watched it disappear down the road. They were heading in the opposite direction from the lake. They were driving toward Death Valley.

"Why'd you call me Jerry in there?" asked Jebediah angrily as the small store receded from view.

"That's the name you used in Chimayo."

"Well, I don't like it. I only use it when I have to."

Mary turned away from him without answering.

"Don't do it again," he added.

"Don't tell me what to do," said Mary, staring straight ahead.

They didn't see another car until they went through Daylight Pass. Jebediah had developed a taste for country, which Mary also liked, so they listened to a Garth Brooks tape. Since they rarely got annoyed with each other, this was a kind of truce. The road was paved as far as Stovepipe Wells, where they turned off onto an old mining road that disappeared after a few miles. Jebediah backed off the accelerator and eased the car up into the low hills. Both he and Mary felt especially good on market days. Though they drove to a different place to shop each time, sometimes making a round trip of two hundred miles, the idea that it was for the family was strong and pleasing. Everything was going as they knew it would. Of course, what sustained them all was their love for their Messiah, their father, Josiah Hummock.

They finally pulled up before an enormous shed made of corrugated aluminum, which gleamed in the sun. It was set in front of an old silver mine. Jebediah pressed the button on the sensor clipped to the visor, and the door rose. He drove inside. The shed housed five other vehicles, all new Jeeps and Land Rovers. A door led into the mine. They walked a hundred feet down a passageway where Jebediah slid back a heavy metal door. They both blinked as a flood of fluorescent light poured out at them.

Inside was a large room painted white and dominated by an immense blowup of Josiah Hummock. The youngest children sat facing a wall while they read the Bible. The six older ones were busy sweeping and cleaning the floor, working in the kitchen, and scrubbing the bathroom. There was no idle conversation as they bent to their tasks. Matthew, who was only a year younger than Mary, sat at a workbench in a corner, cleaning the carburetor from one of the vehicles. Two doors behind him led off to the sleeping quarters and the kitchen. The layout and the furnishings of the room were a mirror image of the rooms at Mesa Blanca.

"How'd it go?" asked Matthew, without looking up from his work.

"Fine," answered Mary. "Now, who's assigned to provisions this week?"

Matthew looked at a piece of paper tacked to the wall. "Solomon, Mark, and Rachel," he said, reading aloud. The three rose and went out the door toward the garage.

"That guy from the Bureau of Lands and Mining was here again," said Matthew.

"What time?" asked Jebediah.

"Little past eight."

"He say anything?"

"Wanted to see the permit and lease. Jebediah, didn't you show it to him last time?"

Jebediah rubbed his chin and then sat down.

"I did. I don't like it. Did he see any of the family?"

"No. Just me. Maybe he forgot you showed it to him."

"I'd like to believe that. We'll have to be real careful. Stay with the rules. The others can go out only after sunset." He took a small notebook from his jacket pocket and opened it. "I've been thinking of the next one." Mary and Matthew watched him closely. Though the young ones still appeared occupied, Jebediah knew they were listening.

"You changing plans?" Matthew asked.

"Yes. Dr. Price has gotten to Agent Barrows. He's begun to look around at where we've been. He's smart. He could be very dangerous to us. Josiah didn't think he was a bad man, just a misguided one. But things have changed. What do you think, Mary?"

"He's a danger to our mission."

"Matthew?"

"I agree. Barrows has to be next."

"Why're you leaving so soon?" asked Sandy, as she watched Nick come down the stairs, suitcase in hand.

It was the morning after his disastrous talk with

LaChance. The minute he woke, he had remembered the ugly scene in minute detail. It wasn't easy to push it back out of his mind.

"Believe it or not, I still have a job," answered Nick, almost curtly. "I've got to get back."

"Come on, Nick. It's Friday. Nobody's going to expect you back until Monday. Stay. It's supposed to be a beautiful weekend."

"My taxi's due in a moment."

"No, it isn't. I heard you calling, and I canceled it."

"Hey, don't I have a say around here?" said Nick, half smiling.

"No, I'm the boss."

"All right, boss. What's on the agenda?"

"A wonderful drive, but not to the airport."

"Then I'll cancel my flight, but"—Nick eyed Sandy closely—"you took care of that, too. Right?"

"You're clairvoyant." She hesitated. "I hate myself for saying this, but it occurred to me the reason you wanted to get to the airport was to knock back a couple of double Scotch Mists in the ultimate privacy of an airport bar."

Nick frowned. "That's a low blow. You know that's over."

"I'm sorry, but don't you realize people are sometimes unfairest to those they care for? . . . Can we agree on one thing, though? Postpone your departure until tomorrow."

"All right, I'll do it."

"Let's get out of this house, then. I know a terrific place in Annapolis for crab cakes."

The crab cakes were every bit as good as Sandy promised.

"Have you ever tried to make these?" she asked, when their order arrived. "It's like trying to make snowballs out of powder snow. They fall apart as soon as you coax them into the right shape."

They were seated at one of a dozen tables scattered over the length of a dock that reached from the grounds of the old inn behind them, out over the water. They were at the edge of the Chesapeake, and a light breeze off the bay cooled them, but they had lingered and the sun had moved, causing the shade of the umbrella to fall on the deck rather than across their table. Sandy wished she had her straw hat. While they waited for dessert, she would run to the car and get it, she told Nick, but he would have none of it. He would do the errand.

"And when I get back, you'll tell me more about the Delaware congressman, right?" The former loves in their lives was a subject they had been circling warily since Nick had arrived in Washington.

Sandy smiled noncommittally. "Maybe," she said.

When he returned, Nick asked her if she minded talking about her ex-boyfriend.

"I don't think so. Not half as much as you seemed to be bothered by talking about Linda the other night."

"She's a bitch. Was, is, and always will be."

"Well, Peter Hayes is not a bitch, that's one thing," said Sandy. "He's smart, funny, fantastically well-read, great company, and a truly able congressman. I'm positive he'll become a senator someday, and from there he'll go on to even bigger things. You watch."

"If you feel that way, why the hell isn't he sitting in this chair instead of me?"

Sandy looked at Nick steadily. "That's only half of Peter's story—the public part. Privately he's a mess. No, that's too strong a word. He's inconsistent . . . totally self-absorbed—and incapable of making or honoring a commitment: everything from returning a phone call to showing up at the theater for a play that took me a month to get tickets for. Oh, sometimes he'd be there for me, but most times he wouldn't. And it wasn't because of his congressional schedule. It's just the way he is. I could never count on him. For anything. He used to drive me crazy . . . because I loved him." Her words were almost inaudible.

"What are we doing, sitting around and talking about these characters?" said Nick after a beat. "Our sorbets have melted and our drinks are finished."

"So let's get the bill and go," said Sandy.

"There is no bill."

"What do you mean?"

"I took care of it. Your bossy habits are catching," said Nick, grinning. "The difference is, you cancel things. I did the opposite. This is too nice a place to leave immediately, so when I picked up your hat I stopped at the front desk and made reservations for us to spend the night."

"How very bold of you!"

"It's for two singles. Down the hall from each other."

"How very proper. But I don't have any—"

"Toothpaste? What do you think all-night drugstores are for?"

That night, after dinner, they sat on the terrace, gazing across the bay at the smattering of lights blinking like fireflies, from the small towns on the opposite shore. There was no more talk of Nick's former wife, or of the congressman, or of Hummock and the children. That afternoon, after a drive through the grounds of the Naval Academy, they had walked for a couple of hours along the beach that ran south of the inn, and though it was early, they were both happy and tired. Without saying anything they both knew it was time to get some sleep.

Upstairs, Nick saw Sandy to her room. They stood by her door for a moment, silent, then Nick pulled Sandy closer and embraced her. Still holding her tight, he looked into her face.

"May I come in?" He asked softly.

Sandy hesitated, then shook her head. "I wish . . . but . . ."

"You're right. I understand."

They kissed again and Sandy slipped into her room, quietly closing the door behind her.

The next day Sandy drove Nick to Dulles. At the main terminal, Nick removed his bags from the trunk, then came around to the driver's side and leaned in.

"Let me park this and I'll walk to the gate with you," said Sandy.

"No, this is easier. I don't think I can handle a good-bye at the gate."

"Nick . . . What's next?"

"The first and most important thing is that I have to see you again very, very soon," he said, bending down and kissing her. "I want you to know something else, though, that's important. I'm not going to quit on you. We have to find out what happened to the children. No more no shows, like that time at the Tulsa airport. I'm here for you on this. I know you're right. Something scary is going on. We have great computer research systems at headquarters that I can access even from my Oklahoma outpost. I'm going to use it and anything else I can lay my hands on, and to hell with LaChance."

When he reached the terminal doors, he turned to look back at Sandy. The taxi driver behind her was leaning on his horn, but she was paying no attention. Her eyes were locked on Nick.

3 As he inserted the key in the front door of his house, Nick kicked aside a week's worth of newspapers and flyers that spread across the mat like a small compost heap. He glanced down and saw the usual announcements of yard sales and church suppers. When he had lived in Washington, the only giveaways he had received were menus from Chinese restaurants which, in turn, had given rise to the strange signs—NO MENUS— taped to most doors. "Welcome back to Tulsa," he said under his breath, as he pushed open the door.

"Excuse me, sir."

Nick turned and saw two young girls, one a little older than the other, standing a few feet away. They were wearing baseball uniforms—and could have taught a Navy Seal a thing or two about sneaking up on the enemy, Nick thought, as he smiled down at them. They had actually given him a start.

"What can I do for you, ladies?"

The two looked back toward the street where a young woman, probably their mother, sat behind the wheel of a Jeep. Nick couldn't make out her face because a large, floppy brimmed hat obscured it. He saw her give the girls an encouraging wave.

"We're raising money for the Girls' Little League."

"An eminently worthy cause. What positions do you play?"

"We're just learning. We don't have positions yet."

"Who's your favorite player?"

They smiled up at Nick nervously for a moment before one of them thrust forward a small box gaily wrapped in green paper with a row of sugar-dusted doughnuts showing through a cellophane covering.

"Would you like to buy some doughnuts?"

"They're very good," the second girl chimed in.

"I really should watch my weight," said Nick, reaching for his wallet. "How much are they?"

"Five dollars a box."

"That sounds very reasonable. I'll take two."

"Well . . . we only have a few boxes left," said the girl holding one box out to him, "and I think we have to give some other people a chance to buy."

"That's good thinking," he answered, as he handed them the money.

"Thank you very much, sir," the two said in unison, and then skipped back to the car.

As Nick was about to close the door behind him he noticed the Jeep drive off. *They must have finished working this block*, he thought, as he walked into the darkened living room. After throwing his jacket on the couch he went over to the answering machine and hit the play button.

"You have . . . twenty-three messages," said the electronic voice.

"Thanks, old buddy. I'll bet half of them are trying to sell me a great new stock or a subscription to *Newsweek*."

He pressed the fast-forward button and skipped to the last three messages. If there were any that were important, that's where he would find them.

"Message twenty, Saturday, nine-seventeen A.M.," droned the metallic voice.

"Nick, where are you?" It was his secretary, Maria Lozano. *"Kevin really has the hots to see you. Call me as soon as you get in. I've been hearing things. Did you really go to D.C. and see LaChance? We have to talk. 'Bye."*

Nick hit the button again. It was another call from Maria. An hour later. He would call her as soon as he had got something to drink.

In the refrigerator his old drinking life stared back at him: a half bottle of Absolut and two six-packs of Coors. *Thank God for mixers,* he thought, as he grabbed a bottle of tonic water. He was headed back to the machine to retrieve the rest of the messages when the doorbell rang.

"Welcome back," said Maria, as Nick opened the door. She reached up and gave him a kiss on both cheeks. Maria was short, with lustrous black hair that tumbled over her shoulders. Standing behind her was her husband, Joe Raven, a Tulsa cop who she had met within two weeks of moving out here with Nick. Joe was half Zuni and half Irish, and still looked like the linebacker he had been in junior college. The two followed Nick into the kitchen. He opened two beers for them, then plopped down into one of the chairs. In one sense he felt good—no, great. There was Sandy, and she had suddenly become very important. And, for the first time in so very long a time, he felt he was really doing something, something that mattered. But he was also dog-tired. The traveling, the emotional ups and downs. He would sleep well tonight.

"Now, what's happening?" he asked Maria after a moment.

"Kevin was asking for you all day Friday. I kept telling him I didn't have your number, you're away on family business, yadda yadda yadda. But he kept coming back. I don't know how many times he said it was a violation of the rules that you didn't leave a number where you could be reached."

Kevin Hornsby, headquartered in Oklahoma City, was the special agent in charge of Nick's district. A straight-arrow, born-again Christian with five children under the age of ten, he was a decent man who played everything by the book and always ran scared.

"Give me the rest, Maria."

"Well, I found out that LaChance called him three times."

"Thank God for the secretarial underground. So the good director is suddenly interested in our little Tulsa office. How nice."

"Say, Nick, mind if I take one?" asked Joe, as he spotted the box of doughnuts.

"Be my guest."

Maria reached out and lightly slapped her husband's hand.

"Joe. Stop that. You promised me. No snacks."

"I just want one, Maria," he answered in his best little boy's tone.

"Come on, I said no." She turned toward Nick. "He's like a kid. If it's sweet, he wants it."

"You're no slouch around doughnuts, either, honey."

"So LaChance called Kevin three times. I have an idea what that's about."

"Am I going to have to find a new boss, Nick?" asked Maria, trying to smile.

"No. We're like Beavis and Butt-head. A team. I might need to take some more days off, but that's about it."

"Well, that's a relief," she said, sighing.

"Hon, remember the game," said Joe, pointing to his watch.

"We have to go, Nick. I promised Joe his tube time and that's one thing that can't be compromised," Maria said, with a laugh.

"Take the doughnuts, Joe. They'll just get stale here."

"Gee, thanks, Nick."

"The pleasure's mine . . . and the Girls' Little League of Greater Tulsa."

An hour after Maria and Joe left, the phone rang. Nick picked it up on the second ring.

"Hello . . . Hello . . . Who's this? . . . Hello?"

He held the phone another ten seconds. He could sense that someone was on the other end. *Some jerks get off on this*, he thought, as he replaced the receiver. Twenty minutes later the phone rang again. Same thing. This time he said, "Hello?" just once and then listened for thirty seconds. "Screw you, creep," he muttered, slamming the phone down.

When he finished unpacking and looking through the mail, he remembered he had forgotten to tell Maria about changing his morning schedule. He dialed her number. The phone rang and rang. Maybe he had misdialed. He punched the numbers again. Still no answer. Nick looked at his watch. The game still had to be on. He tried again. After ten rings he hung up. There was no real reason to be worried, but he was. They could have stopped off somewhere else first, of course, but Nick felt there was something wrong. He put on his jacket and headed out.

Maria and Joe lived in a small ranch house about five miles away. When he pulled up in front, he saw Joe's car in the driveway. Nick leaned on the front doorbell, then started banging on the door. Nothing. He walked around to the back where he found a kitchen window open, and climbed in. Except for a sports announcer's voice coming from the television set, the house was quiet. He followed the sound to the living room. There sprawled on the couch in front of the television, were Maria and Joe.

Nick checked them both and saw they were breathing unevenly. Their lips were tinged blue like children who've been in cold water too long. He dashed to the phone and called 911. As he turned back to Maria and Joe, he noticed the doughnut box, almost empty. He removed the two doughnuts that remained and pocketed them, then anxiously waited for the EMS to arrive.

4 "Hi, Bev. I have to see Kevin," said Nick to Kevin Hornsby's secretary.

"He wants to see you, too, Nick. Go right in."

Hornsby looked up and motioned him to a chair as he finished a phone call, but Nick was too excited to sit, so he paced between the desk and window until Kevin hung up the phone.

"Take a look at this," said Nick, waving a piece of paper as if it were a winning lottery ticket. He pushed it across the desk.

"You were supposed to be here two hours ago," Hornsby said, the anger in his voice tightening his words.

"Sorry about that. I had to stop at the lab first. And there was a lot of traffic between Tulsa and here. You'll understand everything when you take a look at the report."

"I didn't give authorization for any report," he responded angrily.

"Screw the authorization, Kevin. Just look at it, for Christ's sake," Nick said hotly.

"What am I looking at?"

"It's an analysis of some doughnuts I bought from two kids posing as Little Leaguers."

"I don't follow you."

"There was enough atropine in them to kill a marching band.

My secretary Maria and her husband got to them first. Luckily I found the two of them in time. They're at Metro General and they'll be fine. But it was meant for me. The Hummock kids just tried to kill me."

"Whoa! Slow down. I don't want to talk about doughnuts. You have a big problem that has nothing to do with any damn—excuse my language—doughnuts."

"What's the big problem, Kevin? I'm sure it dwarfs this. After all, I'm only talking about a potential conspiracy to assassinate former government officials."

"You were way out of line in going to see the director, Nick. Believe me, he wasn't happy about it."

"That's too bad."

"He recommends, and I agree, that you should take some time off. With pay, of course. We'll call it a medical leave."

"I don't need a leave."

"There's no room here for argument. As of now, you're off duty."

Nick stared at Kevin Hornsby. It would be so easy for Nick to let all the anger and frustration that had been building in him for so long, to burst out now, like hot magma indiscriminately scorching whatever it touched. But Hornsby wasn't the problem. He was just a foot soldier for LaChance. Basically he was a decent guy with a family who wanted to do a good job. Nothing would be gained by erupting now. And Nick realized that maybe this reprimand from LaChance could work for him. A month off to devote himself to finding the Hummock children—this could be just what he needed.

"You know, Kevin," he said, reaching across the desk to shake Hornsby's hand, "I think you might be right. I have been pushing it a bit lately. Maybe I need some perspective on this whole Hummock business."

"Now you're talking, Nick. The director will be glad to hear you're seeing it this way."

"Yes, I do think some time away from here will be good. Maybe I'll travel a bit. See some old friends. Relax. That's just the ticket I need. Thanks, Kevin."

With that, smiling, and with a bounce in his step, Nick Barrows walked out of the office.

5 The front doorbell rang at five o'clock sharp. For all the messiness of his private life, being prompt was something Congressman Peter Hayes prided himself on. When he was late for the theater, say, or didn't show up at all, it was a conscious decision, not forgetfulness or trying to cope with too many commitments. His first commitment, his priority always, was his career.

And his career was flourishing. In the three years since they had gone their separate ways, Sandy had run into Peter at half a dozen receptions, though when they were face-to-face they found it difficult to begin a conversation. Recently he had been appointed to the House Internal Affairs Committee and had started appearing with some frequency on C-SPAN and the talking-heads shows— signs of a rising star.

When Nick left Tulsa, he immediately returned to Washington and Sandy's top-floor bedroom. It would be hard to say which of them was the more angry and frustrated. What could they do next? Was there a "next"? One evening, after a few days of brooding, Nick had had an idea. "Why don't you call Peter? Peter Hayes," he had said.

"Why?" asked Sandy.

"You've told me more than once he's doing fabulously. He certainly has some power. Hell, even I've seen the creep on television."

"If he's such a creep—"

"Stop right there. I want you to appreciate that I'm not thrilled at the prospect of meeting him. But he may be our best bet right now. We need to get some people in government to realize what's going on. He could be extremely helpful. In any case, he'll take your call. And agree to see us. I hope I'm right about that."

"Of course you are," Sandy had said, and had dialed Peter Hayes's office before she could change her mind. And now here he was at the front door.

"Hi, Peter, come in," said Sandy, watching him look around the living room, almost as soon as he stepped in the house, to see what might have changed since he had last been there. "Thanks for stopping by."

"Happy to do it, Sandy," he said, squeezing her hand and kissing her lightly on the cheek, "but I can't stay for long."

"I know. The Gridiron Dinner. And look at you in your tails. You certainly look impressive."

"My opinion exactly. Had this cutaway tailored for me. I see more and more opportunities in my future to wear it."

"Oh, yes?" said Sandy, raising an eyebrow.

"Okay, it's rented. But it does look pretty good, if I do say so myself."

Sandy wasn't sure she agreed with him. It gave him too much frontage. In a number of ways Peter was almost the physical opposite of Nick: He was of medium height with a big frame (and appetite) and fair skin. His light brown hair was beginning to thin, something that was not obvious in his televised appearances, but it didn't detract from his boyish looks. Sandy sensed he was still trading on his youth and, though the reverse was actually true, Peter looked younger than Nick, whose dark eyes, intensity, and emotional roller-coaster rides made him seem older.

"Sarah's having supper now, but before I tell you why I called you, I want her to say hello. She wasn't supposed to be here, but her playdate was canceled. We'll talk quietly, though. I mentioned my friend Nick to you on the phone. He's staying here for a few days and he'll be right down. What would you like to drink?"

"Club soda with lots of ice," said Peter. "I see what's different in this room. You finally finished stripping the mantel. It's beautiful."

"Well, I had some help—I hired somebody."

"And did you re-cover something in here? Maybe that chair by the fireplace?"

"You always had a good eye, Peter."

Sandy pushed in the door to the kitchen. "Come and say hello to Peter, sweetheart," she said to Sarah.

"I want to finish my mashed potatoes. Gina loves them and she'll eat mine if I come in now."

When Sarah didn't make a move to get up, Sandy took the child's hand and led her into the living room.

Gina, who lived in and took care of the little girl, followed them to the living room, straightening her long dark hair with her hands. She had been a major find for Sandy. Before Mesa Blanca, Sandy had met her, then only eighteen, working in a street program for abused children. Gina, whose parents were violent alcoholics, was a graduate of the program. She was so bright and intuitive, and so well-balanced, that she soon began helping out Sandy on other research projects.

"Hey, Mr. Congressman, how're we doing?" Gina said to Peter, with a cool smile. He nodded back to her as he reached down to give Sarah the practiced hug of a politician, warm but not too warm.

Standing beside Peter, Sandy thought he might be thinking the same thing she was. The arrival of Sarah had effectively ended their flirtation with marriage. Peter was more than aware that having a pretty, personable wife like Sandy was a big plus for a politician, but he didn't want his wife to come with a family in tow—and possibly damaged goods as well, with consequences he might not be able to control.

When Sarah and Gina returned to the kitchen, Sandy shut the door firmly and turned up the volume on Chet Baker.

"Before Nick comes down, I want to tell you something—the reason I called."

"I just wish you called me more often, Sandy," he said, as he sat down on the sofa, carefully moving the tails of his jacket to the sides.

"I'm very frightened."

"What's wrong?"

"Someone tried to kidnap Sarah. From her school. It was all worked out. It's a miracle they didn't succeed."

"What did they do?"

"We'll fill you in in a moment. The main thing is they didn't pull it off."

"What are the police doing?"

"Investigating," she said angrily. "They refuse to believe I know who did it."

With the stereo turned up, neither Sandy nor Peter heard Nick enter the room.

"Am I early?" Nick asked.

"No, come on in. Peter, this is Nick Barrows. Nick and I met four years ago when he headed up the FBI's operation at the Hummock compound."

"I think I remember you," the congressman said to Nick.

"You obviously remember what happened there," said Sandy.

"The explosion? Of course. A terrible business. Lots of people dead, and so unnecessary, but I haven't thought much about it since then."

"That's the problem. Nobody has."

"But why should anyone? It was four years ago. It's history."

"But it isn't," said Sandy. "I think you'll understand why, after Nick gives you the whole story."

"I never wanted to get involved in the Hummock stuff again," Nick began. "It was the last thing I wanted to do."

Nick spoke for fifteen minutes. When he finished, there was a long silence. "Isn't it clear?" said Nick finally. "We really need your help."

"We absolutely do," said Sandy. "We've gone about as far as we can by ourselves. We need you."

"What's this got to do with me?" asked Peter.

"Everything, or nothing," answered Nick. "It's up to you. I've taken a month's leave of absence from the Bureau, but—"

"The Bureau, the FBI! It's their ball game, not mine. People in my state don't care what happened four years ago on the other side of the country."

"They *will* care," said Nick. "As I said, I really believe these kids are responsible for killing Ed Trainor and Clayton Bosworth. They even made an attempt on my life."

"Well, I'm sorry to hear that, but that cult has nothing to do with my constituents in Delaware."

"You're wrong, Peter," said Sandy. "From what we've told you, wouldn't you say the FBI botched the job of tracking this?"

"Well, yes, but—"

"And don't you intend to run for the Senate soon?"

"I have been talking to my people about the possibility, that's true."

"Just being a big-shot congressman in Delaware isn't enough. You know that. You want to be as well-known outside your state as in, right? That's how you really raise campaign money. This'll give you the kind of boost you only dream about. It's not a local issue. It's national. And it involves kids. You're perfectly situated in your committee to take it on and I guarantee it will raise your profile— way up! You'll become an expert on a subject that won't go away; that can't be wished away. Isn't it all you've been looking for, in fact?"

Sandy's words hung in the air for what seemed like minutes, before Peter hauled himself out of the depths of the sofa and stood up. "You may have something here," he said, after another pause, looking from Sandy to Nick. "I believe you do. Let me think about it for a few days, and I'll be back in touch. Now"—he looked at his watch—"I'm off to the Gridiron."

6

The crowd inside the Capital Hilton for the annual Gridiron Dinner was in a festive mood. The men, all in cutaways, moved in the tentative way that people wearing Rollerblades do the first time they put them on. Peter Hayes adjusted his collar and smoothed the lapels of his rented outfit. Fortunately, he was a perfect forty regular and his rented ensemble looked as if it might actually be his.

As he moved toward one of the bars flanking each wall, he spotted Phil LaChance at the head of a long line in front of it. He shouted out his name. LaChance turned, saw who it was, and waved.

"How about getting a light scotch for me? I'll meet you over there," Peter continued, pointing to a quiet corner near the entrance to the ballroom. In a few minutes LaChance appeared, holding two drinks.

"Always ready to help a servant of the people," LaChance said, clicking his glass against Hayes's.

"You really run a full service agency, Phil. I'll never argue over your funding again," Peter replied with a laugh. "Everything going well?"

"Pretty much so. What'd you think of the press we got on the Utah train derailment? Didn't take us long to nail them."

"Your people did a first-rate job. You know, I was going to ring you up, about something that my staff brought to my attention. It's about the Hummock clan."

"What about them?" LaChance asked, as he took a long swallow from his drink.

"It seems the surviving children all disappeared from their homes at about the same—"

"Your people have been talking to Nick Barrows, haven't they?" asked LaChance, no longer smiling. "Did he tell them he's on medical leave?"

"What do you mean?"

"I had him placed on a thirty-day medical leave just last week. His recent conduct has been of great concern to both me and the field agent in charge of his district. He's been obsessed with the Hummock case. It's ruined his career, his life, and, I'm sorry to say, his health. He has a real drinking problem. I bet he told them the kids killed Ed Trainor and Clayton Bosworth. . . . Well, didn't he?"

"He might have mentioned a suspicion he had—"

"He's running around telling everyone there's a conspiracy going on. Kids assassinating former top officials of the government? Give me a break! He should be writing for the *X-Files*, for Christ's sake. The man needs help. If you get involved with this, Peter, you're asking for trouble. Take it from me, you'll lose a lot of credibility real fast."

"He didn't mention to us he was on medical leave."

"Of course he didn't. Let me tell you something else about Nick Barrows. Remember those two reporters who made their careers on the Hummock tragedy?"

"Bernie Willis and—"

"Fran Marcum. That's them. Big book contract, Pulitzer prize, the whole schmear. You know, we had an internal inquiry afterward on how the two of them were getting inside information that only we possessed. Well, we couldn't prove it, but everything pointed to Barrows. He was leaking on his own operation!"

"Are you sure—"

"Mr. Vice President," LaChance called out as Big Jim Avery, bookended by Secret Service, passed by. "I got to say something to the veep. Talk to you soon, Peter," said Phil LaChance, darting off in Avery's direction.

Peter Hayes stood in place, motionless, drink in hand, until Rob Chapman, an Assistant Secretary of State for European Affairs, and his wife came over and started to chat with him. Hayes was so rattled by what LaChance had told him, that it was only as the Chapmans left him that he remembered he had been to their house in Chevy Chase for dinner the week before. He quickly caught up with them and thanked them for a truly enjoyable dinner and then headed to the bar for another drink.

7 Whenever it was a moonless night, they left the mine and hiked two miles up to the top of a steep ravine. They walked at a good pace, the young ones at the rear. They all carried walking sticks, each cut to their own size. They didn't use flashlights, so every few minutes one of them would stumble. The young ones fell most often but they knew better than to complain. They just got up and continued on. They walked in single file, Jebediah leading the way, followed by Mary, then Matthew. No one talked, for the most important part of the hike was to move as quietly as possible. Stealth was a vital part of their training. They worked out every day, even the little ones, for at least an hour, so when they reached the top they weren't breathing hard.

Suddenly Jebediah stopped.

"Caleb."

Jebediah's voice sounded immense in the stillness of the dark desert night.

"Yes," Caleb answered from the middle of the line.

"Step forward."

"Why, Jebediah?"

"I said come here. Now."

"I haven't done anything," he said, in a small, frightened voice.

Matthew stepped over to the boy and roughly grabbed him and pushed him forward.

"It's time to confess, Caleb!" shouted Jebediah, clutching the boy's shirt, his face inches away.

"For what?" Caleb asked, trembling.

Jebediah pulled a crumbled sheet of paper from his pocket and jammed it into Caleb's face.

"Why did you write this?"

Mary shined a flashlight into Caleb's face. He blinked his eyes then stared at the ground. "A letter to Mommy?" she said. "You miss her? The love of Josiah isn't enough for you?"

"When were you going to mail the letter, Caleb?" asked Matthew. "The next time we went to town for supplies?"

"I wasn't going to mail it. I just wrote it because . . . because I was lonely."

"When you believe in Josiah, you're never lonely," said Mary, who kept the beam trained on Caleb.

"You were going to mail it, weren't you, Caleb?"

"No, Jebediah. I wasn't. I'm telling the truth."

"Mailing that letter would have given away where we are. You could have ended our mission."

"You know what the punishment is for betraying the family, don't you, Caleb?"

"It's not fair," said the young boy, crying now. "I didn't do anything."

Jebediah clapped his hands and the young ones formed a circle around Caleb.

"Run, Caleb," Jeremiah shouted.

"Yes, run," said Mary.

"You have to run," said Matthew, joining in.

And then the young ones began to strike Caleb across the legs with their walking sticks.

"Run, run, run," they shouted in unison.

Caleb turned and ran. The group followed, chanting, "Run. Run, Caleb. Run." He fell roughly to the ground and the young ones were on him before he could get to his feet. "Run, run," they bellowed, as they beat him with their sticks. They lashed at his legs and body, the noise of the sticks striking his flesh sounding in the vastness of the valley like applause from hell. He tried to plead but then Mary hit him across the mouth; teeth broke off with the speed of a finger snap. He pulled himself up and started running again. He knew he had to get away, so he ran as fast as he could, falling again and again. Each time, the group fell upon him and beat him with remorseless efficiency. Caleb rose unsteadily and stumbled on, the group right behind him.

"Why aren't you running, Caleb?" they shouted. "You have to run. Run!"

He finally fell down at the lip of a steep ravine. They knew he wasn't going to get up this time.

"Please," he whispered, his mouth awash in blood. The group stared down at him. "Don't hit me . . . any . . . more. I love . . . Josiah."

"You don't love Josiah," shouted Jebediah.

"You love the devil," said Matthew. "He's your father, not Josiah."

"Caleb loves the devil," echoed the young ones.

"Let's help Caleb find his father," said Mary as she dug her stick into Caleb's midsection and started to push him closer to the edge. The others joined her. And then the earth fell away from Caleb. He was barely able to scream as he dropped down into the ravine. They stood there for a long time before Jebediah turned and started to walk back to the mine. No one spoke, but they all knew that Josiah was with them. They had done what he wanted them to do.

8 From a back booth at the Shanghai Dragon, Nick Barrows looked up every few minutes from his newspaper to see if Nelson Stagg had arrived. Nelson always ran late. He hadn't wanted to meet at all until he remembered this obscure, out-of-the-way spot in D.C.'s Chinatown. It looked like the kind of place where operatives in film noir movies passed secrets. The only difference was that it was well-lighted, and instead of wine bottles on the tables there were small containers of soy sauce.

After twenty minutes, Nelson materialized in the entrance to the restaurant. He was short and overweight, with a round, good-natured face and a prominent nose. He wore his black hair cut so close to his scalp that it appeared as if it had a perpetual five-o'clock shadow. After carefully surveying the other customers in the restaurant, he walked toward Nick.

"Good to see you, man," said Nick, smiling as Nelson slid into the booth. "I know you have reason to worry, but I swear I'm not Aldrich Ames."

Nelson did not laugh. "Yeah, I'd probably run less of a risk meeting him. You wouldn't be so amused if you had LaChance hanging over your shoulder and haunting your dreams. Now he's saying that anyone—and I swear he was looking at me when he said it—anyone caught talking with you will be sent to Nome, not Tulsa. *Nome.* I don't know what's set him off again. But, hey," he continued, breaking out of his mood, "you're looking good."

Nick, surprised, sat up a bit straighter and reflexively tightened his gut. "I've sort of become a yuppie. I go to a gym now, run every morning, and I've stopped drinking. I haven't taken up carrot juice yet, but I may, just for a change. Listen, the reason I called you is I've reached a dead end on the Hummock kids. I need more info. I've studied the files you gave me I don't know how many times, and there are huge gaps. Things are missing. I know it."

"That was all that was there, Nick. If there's anything else,

LaChance vacuumed it up a long time ago and he's been sitting on it ever since."

"I can believe that. He's capable of anything," said Nick, keeping his anger down. Then he added, "I thought a little while ago we were going to be able to jump-start the investigation with Peter Hayes, Sandy's ex-boyfriend—you know, the congressman from Delaware."

"Mr. C-SPAN. I see him all the time."

"Yeah, that's him. He heard us out, saw the benefit to himself to hold hearings, said he'd get back to us in a few days, but that was over a week ago."

A waiter in a bright green jacket with an assortment of stains that resembled a Jackson Pollock painting approached the table.

"Let's order," said Nelson. "I got the menu memorized, so if you don't mind I'll tell him what we want. First," he said to the waiter, almost trembling with pleasure, his fears about being observed by LaChance's spies drowned in the cascade of delicious odors coming from the kitchen, "we'll start with soup buns—you're going to love these, Nick, a fabulous variation on dumplings, a Shanghai specialty—and then we'll split a couple of main courses. Sautéed string beans and crispy beef and sea bass with ginger. Okay with you?"

Nick nodded.

"And chopsticks," Nelson shouted to the waiter as he retreated.

"This is what I wanted to tell you," said Nick. "Something happened to me when I got back to Tulsa. It started out so innocently—and I fell for it. I can't believe it, but I did. Maybe the Bureau *should* put me out to pasture . . . permanently."

Then Nick told Nelson about the Little Leaguers in uniforms and the doughnuts. "Can you believe it?" he said, his voice rising. "The Hummock kids tried to poison me!"

"You're joking."

"I wish I were. Those doughnuts were loaded with atropine. It would have done the job. Killed me! They're going after everyone on some list they have. A death agenda. God knows how many are on it. They've got to be stopped."

Nelson looked stunned. "This is awful."

Nick laughed in spite of himself. "Now you're finally hearing me, Nelson. At last."

The waiter arrived with the soup buns steaming in a bamboo basket, and the conversation ceased. Nelson was in his element, his eyes gleaming like a kid eyeing his Christmas presents under the tree. "This is how you eat them," he said. "Place the bun in your spoon. Bite off the little twist at the top that seals it, let it cool a sec, and then sip and eat. Voilà, you will experience an ambrosia that will make you forget all your woes."

The two friends fell silent as they consumed the food.

When he finished, Nick spoke again. "Back to the real world. I've got a new angle to pursue. Money. I asked myself how these kids are paying for the groceries—and the plastique: with money that Hummock put away for them! When they left the compound, he must have told them where it was stashed. If I can locate the money, maybe I can trace it back to the kids."

"Makes sense, but I have nothing more to give you. Remember, back at headquarters during the siege we were only interested in getting the children out and getting our hands on the weapons inside. We didn't care where Hummock got his money."

"I was afraid you'd say that."

"You get anything out of that book on Hummock?" Nelson asked.

"You mean by those fucking reporters?"

"Yeah, the two who always seemed to know things they shouldn't have known."

"They were in the know for a very good reason. Someone was feeding them. I never could find out who it was. After it was over, I didn't want to have anything to do with them, though I did read their so-called reportage. Sensationalist shit. Nothing else," said Nick with contempt.

"That's their reputation."

"Brenda Rawlins," said Nick, after a beat.

Nelson gave him a puzzled look.

"You remember, Brenda Rawlins of the Rawlins Brake and Engine family. She was the poor, misguided soul who gave Hummock the big money. Twenty million, I think it was. Maybe the parents know something about where Hummock put it. Maybe there's still a trail."

"It's possible, Nick. I think it's worth going for."

"First I have to find them," said Nick, thinking aloud, "where they live."

"With a corporation that size, it shouldn't be difficult."

"Or maybe it's in that fucking book. I'm pretty sure I saw it sitting on a shelf in Sandy's study."

The minute they had finished, Nelson stood up. "I have to get back," he said. "Let me know how it goes, and if you want to talk to me, call me at home. *Home*. Got it? By the way, wasn't this food great? Now, wait here five minutes or so. We shouldn't walk out together."

Before he headed for the door, Nelson leaned down and whispered to Nick. "You know what they say about really good Chinese restaurants?"

"What?"

"Never—I mean, *never*—look in the kitchen," said Nelson, and then he was out the door.

9 When he returned to Sandy's house after lunch, Nick went directly to the study, where she kept her research, books, and papers on the Hummock children, and removed a copy of *The Evil Messiah* from the shelf. It seemed odd to see Fran Marcum's and Bernie Willis's names sharing the cover of a book. Bitter rivals united in print. Nick reasoned that each had needed information that the other had and thus the collaboration. It had proved a lucrative pairing: the copyright page showed that the edition he held was the fourteenth printing.

Nick sat down on the couch and opened the book. He quickly found a mention of Brenda Rawlins. He found several references that were not confined to just a few paragraphs, but ran for several pages. The reporters must have visited Key West, where, according to the book, the parents lived. It appeared they had, to some extent, cooperated. Maybe the notion he had floated to Nelson about looking for the money the kids were using would pan out. Just maybe.

Nick was writing on a pad in the study when he heard Sandy's key in the door.

"How was your lunch with Nelson?" Sandy asked, as she put a shopping bag down on the counter.

"Good to see him, but I don't see us getting anything more from him. Nelson swears there's nothing. He gave me absolutely everything in the files. He was vehement about it. And scared to hell of being seen meeting me."

"Too bad. I was hoping. . . . What're you writing?"

"I have an idea about Brenda Rawlins, the one who gave Hummock a load of money."

"Tell me," said Sandy. "But before I forget it, I accepted an invitation for a reception at the Canadian embassy tomorrow. It's guaranteed to be D.C.-dull, lots of north-of-the-border wonks, but Peter might be there. I'd like to know why he hasn't gotten back to us."

"Can't do it," said Nick, who had gone back to his writing. "I'm going to Key West tomorrow. To see Leland and Wendy Rawlins."

"Brenda's parents?"

"Yeah. If we can find out where their money went and who's

withdrawing it, we might get a lead on where the kids are. They need a lot of money to pay for bread, butter—and bombs. I bet those're the funds they're using. Hummock set it up for them before the explosion."

"You could be right. There might be something there. You booked a seat for me, didn't you?"

10 The following afternoon Nick and Sandy pulled up in a taxi in front of a large pink house in Key West. A maid answered the door and led them through the house, over polished dark-wood floors. At the back was a verandah that ran the length of the garden and provided a generous shaded sitting area. Dominating the garden was a pool, marked at its four corners with clipped hibiscus trees in large terra-cotta pots.

Sandy and Nick were standing with their backs to the house, staring at the water in the pool and the wall of tropical plants that curtained the garden, when they heard the voices of Leland and Wendy Rawlins. After introducing themselves, they sat in chairs grouped around a table, their eyes fixed on the maid wheeling in a tea tray as if she were a performer making a stage entrance. A palpable awkwardness enveloped them as they all waited for one of the others to speak first. It was Wendy Rawlins who broke into the conversational void with the first and almost the last words she would utter that afternoon.

"I'm sorry your plane was late," she said. "But if you'd been on time I still would have been in the pool, doing my laps. I, too, got off to a late start today."

Leland Rawlins smiled at his wife. "Twenty-six laps a day, every day. Half a mile." The Rawlinses, slender and tanned, were in their seventies but looked younger.

"We haven't talked to anyone for a long while about what happened," said Leland Rawlins, after tea and sandwiches had been served. "Why would we? There's no comfort in it for us. But what you said about the children made us agree to see you. The young survivors. That word makes them sound so innocent, but you say they're far from it."

"Dr. Price and I are convinced they have to be found before another tragedy occurs, but it's been uphill all the way."

"And the FBI?"

"They think we're cranks with a crazy theory about a children's conspiracy. They've dismissed us from the beginning. That's why we're here."

With a nod to Nick and Sandy, Leland Rawlins told them how their daughter, Brenda, had become involved with Josiah Hummock. How Brenda, then a senior at Stanford, had stopped with her friends at a motel in Bluff, Utah, the night before a rafting trip on the San Juan River. How she went out for a walk after dinner and had never returned. Two days later, the local police found her at Hummock's retreat, a large adobe building outside Flagstaff, Arizona. She refused to talk to her friends, and when her parents arrived, she would only see them in Hummock's presence. They had learned that three years after this, she bore a child of Hummock's.

"That trip to Arizona was the last time we saw her alive." Rawlins paused, then cleared his throat and continued. "It still mystifies us what attracted her to Hummock. How did she even know about him? Why did she fall under his sway? We thought she was a strong and independent girl and we were proud of her, but somewhere we missed something. We've asked ourselves, Were we to blame for what she did? We've thought about this often, but I don't think so."

"Mr. Rawlins, when did you hear that Brenda had transferred her trust fund to Hummock?" asked Nick, after a moment of silence.

"She came into her trust at twenty-one. She took a year off from college to travel, but otherwise I don't think she gave any thought to her . . . wealth."

He glanced at his wife, whose head was bent, eyes trained on the gleaming floor. She did not look up.

"Our accountant provided her with what she needed," he continued. "But two months after we last saw her, he called to tell us she had asked him to transfer the balance of her trust to Hummock. I doubt Hummock had any idea what she was worth. He just got lucky." His voice was bitter. "We tried to stop her, but there was nothing we could do. There were no restrictions on it. She could do what she wanted with it. We had had no trouble with her two older brothers. I've always believed that responsibility with money should start at a young age. With Brenda, it didn't work out. It was a mistake."

Rawlins looked again at his wife, who still had not lifted her head. She had begun to move her lips soundlessly. Sandy watched her closely.

"Mr. Rawlins, sir," Nick asked quietly. "Do you know where the money was sent?"

"To a Swiss bank, and then to an offshore bank. The Bahamas, I think. But that's as far as we were able to trace it."

"My little girl," said Wendy Rawlins, in a low monotone, still staring downward. "My little girl." This was what she had been repeating to herself, Sandy realized.

Leland Rawlins reached out for his wife's hand. "Not much longer, dearest."

Nick knew he had hit a brick wall, but then he had another idea. "Just one or two more questions, Mr. Rawlins. I promise this will take only a minute." He was beginning to feel like an ambulance chaser, and was acutely uncomfortable.

"My little girl," repeated Wendy Rawlins mournfully. Her husband squeezed her hand.

"By any chance, did your daughter have other assets? Of a lesser kind perhaps."

"Well, she had a car and a checking account where she kept enough money to pay her bills." Rawlins stopped abruptly and turned to his wife, who was still murmuring her mantra. "Wendy, look at me, darling," he said.

Slowly Wendy Rawlins raised her head. Tears coursed down her cheeks. "My little girl," she said.

"Wendy, sweetheart, let me help you upstairs," said her husband, wrapping his arms around her and lifting her out of the chair. "Excuse us, please. I'll be right back."

"That was awful," said Sandy, as soon as the Rawlinses were out of earshot. "I think we should leave."

"We're going to, but I have to ask Rawlins another question."

In a matter of minutes, Leland Rawlins returned to the verandah. This time nobody sat down. "I took the liberty of calling you a taxi."

"Thanks," said Nick, glancing at his watch. There was a plane at six-thirty. "I'm sorry we upset Mrs. Rawlins," he added.

"She'll be fine."

"Just one more question, Mr. Rawlins. Getting back to the car, do you have any idea if your daughter gave it to Hummock?"

"I guess so. Right after she joined his cult, our accountant informed us the insurance on it had been canceled."

"Your accountant?"

"His name is Arnold Proctor."

"Does he still work for you?"

"Yes. He's in Boston." A taxi honked at the front of the house. "Wait a moment and I'll give you his number."

As they left, Nick asked Rawlins if he wanted to know what they might find out.

"Yes, I would. Let Proctor know, and I'll make a point of calling him to follow up. I'd like not to involve Mrs. Rawlins. I think you understand."

As they cut through the old section of town, Nick peered at the houses they passed, many almost buried in the lush plantings surrounding them. The visit had depressed him and the claustrophobic scenery matched his mood, which only began to lift when they reached the open, ocean-fronted road to the airport.

"I'm glad we're out of there," Nick said to Sandy.

"So am I. It was all so very sad. Why did we put them thorough it? And ourselves? It wasn't worth it."

"Maybe, maybe not. I think we might actually turn up something. The big money is untraceable, I'm sure. Switzerland? The Bahamas? Those places are virtual black holes for money. But the car and the checking account may not have been so carefully hidden. As soon as we get back, I'm going to call Arnold Proctor."

11 Arnold Proctor's voice was thin, with a strong hint of a New England accent. His tone was formal and guarded. He sounded like he was close to his client's age, and had been handling Leland Rawlins's affairs for over forty years. As Rawlins's principal lawyer and accountant, he was as adept as a priest at keeping confidences.

"Thank you for taking my call, Mr. Proctor."

"My job is to expedite the wishes of my client, Mr. Barrows. Mr. Rawlins instructed me to give you whatever information you required."

"He told me you were never able to trace the bulk of the money that was transferred to Hummock. Is that right?"

"Unfortunately, yes. Several of my associates and I worked on the matter for months. We traveled to Geneva, Nassau, and finally to Panama. It was like chasing a vapor trail. Ultimately, we found nothing. After that I hired a firm that specializes in electronic transfers to offshore banks. They worked on it for the better part of a year and came up with little more than we did. This man Hummock was extremely skilled. Either he had sophisticated help, or somewhere in his past he learned a very arcane aspect of banking. The outside firm believed that the final depository of the funds was somewhere in East Asia. Either Indonesia or Singapore."

"Didn't Brenda Rawlins also give Hummock a smaller sum of money when she joined his congregation?"

"Yes, and a car. There was, I think, a few thousand in her checking account."

"Do you know where that went?"

"I don't remember. As you can understand, we were more concerned with the much larger amount she gave to him."

"I don't want to put you through a lot of trouble, Mr. Proctor, but if you would check your files and see what happened to the car and the checking account, it might prove to be very helpful."

"I'll have someone on my staff work on it. Leave your e-mail address with my secretary and I'll send you whatever we turn up."

"I'd appreciate that."

There was a long pause before the older man spoke again.

"How did Mrs. Rawlins seem to you?"

"She looked good. Quite healthy, I'd say."

"I meant how did she . . ."

Nick didn't know how to answer. Seeing Wendy Rawlins stare into the past and repeat "my little girl," over and over again—a cry of loss and hopelessness—played out again in his mind.

"I would guess she's pretty much the way she's been for a while." What else could he say?

"Leland and Wendy Rawlins are my oldest clients *and* my closest friends. No one deserves what they went through. What that man Hummock did to their lives and to those of so many others goes beyond words." Proctor paused, and then continued. "I'll look into the matter myself, Mr. Barrows. I will get back to you as quickly as possible."

FROM: APROCTOR@EARTHLINK.NET TUE MAY 4 01:55:16 1999
RETURN-PATH: APROCTOR@EARTHLINK.NET
SUBJ: B. RAWLINS
TO: N. BARROWS

TITLE TO 1993 TOYOTA LAND CRUISER (CA REG. F2781076)
TRANSFERRED TO DUANE HUMMOCK, LONG BEACH, CA.
CHECKING FUNDS ELECTRONICALLY SENT FROM B. RAWLINS
WELLS FARGO CHECKING ACCT. (570 1 312173) TO BANK OF
AMERICA ACCT. (245 3 467389) IN NAME OF HUMMOCK'S
WASH-O-MATIC, INC., LOCATED IN SAME TOWN. HOPE THIS
HELPS.

ARNOLD PROCTOR

12

Esther Blum was Sandy's best friend on the faculty, a full professor of theology. Sandy had met Esther on her first day at the school. As soon as they discovered a shared passion for opera, gossip, and chilled vodka, a strong friendship was struck. Esther had been after Sandy to come to dinner at her place in Virginia ever since Sandy had confided that she and Nick had become lovers. The crisis they were in with the Hummock children had drawn them closer and closer until the next step seemed almost inevitable. And they had always liked each other from the beginning.

"I want to meet him. It's hard to believe there's an available, attractive, heterosexual male, who's not massively fucked up, alive in the lower forty-eight. He'll give me hope for myself. And I surely need it."

Esther was a large woman who always seemed to smile. She had wiry dark hair with pencil-thick bands of gray running through it. She was in her early forties and dressed in a style that could charitably be called "vintage ecletic." Her house, though only twenty-five miles from the heart of D.C., was deep in the country. It adjoined the Prince William Forest Park and there wasn't another house for almost a half mile. The house itself was decorated with Esther's finds from her constant trips to antique fairs and flea markets. Everywhere one turned there was a "collection": salt and pepper shakers shaped like animals; shelves of Big Little books; ashtrays depicting state capitals.

After a huge meal and a couple of pitchers of sangria, the three talked until almost one in the morning. Esther, who was a true night person, then started to search for a tape of *Double Indemnity* to watch.

"This has been great, Ess, but tomorrow's Gina's day off and I have to get up early. We really have to go."

"How about we watch *Mildred Pierce*? It's even better than *Double Indemnity*. And the dresses Crawford wears are to die for."

It took another fifteen minutes, and further entreaties to play Scrabble or Monopoly, before Sandy and Nick were able to get out the door.

"She's amazing," said Nick, as they pulled out onto the road from Esther's driveway.

"A true original," said Sandy, stifling a yawn. "I just wish she'd find a man. She's so smart and loving."

"She'd probably have to jettison a collection or two to fit him in," said Nick, laughing.

He drove down a narrow road bordered on both sides by dense stands of trees. A light rain had fallen earlier and the tar surface of the road looked as smooth as vinyl. They probably wouldn't see another car until they reached the interstate, which was five miles away.

"I have an idea," said Sandy. "Tomorrow let's take Sarah to—"

"Hold on!" shouted Nick, as he jammed on the brakes.

A hundred yards ahead was a car half off the road. Something was lying on the road. As he slowed the car, Nick saw it was a man.

A boy came running out of the woods from where the car had run off the road.

"Help! Please! We need help! My dad's hurt real bad," yelled the boy as he ran toward their car.

"Wait here," Nick said, as he undid his seat belt.

Nick started to open his door, when Sandy screamed out, "Stop, Nick! Don't get out! It's Seth."

He looked up and saw the boy, now thirty feet away, as he held up a pistol and fired. There was a deafening roar and then the front windshield cobwebbed.

"Get down," he said, as he jammed the car into reverse. The back end of the car fishtailed from side to side like a banner in the wind as Nick stood on the accelerator. The boy continued to fire, one bullet exploding against a headlight, the rest snarling harmlessly into the night. When he could no longer see the boy, Nick whipped the car around and sped back toward Esther Blum's house.

"Are you going to call the police from Esther's?" asked Sandy.

"No. By the time the cops get here, they'll be gone. We have to get back to your place to check on Sarah and Gina."

The trees whipped by as Nick raced the car down the deserted road. He remembered from the map he had looked at before they'd set out, that there was a small town nearby. He'd be able to find the highway back to the city from there. It couldn't be very far away. The road was pencil-straight. Nick glanced at the speedometer. Eighty. He eased off the accelerator a bit. They should be there in a couple of minutes. The road turned slightly to the right, then straightened again.

"Nick, what's that light? There. On the right."

He peered through the shattered windshield and saw two shafts of light stabbing out from the trees.

"Brace yourself!" Nick called out.

And then the lights moved out of the forest onto the road. It was a truck. Behind it, a Land Rover moved out to block the other lane.

Nick smashed the wheel to the left; the car almost tipped over. A tree snapped off the mirror like an icicle. The car continued to tilt, its side raking the trees with a mad grinding sound. And then they were past the blockade. Nick battled the wheel as the car slid crazily on the narrow road.

"Are they behind us?" he asked.

"I can't tell. . . . Oh my God. Yes. They are."

"I don't think I can go any faster."

"Now they seem to be . . . They're dropping back."

"Wait a second. What's that ahead of us?" Nick groaned.

He tightened his grip on the wheel.

"It's all right, Nick." She reached across and squeezed his hand. "Those're the lights of the town. We're okay now. They've given up. They're not going to get us."

Nick went out with two detectives from the Maryland State Police the next morning. They walked both sides of the road in the area where the two attacks had occurred. They didn't find any sign of the first car, or of the truck. Nick spotted a few trees with fresh scarring on their trunks but that was all. The troopers asked him if he wanted to lodge a formal complaint, but what was the point?

That afternoon he purchased another pistol to keep in the house. He would try to remember to carry his Bureau gun on him at all times from now on.

13 By this time Nick knew each stair by heart. The fourth stair was as squeaky as a car that had been up on blocks for years. The seventh emitted a raspy groan. The bottom step was so loud that Nick always hopped over it.

He usually came down to Sandy's bedroom well after midnight, but no matter what time it was, he made sure both Sarah and Gina were asleep. He stood outside his room on the top floor, listening intently to the sounds of the house. Sarah was a good sleeper and the chances of her wandering into Sandy's room were small. Gina was addicted to the TV in her room and always watched Ted Koppel. But, luckily, that was the limit of her viewing and she usually turned the light off when the show ended.

Nick opened the door to Sandy's bedroom without knocking. She was sitting in bed, two large pillows propping her up, reading. Her hair, backlit by the reading light, shone like a piece of silk.

"You know," he said, after he'd kissed her, "you're the only person I know who can look sexy reading a psychiatric journal."

"You don't have to flatter me to share my bed, darling."

"I wasn't. I just brought it up because it's true," he answered, kissing her again. "I don't know what I love more about you, your skin, the way you smell, or your eyes . . . I guess I love all of you," he said, getting into bed.

"Did my favorite late-night visitor make the trip unscathed?"

"A miracle, but yes, Doctor. Neither barked shin nor bruised knee tonight. I looked almost balletic prancing down the stairs."

Sandy giggled.

"What's so funny?"

"I just had this image of you in tights, pirouetting from step to step," Sandy said, as she snuggled next to Nick.

He pulled her close.

"I wonder why I like it so much when you don't wear your pajama bottoms to bed."

"But you still have on yours."

"I can correct that easily."

"That's better," Sandy said as she ran the tip of her tongue around the outside of Nick's ear.

"Did I tell you that I love you?" asked Nick.

"I think so, but it's the kind of thing I like hearing more than once."

Nick arched his body over hers.

"Then hear it again. I love you, Sandy."

Sandy smoothed the sheets to create a flat area in the middle of the bed and then set down a tray of chocolate-chip cookies and mint tea. "Have some of this, but be careful with the crumbs," she said, easing herself back into bed.

"I'm careful with everyone, particularly crumbs."

Sandy smiled. "I'm setting the alarm for five, darling," she said.

"How about five-thirty?" Nick pleaded.

"Too close to when Sarah wakes up," she answered, twisting the alarm on the clock. "But, okay. I'm feeling magnanimous. Five-fifteen."

"Oh, thank you," said Nick teasingly. "You know, Sandy, some-day soon we have to tell Sarah about us. She knows there's more between the two of us than just my being a boarder."

"And that time is almost here, darling. But not quite yet. Just as soon as this situation is resolved."

"That might take awhile."

"Did you get any further with the information Rawlins's lawyer gave you?"

"Not so far. Just what I told you, the account was closed two months after the transfer. The car was sold, and I haven't been able to trace it."

"And what about Linda?"

"What are you trying to do, Sandy," he asked, laughing, "drive me back into her arms?"

"You told me she knows everyone in town. She could help us."

"Just like your old boyfriend."

"We have to try everything and everyone. That's your theme song, not mine."

"I've called her twice already, but I'm probably so far down on her callback list that the Unabomber would get a response before me. But I'll try again tomorrow."

"I know you don't want to see her, Nick, but it's worth a shot."

"I guess so," he answered glumly.

"I spoke to all the families today. Still no word from any of the children. To tell you the truth, it puzzles me. I can't believe all of them are still that much under the control of Hummock's persona. There's nothing in the literature that shows that kind of total domination, and trust me, I've read everything in the field. There's got to be *one* of them that misses his family. And one day that kid will call home and we'll have what we need to track them down."

"We can't wait."

"I know. Hey, watch the crumbs! They're getting on my side."

"Sorry, madam," said Nick, brushing them away. "I got an idea today," he said, looking over at her. "I went back to the book by the reporters. There's a whole chapter on the town Hummock grew up in. Darnton, Texas. When the book was published, his mother was still living there. It might be worthwhile for me to take a trip down there."

"That doesn't sound like fun."

"No, it doesn't, but if I go, you'll owe me something for my self-lessness."

"Anything your heart desires, Agent Barrows," Sandy whispered as she leaned forward.

"Anything?"

"For you? Of course. But in that case, I think you should put the tray on the floor."

14 (From the preface to *The Evil Messiah* by Francine Marcum and Bernard James Willis, 1995)

The Hummocks first came to Darnton, Texas, in 1869. Luther Hummock, who had been wounded at the battle of Spotsylvania, brought his wife, five children, and four horses to two hundred acres of flat, sandy soil that most years was dry as tinder. Three years later he had lost two of his children and one of the horses, but he stayed on. The Hummocks always thought of themselves as a tough lot, and the early years in Darnton certainly proved it. Though barely able to eke out a living from the land, the Hummocks stayed through bad times, and the other times that were only slightly better than bad.

July 17, 1961, was a particularly hot day in a town where hot days were as common as the bluebottle flies that roared through the still air. On that day, a Sunday, Wendell Eugene Hummock was born. Twenty-seven years later he left Darnton and changed his name to Josiah. Six years after that, he caused seventy-one innocent people to die in an explosion that was heard around the world.

The ride from San Antonio to Darnton took three hours. Once Nick left the interstate he drove through a series of small towns that looked marginal at best. Darnton was even sorrier than the neighboring towns. The center of the town was one broad main street where a third of the stores were boarded up, and Nick sensed they would never reopen. The town's one motel was located across from an empty feedlot and looked like a set for a low-budget remake of *Psycho*.

"Could you tell me how to get out to the Hummock place?" Nick asked the old man at the registration desk after he checked in.

"You a TV fellow?"

"No. Insurance."

"Well, maybe she'll see you. Elvira Hummock sure won't talk to anybody from the TV. No chance of that."

The fence that bordered Elvira Hummock's house was festooned with handwritten signs, like stickers on a well-traveled suitcase: NO TRESPASSING—THAT MEANS YOU! NO, I DON'T WANT IT! MY DOG IS MEAN AND LIKES TO BITE!!!! WHO THE HELL INVITED YOU?

The clapboard house looked like it had last seen a coat of paint around the time *Bonanza* had been the number-one-rated show in the country. In the front yard, an old tractor rested on boxes, its engine cover open like the mouth of a huge predator. The mean dog didn't seem to be around so Nick walked up to the door and rapped on it forcefully a few times.

"Mrs. Hummock!" He knocked again. "Mrs. Hummock. My name is Barrows. Nick Barrows. I'd like to talk to you."

He heard someone move inside, so he rapped on the door again.

"Please, Mrs. Hummock. I'd like to see you. It'll only take a few moments of your time."

A voice, thin as string, snarled, "Go away!"

"I'm not a reporter, Mrs. Hummock. I only want to talk to you for—"

"Damn you, I said get away from here," she yelled, her voice suddenly growing in strength. "I'm going to call the sheriff. You're on private land. Now go, or you'll be sorry."

After standing there for ten minutes Nick could make out the old woman talking on the phone. The sheriff? Probably. He hadn't come all this way to talk to a closed door, but nothing was going to happen now, so he turned and walked back to his car.

That evening, as Nick was getting ready to leave his motel room to find a place for dinner, the phone rang. He picked it up and was about to say, "Hi, Sandy"—for that was the only person who knew he was in Darnton—when a man's angry voice barked, "You stay the fuck away from Elvira Hummock. You hear me? She's a tired old woman. She's been through enough already."

"Who's this?"

"Wouldn't you fucking like to know," the man answered, the words bracketed by explosive coughs.

"You'll be happy to hear that I've decided not to try to see her again."

"That's good."

"Now, who are you?"

"I'm somebody you probably should talk to. I might be able to help you."

"How would you know what I'm looking for?"

"We live in a small fucking world," the man said, laughing.

"Not that small."

"I know who you are, Mr. Barrows. Or is it still Agent Barrows? My memory isn't what it used to be, but you got an awful lot of TV time four years ago. The vodka hasn't completely flattened the ridges of the old brain quite yet. I'll admit it's done some damage, but I'd never forget you."

"So you know my name. What's yours?"

"Bascombe. Duane Bascombe. It used to be Duane Hummock until I changed it a few years back. It wasn't that great a name for doing business. I'm Josiah Hummock's brother. My mother doesn't talk to anyone outside the family."

"And you do?"

"I might."

"How about tonight?"

The man on the other end started to laugh, but that quickly became a salvo of rumbling coughs.

"Is tonight okay?" Nick asked again.

"Sure. Tonight's fine. All you have to do is get yourself to L.A., 'cause that's where I live."

15

"If I was a piece of ass I'd be flattered, Mr. Barrows."

"What do you mean?"

"The way you're staring at me. I don't think Madonna's butt gets this close an inspection."

"I'm sorry," Nick said quickly, and then looked down at the glass on the table in front of him.

"Doesn't bother me much anymore. For a while back then, I'd get lots of weird looks from people. But that's past. Shit, today most people hardly remember him."

Nick couldn't keep his eyes off the man who sat opposite him. It was as if all his nightmares of Josiah Hummock over the past four years had been dropped into a blender and the result was the changeling in front of him. Duane Bascombe was a much shorter man, maybe five foot ten, and weighed a good seventy pounds less than Josiah. He wore his gray hair as short as a marine's, and his eyes were a dark brown that almost seemed black. His cheekbones were high, and his lips thin. He had a smile that a policeman would call shifty, and seemed to have a cigarette stuck permanently in the corner of his mouth. But the eyes—even though the color was completely different—and the voice, which was much deeper, reminded him unpleasantly of Josiah Hummock's.

"I know what you're thinking," Duane Bascombe said, as contrails of smoke flowed evenly from his nostrils.

"What's that?"

"The resemblance. It's sort of there but it isn't. That's it, isn't it? You know why?" Nick looked up and didn't say anything. "Same mother, different pappy. My old man adopted Josiah."

"What do you do, Duane?"

"I'm in a clean business, Mr. FBI," Bascombe said with a laugh. "I own a car wash just down the road in Gardenia. Used to call it Hummock's Wash-O-Matic. That was before the fucking explosion. Then I moved and changed my name. I want people to know that I clean cars, not blow them up."

The two were seated in a cocktail lounge that was outside the main room of one of Gardenia's card casinos. The way Duane Bascombe had been welcomed by the waitress made it obvious he was a regular. He signaled to the waitress again.

"Delia, another Wild Turkey and water for me," he said, when she came to their table. "And another—What was that you're drinking?"

"Ginger ale. Lots of ice."

"You heard the man." Bascombe waited until the waitress left the table and then, his voice mock friendly and conspiratorially low, leaned toward Nick. "Now, Mr. Barrows, what's suddenly got your joint stiff about my family?"

"It's not your family. It's Josiah."

"Of course. The guy was blown to a few thousand pieces and the FBI is still interested in him. Good way to spend my tax dollars."

"Were you in touch with your brother—"

"*Half-.*"

"Did you speak to him during the last year of his life?"

"Yeah. A lot. He was always trying to get me to join his fucking flock. Same kind of shit he went on about when he was living in Darnton. Couldn't get a congregation going there, though. People were on to him. Had to leave the state to find enough dumb schmucks he could manipulate like fucking hand puppets. The son of God! Give me a break."

"So you were not tempted to join him?"

"That was all I needed. A place where I couldn't smoke or drink and the only time I could get laid was when my half-brother said so. Thank you, but this boy will take a Pasadena on that."

"Did Josiah ever talk to you about the congregation's money?"

"Sure. Most of the time it was about small things, because they didn't have a pot to piss in. Then some rich broad gave him a bundle and I handled some things for him. For a fee, of course."

"Like what?"

"I bought some properties for him. A ranch. Grew walnuts there, I think. A small apartment building. A chicken farm. A bunch of parcels of land. Mostly here in California. Even a played-out silver mine."

"Can you remember where these properties were located?"

"Jesus, Barrows, who the fuck do you think I am? Houdini? That was years ago. And I used real-estate agents to handle the details." Bascombe fished an ice cube out of glass and cracked it between his teeth. "I might be motivated to take a look through my files if there was something at the end of the rainbow."

"What are you talking about?"

"I know the FBI has money for these things."

"Let's suppose I can get you something."

"I don't work for chump change, Barrows. What are you talking about?"

"I can't promise anything until I see what you turn up. But I think a thousand dollars might be possible."

"See that napkin under the peanuts? Why don't you write down where I can reach you and maybe you'll get a call from me one of these days."

16 They held hands in a circle, all of them kneeling, the flinty ground pinching at their flesh, heads bowed, eyes closed tight as fists. The sun had dropped beneath the ridge above them, now colored a deep purple, like an overripe plum. They always prayed like this at sunset, before dinner. They opened their eyes and raised their heads almost as one, sensing, like a company of dancers, the end of this part of their prayers.

"Josiah," intoned Jebediah in a clear rising voice, "we know you are with us every second of every day. We are one with you. Nothing can harm us because you watch over and protect us. We ask you to keep our hearts true and our steps on the path that will lead us back to you and then to Paradise. We are your devoted messengers and nothing will stop us from delivering your judgment."

They bowed their heads again, just for a moment, then rose and walked, still holding hands, back to the mine.

That night, while the young ones memorized their daily portion of the Bible, Jebediah, Matthew, and Mary left the mine and walked down the rough track to the floor of the valley. There was enough moonlight to see the rocks that studded the way. The sky was ink-black, and strands of stars looped above and then dropped behind the mountain ranges that fenced in the valley.

They walked for a half mile before Matthew spoke.

"If we keep on this way, it won't work. Josiah entrusted us with a mission and if we continue this way, we'll fail." Matthew dug his hands deeper into his pockets and stopped. He looked at Mary and Jebediah. "We're going too slow."

They both knew Matthew was angry. That's why they hadn't wanted the younger ones to hear him. Dissension could rip them apart. Josiah had anticipated this and warned them to be alert for it. Whatever friction there was, always came from Matthew. He thought of himself as Jebediah's equal in every way. Matthew was constantly challenging Jebediah's authority. It was Jebediah's inner strength, derived from the fact that Josiah had annointed him the family leader, that enabled him to stand up to Matthew and make him back off. But lately Matthew was becoming more difficult and harder to handle.

"I know I'm right. Barrows is still out there. He won't stop until he finds us. And what about Sarah? Why did we quit after only one attempt to get her? She's as important to this family as anyone. The most important. She's the seed of Josiah. His only real child. She's the living remnant. She's his blood."

"Yes," said Jebediah quietly, moving closer to him. Matthew's long, blond hair fell down his back, shining in the moonlight like a waterfall. "But we haven't quit. We'll get Sarah away from Dr. Price as soon as we can. She belongs here."

"Trust us, Matthew," Mary joined in. "She'll be back with us very soon. Jebediah has a new plan."

"Why does he tell you the plan first?" he shouted. "I thought the three of us were the Elders. I should be part of these decisions."

"You're right," said Jebediah, putting his arm around Matthew's shoulder. He began to pull away and then stopped. Jebediah knew that Matthew needed the attention they were now giving him. Had to have it, in fact. Of all the family members, Matthew demanded the most from them. And it was never enough. "I was going to tell you about it tonight. I need your help most of all. You were the most important person in the first two missions. They worked because of you. What we have to do now is take care of the reporters and get Josiah's daughter away from Dr. Price. It will mean that you and I, and maybe one or two of the younger ones, will have to be away for quite a while. It won't be easy on the rest. Especially Mary." Jebediah pulled Matthew a little closer. He didn't resist. "Soon, before any of us realize it, we will have fulfilled all of Josiah's commands. We have almost completed the first ones. Then we will deal with the ultimate retribution."

Mary moved to Matthew's other side, her arm around his waist. The three stood that way for a long time. High above, a dot of light from a plane scratched a line against the blackboard of the sky. Nothing else moved. At that moment all three felt incredibly close to each other and to Josiah Hummock. They finally walked back to the mine, a soft wind from the west the only sound in the immensity of the emptiness that surrounded them.

"What did you do at Cafe Adobe?"

"I started as a busboy and then waited tables for a year."

The small man again bent over the application on his desk. He didn't like to use his glasses. His wife said they made his eyes look like a ferret's.

"And at Mission Hills Restaurant?"

"I worked in the kitchen at first. Prep work. Then they were short-handed, so I went back to waiting tables."

"Still going to school?"

"I'm hoping to enroll at NYU next semester. Film school."

"You're totally available to work any night we need you? That's right, isn't it?"

"Absolutely, Mr. Kraft. I need the money."

"These references can be checked?"

"Of course. I can also give you personal references if you need them."

"I don't think that will be necessary."

Albert Kraft, senior banquet manager for Sumptuous Cuisine, New York's most successful and toniest catering company, looked down again at the young man's job application. Gary Linnett would be twenty-two in a few months, though he looked younger—nineteen, maybe twenty. Kraft smiled to himself. It was true, as you get older everybody else looks younger than they are. Gary Linnett was an attractive young man. Tall, over six feet, with a lean physique, like a swimmer. He stood before Albert Kraft's desk with an assurance that belied his years. Hands at his side, he hadn't fidgeted once during the interview.

"There is one small problem I have, Gary."

"What's that, sir?"

"Your hair."

"My hair?"

"It's not me. Company policy. Personally, I think your hair looks fine. It's just too long. Would you mind having it cut back a bit? I'm not talking about a buzz cut. Just slightly past your collar would be fine. Is that okay?"

The young man smiled.

"Mr. Kraft, your company pays well enough for me to get a haircut. It's not a problem. Good jobs don't grow on trees, but hair does, even when I sleep."

"I like your attitude, Gary."

Kraft thought there was no need to check Gary Linnett's references. He could see that the kid was all right. A call next week to one of the restaurants he had worked at would be sufficient.

"We have a benefit tomorrow at the Regency. It's for macular degeneration—that's an eye problem. The following night we're doing a party under a tent at Tavern on the Green. For the Broadway Producers Guild. Then, if you still have the energy, we could use you a little later at the Public Library. Their party will be held in the Bartos Conservatory. It's an award dinner for journalists."

"I'm sure I can do all of them."

Albert Kraft gave the young man an additional form to fill out and then stood and shook his hand.

"I'm sure you'll do a good job, Gary."

"Thank you, Mr. Kraft. I'll do my best."

"I know you will."

Albert watched Gary Linnett, whose real name was Matthew Hummock, walk out of the office. *Young people get a bad rap these days,* he thought. *So many of them are decent and hardworking.* He saw a lot of them and he knew.

18 Nick tried for a week to see Linda. His calls were politely noted by both of her overefficient assistants: "Ms. Douglas is tied up in meetings all day. I'm sure she'll get back to you as soon as her schedule permits." Linda's life hadn't changed, it was still a merry-go-round of meetings, lunches, conferences, and dinners. When they were married, Linda, who always used her maiden name, had barely managed to take Nick's calls. Once a year, on their anniversary, she'd found time to have lunch with him at the Madison where—so many years ago it seemed like someone else's life—he had proposed to her. They hadn't spoken in over two years. His only contact was a Christmas card, the same one she sent out to over seven hundred people, signed in green ink with a personal touch, a postscript: *Hope all is well with you . . . much love, always.* Nick had recently read in a gossip column that she was engaged to Dwight Cutler, a telecommunications CEO. They would get married as soon as his divorce became final. Cutler had recently appeared on the covers of both *Business Week* and *Fortune* and was known as a tough corporate samurai capable of cutting thousands of jobs with ease. His sobriquet in the business press was "Cutler the Cutter." Nick sensed the pairing of Linda with Dwight Cutler was a perfect match.

He wasn't interested in discussing old times with her. It was Linda's supreme access to the power brokers in Congress and the executive branch that he was interested in. She was a lever he could use to open up those parts of the government that could help them find the Hummock children before they struck again. They were running out of time.

By week's end Nick realized his only chance of seeing Linda would be to "bump into her" when she least expected it. To wait for her in the reception area of her office would be like waiting for a bus in Los Angeles. Eventually, she would rush out to greet him with the obligatory kiss on each cheek, and tell him she'd love to see him but "it was just a truly terrible day" and maybe they could "get together next week." She'd call as soon as things calmed down. "That's a promise, hon."

After some reflection, Nick realized the place to meet Linda was obvious. Where, he asked himself, did she go every day no matter what? Her gym! Though her body was as tight as a python's, Linda was addicted to her daily workout. A call to the gym using Dwight Cutler's name yielded the information that Linda had booked a trainer for an hour at seven-thirty that evening. That meant she'd be there at seven to start her warm-up.

Posing as a prospective member, Nick was given an introductory session, including an evaluation by a trainer and the use of the pool and steam room, for twenty dollars. Nick passed up the evaluation and got on a stationary bike and waited for Linda. Promptly at seven she showed up. A bright green spandex leotard clung to her as closely and smoothly as a seal's skin. A purple sweatband bisected her forehead and the earphones of a Walkman were dug into her ears, the tape part secured to a belt at her waist. What was she listening to? Knowing Linda it had to be either information or motivation. No Bach fugue or Grateful Dead riff for her. Improvement, not enjoyment, was her game.

She got on a Stairmaster, set the speed near the top setting and the resistance at a level that would make a trained athlete pant, and started off. From his bike in the corner of the gym, Nick watched her closely. What was she thinking? Just taking in the words spilling out of the headset? Not likely. Linda's mind went in several directions, even at rest. Planning her new home with the CEO from hell? Probably. Thinking how to hustle a new client? More than likely. Speculation on why her ex-husband had been trying to see her for the past week? Highly unlikely.

He waited for her to get halfway into her workout—drops of sweat drizzled down her forehead and a half moon of wetness stamped her lower back—before he walked over. He stood alongside her for a moment, but Linda was gazing into the middle distance like a devotee of an Eastern religion. He reached to her waist and unplugged the earphones. A sudden look of confusion flashed across her face and when she looked down at her belt she saw Nick, head canted at a silly angle, smiling up at her.

"Hey there, beautiful lobbyist lady, got a minute for your last husband?"

She shut off the machine and jumped down.

"Nick, what a surprise," she exclaimed, as she hugged him and lightly kissed him on both cheeks.

"I hate to break into your workout but you're a hard person to see."

"It's been a killer week. Believe me, you were on the top of my call list. You understand, don't you?"

"Of course, Linda."

"I must say you're looking good, Nick."

"The fitness bug seems to be biting everyone these days."

"I don't have much time, Nick. You see, my trainer—"

"Scott, I think that's his name, is not scheduled to begin your session"—he looked at his watch.—"for another eleven minutes. Let's sit over there. I'll buy you a juice."

"Sure. Though I'd prefer an Evian. And I see your Bureau training still comes in handy."

They sat silently sipping their drinks for a moment before Nick spoke.

"I guess it's a little premature but I'd like to congratulate you on your upcoming nuptials."

"Thank you. Dwight's a sweetheart. You'd like him."

"I imagine the ten thousand employees he cut last year missed that aspect of his personality."

"I see you've been reading the business press. Dwight operates the way most CEOs have to today. Those cutbacks were a wrenching experience for him, believe me. But to be competitive and succeed in today's business climate you have to make tough decisions. But I don't think you waylaid me to discuss Dwight Cutler's corporate ethos. Isn't that true, Nick?"

"You always could read me like a Dick and Jane primer. I need your help with something. At least, I think you can help me."

Nick quickly sketched out the disappearance of the Hummock children, leaving out the murders, but playing up his worries about the safety of the younger children. That perhaps some crazy idea might have been imprinted on them by Hummock that could lead them to a similar tragic end.

"Fascinating. But why do you think I can help? You seem to work for the agency that's perfectly equipped to deal with it."

"I do, but my colleagues don't see the urgency I do."

"Oh, that's too bad," she answered, as she drained her glass.

"You know most everyone in government, and my contacts begin and end with the FBI. I've written down several names in the House and Senate that I'd like to see. As soon as possible." He handed Linda a folded-up piece of notepaper. "Do you think you might be able to set it up for me?"

She opened the note and smiled.

"I actually played doubles with Senator Hoge last week. For a man his age he's a very good player. Let me see what I can do. Is this the number you're staying at here?"

"Yes."

"I can't promise anything, Nick, but I'll try." Linda looked up and saw a tall, lean young man dressed in a T-shirt and shorts beckon from across the gym. "That's my trainer. I have to go. It was great seeing you, Nick. And you really do look great. No point in trying to reach me next week because it's going to be frantic. Regulatory meetings, an all-day Internet conference—you know, the usual things. I'll be in touch." She got up, this time not kissing him, but pressing his hand between both of hers, then bounced over to the trainer.

As he watched her do set after set of abdominals, he knew he wouldn't be hearing from her next week. Or the week after. The little favor he'd asked her for couldn't possibly help her and, who knew, the damaged piece of goods known as her ex-husband, might actually do her some harm. Linda wasn't a bad girl. She just didn't have room for him on her dance card any longer. That's the way it was.

 "Seven. Well, Nick, it looks like you'll be visiting our hotel on Atlantic Avenue. We're certain you'll like the decor," said Gina, rubbing her hands in glee. "Sarah and I just redecorated the rooms and we'll be sure to tell the staff to leave an extra mint on your pillow. Unfortunately for you, your stay will be pricey," she paused as she turned the Monopoly card over, "to the tune of twelve hundred and forty dollars. That's cash, Nick. We never take plastic at our hotel."

"I've found over the years that Monopoly brings out the worst character flaws in a person," Nick answered, as he counted out the money and handed it to Sarah, who kept the bank and carefully stacked the bills into neat piles.

"Nick, I think I detect a hint of . . . What's that phrase I'm looking for?"

"Sore loser!" yelped Sarah, laughing and high-fiving Gina.

"Okay, smart guys. I'm set to make a comeback."

The phone in the kitchen rang.

"Gina, could you get that?" Sandy yelled out from the kitchen. "I'm knee-deep in chili con carne right now. And Esther's due here in ten minutes."

"Yippee," shouted Sarah. "I didn't know Aunt Esther was coming. I bet she brings me a present from a flea market," she said to Nick.

"Sure thing," Gina said, as she got up from the dining-room table littered with the game's detritus and headed for the phone.

She reached it on the third ring. Within a few moments she was back at the table.

"Whose roll?" she asked.

"It's ours," shouted Sarah. "Don't roll a four. We don't want to land on Kentucky. He has three houses on it."

"Who was that?" Nick asked, as Gina tossed the dice like a professional crapshooter.

"Same old, same old," she replied without looking up.

"Five! Electric Works. That's ours," said Sarah, as she reached over to move their piece.

"What do you mean?"

"Some asshole—"

"You're not supposed to use that word, Gina," Sarah piped up, with a mock scowl.

"Right you are, Miss Sarah. I'll try to remember," she answered, then she turned to Nick. "We get these hang-ups from time to time."

"How long has it been going on?"

"Come on, Nick," prodded Sarah. "It's your turn."

"In a sec, Sarah," he said. "For how long?"

"Couple of months."

"How frequently?"

"Once, sometimes twice a week."

"Does the person say anything?"

"*Nada.* Just the usual. Heavy breathing. Then a hang-up."

"That's it? Nothing else?"

"That's it. You think—"

Nick quickly glanced toward Sarah and shook his head at Gina. He picked up the dice and threw them.

"Yahoo!" whooped Sarah. "Nine. Nick's on Park Place, where we have two very expensive houses. How much does he owe us, Gina?"

Later that evening Nick called Nelson Stagg at his home.

"What now?" he asked with resignation.

"I need a phone drop."

"Give me a break, Nick. You know I need a sign-off for that."

"It's no big thing."

"It is now. Especially in the District. That's where you want it, right?"

"You're a mind reader."

"This is absolutely the last time, Nick. Write this down—I have a friend with the D.C. phone company who might help you. Dennis Ashbaugh. 877-5774. He's the Metro manager."

"I can use your name?"

"I guess so," he said reluctantly. "And do me a favor, Nick."

"What's that, Nelson?"

"Next time you call, please just ask to borrow my hedge trimmer. Okay?"

Dennis Ashbaugh was more than happy to put a drop on Sandy's phone. Two days later Nick received a six-page list of all incoming calls received over the past two months. It didn't take Nick long to find a pattern. There were regular calls, once, sometimes twice a week, from two small towns in Nevada: Beatty, and Scotty's Junction. A quick look at a map revealed that the two towns stood on the edge of Death Valley. And then Nick remembered something Duane Bascombe had told him: Bascombe had once bought a defunct silver mine in California for Hummock. Nick picked up the phone.

"If it isn't my FBI friend. How's it going, Mr. Barrows?"

"Not bad. I got something I think you might be able to help me with."

"Not even a hello for your old buddy Duane?"

"You told me that Josiah had you purchase an old silver mine in California."

"I guess I did."

"Could it have been in Death Valley?"

There was a long pause before Bascombe spoke.

"Sounds familiar."

"I'd like to see if you can find out for me *exactly* where it was, Duane."

"A little something might give me some extra motivation."

"You did receive the thousand dollars I sent, didn't you?"

"And I appreciate it. I surely do. But I got to go through quite a few boxes of documents to find what you're looking for. I might accelerate my efforts if you—"

"I'll sent you an additional five hundred tomorrow. But that's it. This money is coming out of my pocket, not the Bureau's."

"I'll get right on it, Mr. Barrows. You'll hear from me soon. Real soon. Have a good day now."

20 Fran Marcum still lived in Washington, D.C., but her lifestyle had changed dramatically in the past four years. She had traded in her studio apartment for an 1864 Federal style townhouse in Georgetown. The Ikea furnishings from her years in the journalistic wilderness had been replaced by professionally decorated rooms of chintz and period furniture. The advance and royalties she had received from the book on the Hummock clan (it had been number one on the *New York Times* bestseller list for seventeen weeks)—even when split with Bernie Willis—gave her enough for all of this, and a small house on the Maryland shore that she was renovating. She had decided to stay at the *Washington Post* when the paper, in order to keep her from leaving for the *New York Times*, gave her a column. She had recently signed a book contract for over a million dollars, on the history of cults in the United States.

Since the time Fran had won the Pulitzer prize with Bernie Willis, their contact with each other had been infrequent and formal at best. Frankly, each despised the other. Both felt they should have won the Pulitzer alone and both believed they had done the lion's share of the work on the book. They regularly popped up together on news shows whenever there was a need for authoritative voices to comment on that day's incident of mayhem or disaster. The disdain they felt for each other was barely masked on these shows, which added to their popularity with producers.

The one thing that hadn't improved in the years since the Hummock tragedy was Fran's still-futile search for a man. She had had more dates since becoming famous, but most stemmed from curiosity. Fran placed the blame on the absence of a man in her life to the generally low state of males. She was hardly introspective and any thought that her single state might have something to do with her bossiness, sourness, and basic meanness never entered her mind.

She had gone to a cocktail party at the Brookings Institute earlier that evening, prowling the crowd for a potential man. She didn't set her sights high, just someone to have dinner with and the possibility of some sex afterward. It wasn't a tall order, but one that seemed out of reach with this crowd.

When she got home she retrieved her phone messages. (One from her sister, complaining as usual; the other from the alumni office of her college looking for a contribution. Fat chance!) Then she plopped down in front of the big-screen TV she had bought with her first royalty check and surfed until she found an old Bette Davis movie she remembered liking. Then she realized that she was hungry—very. The hors d'oeuvres served at the party had been policy wonk fare: lots of biopsy-thin slices of cheese on crackers, topped with commas of pimento; a dip the color of pond scum surrounded by platters of carrots and celery which looked like they had been cut the previous week. Fran picked up the phone and dialed Papa Vinnie's, the local pizza parlor.

"Papa Vinnie's," a man answered cheerfully.

"Aldo? It's Fran Marcum."

"*Signorina* Marcum. What can I do for my favorite customer? The usual?"

"I'm feeling adventurous tonight. How about a *quattro formaggi*?"

"*Bellissimo!* Some fried zucchini with that?"

"Why not. I'm in a mood to splurge."

"It'll be there in fifteen minutes, *signorina*. Enjoy."

The young man stood motionless behind a curtain of rhododendron. The massive shrub was planted next to the front steps of a lovely Federal style house. If a person stood at the front gate, some thirty feet away, and peered intently at the foliage, they wouldn't have detected the man hidden behind its cascading branches. He had taken his place after he saw the owner, Fran Marcum, return for the evening. It was his third night of waiting, standing still for hours, but he had been trained to do it. His father had taught him and all his other children how to watch others without their awareness, remaining dead still in some recessed spot for as long as it took to accomplish their objective. Anticipating what was to come, and shaping it to their own ends, made all the difference.

The house was on a quiet street filled with well-tended old brick and clapboard houses separated by narrow alleys. Then he saw someone on a bicycle. He was a heavyset teenager in a jaunty white cap. He pulled up in front of the house, chained his bike to the iron fence in front, and then removed a large pizza box from a basket on the back. As the delivery boy walked up the pathway to the house, the man who had been waiting stepped out quickly from behind the shrubbery.

"Is this for Ms. Marcum?" he asked.

"Jesus! You shouldn't pop out like that. You scared the shit out of me."

"I asked you a question. Is this for Ms. Marcum?"

"Why . . . yeah."

As soon as he heard the answer, the young man quickly pushed a long, thin knife underneath the delivery boy's ribs, upward into his heart. He had practiced this many times before, on the carcasses of animals, and he made an easy job of it. He grabbed the pizza box before it hit the ground, lifted the white cap from the boy's head, and then dragged the body deep into the shrubbery. The lettering on the cap read PAPA VINNIE's. He flicked the crease that ran across at the top, and with a satisfied smile, put it on.

When Fran Marcum heard the doorbell, she padded to the front hallway, a twenty-dollar bill in her hand, and opened the door.

"Marcum?" asked the attractive young man wearing a Papa Vinnie's cap. Fran hadn't seen him before, but he was certainly a step up from the overweight, acne-challenged delivery boys she knew all too well.

"You're at the right place," she replied, smiling brightly. *Ah,* she thought, *if only he were ten years older.* "Put it right over there on the table," she said, pointing to a console set against the wall. "Your timing's perfect. I'm so starved I could—"

The cloth that had been drenched in chloroform covered her nose and mouth. She barely had time to struggle before she was unconscious, her limbs as lifeless as a rag doll. Jebediah eased her to the floor, and then went back to the door where he slid the bolt back into place.

The room was dark when Fran awoke. She tried to move but couldn't. It only took a moment for her to realize that her hands and feet were tied to the posts of the bed. A draft came from some-where and she shivered. She was stripped naked. A wide piece of tape pressed tightly against her mouth. Her mind was frozen with fear. Dark, horrible thoughts tumbled through her brain, each more frightening than the last. Then she heard a sound. Footsteps on the stairs. The door opened and Jebediah walked in.

"I had to get rid of the bicycle," he said, as he sat down next to her. "Then I had a few others things to do. I'm sorry."

Fran twisted violently against the ropes that bound her. She tried to scream, but only a muffled cough seeped under the tape.

"That's not going to do you any good. I know how to do these things, and until I release you there's nothing you can do. I'd take off the tape but I'm pretty sure you'll scream. Houses are close to-gether here and someone would probably hear you."

He didn't tell her that before he left he had smeared some of his own semen on the insides of her thighs and in her vagina. He also had scraped the area with his nails.

"I am going to ask you a few questions, and if you answer them truthfully, I'll leave you alone. Do you understand?"

Fran Marcum nodded vigorously.

"Did Agent Barrows give you information about Josiah Hum-mock and the congregation?"

She shook her head no.

"Was it Dr. Price?"

Again no.

"One of the other agents who was there?"

She shook her head.

"Was it Trainor, the head of the FBI?"

Again she indicated no.

"You're telling me the truth now, right?"

Fran nodded.

"I think I believe you." He got up and went to the desk that was in the corner of the room. He came back with a notepad and pencil. "Which hand do you write with?" She turned her head to the right. He untied her hand and gave her the pencil. "Write down the name of the person who gave you the information."

Fran Marcum awkwardly wrote on the pad. Jebediah held it up to the light that fell into the room from the hallway. There in an awkward scrawl was the name of Phil LaChance.

"The man who succeeded Trainor," he said, almost to himself. Fran beckoned for the pad again. Jebediah placed it down before her. He looked as, with difficulty, she wrote, *Will you let me go now?*

"Yes, I will." He took the pencil out of her hand and leaned close to her. "I'm going to free you from all the troubles of this world," he whispered in her ear.

Before she could comprehend what he meant, Jebediah had her throat between his young, powerful hands, and as he prayed to the darkness above, Fran Marcum quietly left this world.

21 Nick telephoned Bernie Willis a few days after Fran Marcum's death—partly for selfish reasons, partly not. He knew he had to warn Willis that his life was in serious danger. No one really understood that except Sandy and himself. It was also true that Willis, with his aggressiveness and persistence in nailing down a story, in a manner akin to a hyperactive Jack Russell terrier pursuing a fox, might be extremely useful to them. His skill at digging up information was exactly what they needed. He should have thought sooner of going to him, and for that matter, Fran Marcum.

Willis was chilly and abrupt when Nick reached him on the phone. He was in the midst of a whirlwind tour of the television talk shows, in the aftermath of Fran's death. When Nick asked to see him about an important matter that could not be discussed on the phone, Willis professed astonishment and implied that it was almost humorous to think that a failed and disgraced FBI agent like Nick could have anything of importance to tell him.

At once Nick cut sharply to the point. "I believe I know who killed Fran Marcum."

There was a long silence on the other end before Willis spoke. "You do? I haven't seen anything from the police saying they were near solving it. I've been combing the papers. I just talked with a former colleague at *Time* who's covering it. He says the D.C. police are still at ground zero."

"What I have is not part of a police report, Willis."

"Inside information?"

"You could call it that. *Way* inside." Again Nick waited for his words to sink in. He could almost hear the reporter scrambling on the other end of the line, for a response that would put him back in charge of the conversation. This was the position he had been accustomed to holding in Nick's press briefings four years ago.

He finally said, rather lamely, "Yes, I see what you're saying. We should talk in person about this. If you're not too far away—"

"I'm in New York City."

"Then come for lunch. I'm at my beach house. Say, one o'clock."

Bernie Willis's house was two miles west of the village of Sag Harbor. It was a substantial, white clapboard house set next to a brook and looking across a broad expanse of Peconic Bay to Shelter Island. A sign at the front of the circular driveway announced the house as Bay Lodge. An older man in a butler's jacket answered the door and led Nick into a sunporch blazing with light and lined with tubs of flowering orange trees. There sat Willis, ensconced in a large, vintage wicker chair with built-in magazine and book holders on each side, like saddlebags thrown across the back of a horse.

"You can understand why I don't like to leave this place," said Willis, standing to greet Nick.

Nick could see what he meant. The room was suffused with the reflection of the nearby water, almost making it seem as if they were bobbing about on it themselves, and the furniture and pale, thin kilims were old and well-chosen. "It's charming," said Nick, though charm was not what he was looking for in Willis.

"Jorge," said the master of Bay Lodge, to the man who had ushered Nick in, "tell Carla we'll dine in half an hour. It's good to see you, Nick," he said, turning back to his guest. Willis was dressed in an expensive cashmere jacket and well-tailored trousers that streamlined his overweight form. He was short, with a round face emblazoned with freckles mixed with age spots, had thinning hair, and a bulldog's pugnacious lower jaw, which he frequently thrust out to underline a remark—and to diminish his double chin.

"I saw you last night on *Charlie Rose*. I thought what you said—"

"Wasn't it a shame about poor Fran? I miss her so."

Nick bet he did.

Willis paused in respectful silence, then continued with a litany from the past: How unfortunate it was that he and Fran hadn't been able to talk with Nick after the explosion (to help with the book, what else?), but he understood what Nick was going through and didn't want to intrude (tell me another), and what a travesty it was that he got stuck with the blame for what happened (oh, sure). Mercifully, Jorge cut short this saga with the announcement that lunch was served.

As soon as they sat down at a dining table in a corner of the sunporch, the butler held up a bottle of wine to Willis for his approval. Nick, seeing the label over Willis's shoulder, called out, "Oh, no, that's a notoriously bad year for merlots. I'd send it back."

Willis stared at Nick. Nick started to laugh. "Only kidding, Bernie," he said. "Just joking. But don't open it for me. I'm not drinking."

"Oh, but you must," said Willis, nodding to Jorge to uncork the bottle. "It's a favorite of mine. A light, simple, quite wonderful merlot."

"Sorry, no dice, Bernie."

"Well, don't mind if I do," said Willis, drinking deeply from his glass. "Wines are a passion of mine. When I was just starting out and had no money, I'd go to a wine store on Madison, a ridiculously expensive place, but they had the best, and buy wines as Christmas and birthday gifts for myself. That was how often I could afford them. And now I have my own wine cellar. Funny how things change."

With the arrival of bowls of velvety cream of asparagus soup (Carla in the kitchen knew how to cook), Willis turned serious, asking Nick why he hadn't gone to the police with the information about Fran's killer.

"I have, but the police think like the police. They lack imagination, but you, I feel, will understand. And the FBI doesn't want to hear the name Hummock ever again." Willis nodded. "But the principal reason I came to see you, is that I believe your life is in real jeopardy. In fact, you could be the next victim."

Nick had the reporter's full attention now. Willis looked shocked. "Explain," he said in a tight voice.

Watching all the while for Willis's reactions, Nick ran through the story he knew so well, from the disappearance of the surviving Hummock children from their homes, to the deaths of Ed Trainor and Clayton Bosworth, the attempts on his own life, and now, the death of Fran Marcum. By the time Nick finished talking, Willis was transfixed.

"This story, the story of the aftermath of the explosion, the end of Hummock's congregation, is *the* story," said Nick. "Haven't you ever wondered—I think we all have—what happens in the long run to children exposed to trauma at a young age? This is one outcome, a very tragic and horrifying one. I'm positive it could lead you to write a much bigger book than the first."

"I agree wholeheartedly," said Willis excitedly. It was easy for Nick to imagine what was dancing now before Willis's mind's eye. More money and more fame—fame for him alone! No more need to share the glory with a co-author.

"I hope you understand: It's quid pro quo. Sandy and I will tell you all we know, but we need your investigative skills in return. First, we need to find these children. Before they strike again. We need your help."

"Oh, absolutely. You have my word."

Now that they had finished lunch, Willis asked Jorge to bring him his special bottle of port. "I can arrange to work solely on this. I'll renegotiate my book contract to substitute this idea for the one I was doing. I have a big piece I'm doing for *Vanity Fair*, but I'll delay it. In other words, no problem."

Nick and Willis agreed to meet in a few days in New York City, where Willis would be accepting an award. They would get down to work the following morning at Willis's apartment in the Carlyle.

"Before I leave," said Nick, "I must caution you again about the danger I believe you're in. It's real. You have to be careful."

"Oh, right, right," said Willis, cavalierly brushing aside the warning as he savored his glass of port. He raised his head and thrust his jaw toward Nick. "Of course," he added, revealing what was really on his mind, "I hope you and Dr. Price realize that I can give you only an acknowledgment in the book. You'll have no monetary participation."

"I'm not interested in the money," said Nick, as he rose to leave. "But remember what I told you. Watch your back. Keep an eye out for anything that seems out of the ordinary."

As Willis said good-bye he had the closest thing to a pleasant expression that Nick had ever seen on the man's round face. But why not? What Bernie Willis saw before him was not mortal danger but a merry-go-round of prizes and royalty checks, movie deals, and myriad foreign editions. Willis was already thinking how he would start the book: Nick Barrows coming to lunch and telling him that his life was in mortal danger. What a beginning!

"This is 364-5227. The Stagg family is out right now, but you're not, so leave a message and we'll get back to you as soon as possible."

Nelson Stagg's answering-machine voice was deeper than his normal tone and full of a talk-show host's bonhomie.

"Nelson, this is Nick. I really need to talk to you. Call me ASAP. I'm sure I gave you my number but I'll give it to you again anyway. It's 763-4487. Talk to you soon, I hope."

Over the next day and a half Nick called Nelson an even dozen times, his messages becoming terser ("Call me back for Christ's sake!") and nastier ("I'm not calling you at your office, Nelson. This is where you said I could call. I always thought you understood that a backbone should be used for something beyond posture."). Nick knew Nelson was at home screening his calls, listening intently like a spy in a World War II movie hunched over an illicit shortwave radio.

When Nelson Stagg pulled out of his driveway a couple of mornings later, he had to stop abruptly for Nick Barrows, who suddenly stepped out of the bushes lining the blacktop and blocked his way.

"Hey, old buddy," said Nick, his voice laced with sarcasm as he opened the passenger door and got in. "You seem to be a very busy guy these days. Or maybe your answering machine's on the blink."

"What now, Nick? The Hummock kids doing a sitcom? Something like *The Brady Bunch*?"

"That's pretty funny for this time of day."

"I'm late, Nick. What do you want?"

"It's about the Fran Marcum murder."

"Don't tell me. One of your kids offed her."

"Maybe."

"You know something, I'm really worried about you. I think you've lost it. You've become one of those conspiracy nuts. You know, everybody did it but Oswald. You probably believe Vince Foster was murdered."

"I need a contact with the D.C. police."

"Jesus, Nick, can't you give it a rest? You're supposed to be on leave. If LaChance gets wind you're still messing with Hummock, your medical leave will be permanent."

"I guess that's my worry, Nelson, not yours."

"You're my worry. I told you to leave me alone on this. I've got a career that can turn to shit real fast if the director thinks I'm helping you."

"I thought you told me I could contact you at home."

"Well, I've reconsidered that."

"Thanks, friend."

"You're so hell-bent on this wacko mission of yours that you don't care if you take me or ten other people down with you."

"As I just said, I need someone to talk to in the DCPD."

"This is the last time, Nick."

"Don't worry. It will be."

"Pender. Woodrow Pender. Everybody calls him Woody. He's number two in Homicide. I've worked with him a couple of times. He's solid." Nick wrote Pender's name in the notepad he always carried. "I'll call him this morning. He'll be expecting your call."

"Thanks."

"Remember. This is the last time. I mean it. Stay away."

"How can I forget."

The two men stared at each other for a long time before Nick got out of the car. Nelson Stagg pulled away quickly and headed down the tree-lined street. If he stole a glance at Nick standing there watching him, Nick didn't notice.

23 "Jamil! I said box-on-one. Why you playing man-to-man? Jesus, boy, listen to me."

The tall black teenager hung his head for a moment and muttered, "Yes, Coach."

"Now get with it. I want to see some real D."

The young men started playing again. They passed the basketball swiftly around the outside of the defensive perimeter.

"That's more like it. Rashad, keep those hands up. Marquise, play Tyrone more to the left. You know why."

Woodrow Pender watched his players for a few moments before turning back to Nick, who sat next to him on a bench just off the court in the drafty high-school gym. He had asked Nick to meet him at the gym because he was jammed up at work. As luck would have it, he was heading up the Marcum investigation.

Pender was a huge man, six foot six and over three hundred pounds. His skin was the color of a well-oiled dark-wood table. He was the kind of man who wanted to be seen as tough, but he smiled too much for that.

"What do you think of my guys?"

"They look pretty good to me."

"They got the ability. What I'm trying to give them is the discipline to use their basketball skills to get a leg up and maybe get a shot at a decent life. None of them completed high school and most of them have rap sheets as long as the half-court line. I got them being tutored in reading and math and several of them even have a shot at a junior-college scholarship."

"How many evenings you work with them?"

"I try for two but—Ahmad! Watch the ball, not his eyes—sometimes all I can fit in is one. I'd like to give them three but I have a family, a job. You know the story. Anyway, Mr. Barrows, what can I do for you?"

"How's the Marcum investigation progressing?"

"I've got sixteen men on it. So far it looks pretty straightforward. We should have the perp pretty soon." Pender kept turning away from Nick to watch his team practice. He kept up a string of pointers and admonishments until he finally told them to do laps for fifteen minutes around the gym and then take a shower.

"Why you so interested in the Marcum murder? You know her?"

"A bit."

"Stagg told me you got a theory that it has something to do with that nut from the explosion a few years back. What was his name?"

"Hummock."

"That's it. I thought he was blown to bits with the rest of those fools who believed in him."

"He was."

"Well, I guess if you want to spend your time with your theory, it's your call. My wife can't understand why I give so much time to these kids. She thinks I should at least be out there playing with them. Take a few pounds off. It's hard to believe I was rail-thin in college. I'm the happy by-product of marrying a woman who can really cook."

"You said you thought you were close to finding the guy."

"Yeah. The case is pretty straightforward. A couple of murders, a rape, and a little burglary thrown in. Rape's definite. Lab found semen, abrasions on the genital area. Her credit cards are missing. Probably cash, too. No prints, though. Perp must have been wearing gloves. There's no way we won't find this guy. Though our arrest rate here in the District sucks, we'll nail this one. We have to. The whole fucking country is tuning in to CNN to follow it."

"You don't seem to have much to go on."

Woody Pender leaned toward Nick and smiled.

"Mr. Barrows," he said in a lowered voice, "we have a partial ID." Pender noticed one of his players tying a shoelace. "Artis! I said jog, not lace up. Get your sorry ass moving." Pender turned back to Nick. "A neighbor across the street noticed a guy hanging out by the house on and off during the day. A white guy."

"What else?"

"The woman thinks he was young. Twenties to thirties."

"That's doesn't sound like too positive a make."

"We're working the street real hard. Someone will make this guy pretty soon. Plus he's got Ms. Marcum's credit cards and he'll start using them, sooner or later. Mutts like this are not known for their brainpower. We'll find him."

"Not here in D.C. This guy is long gone."

"How you know that?"

"I've been tracking him for some time. The neighbor was right. He is white. He's just twenty. He uses either the name Jerry Howland or Alan Stone."

"Keep talking."

"His real name is John Phillip Harris. He was baptized and renamed Jebediah Hummock by Josiah Hummock in 1994. Howland is the name he used when he lived in Chimayo, New Mexico. He killed Alan Stone earlier this year after picking him up in a gay bar in Albuquerque. And, no, he's not gay. I just think he thought the pickings were better in a bar of that sort. He was looking for someone who could pass for him after the body was consumed in a fire. It worked."

"So who am I looking for?" asked Pender.

"I'm sure he never uses the Hummock name except with his group. I'd put out an APB using the other two names. And yes, I can get you a photo. It was taken four years ago but it's probably pretty close to how he looks now."

"What can I do for you, Mr. Barrows?"

"It's Nick, and you can do a lot for me by keeping me in the loop and finding Jebediah Hummock. I can't tell you how important it is to find him. He killed two others before Fran Marcum and he's going to kill again."

24 When Bernie Willis approached the microphone after accepting the Ike Lasher Award, named for a reporter killed during the Tet Offensive, a hush descended on the crowd. No sound of cutlery hitting against plates, no whispered conversations. Four hundred people in the business of writing and disseminating the news stared at the lectern and held their breath. The news only days before, that Fran Marcum had been found raped and murdered in her Georgetown home, was the number-one story in the country. Bernie Willis had already appeared on all the networks and would be seen that night, albeit on tape, on various talk shows with Larry King, Charles Grodin, and Geraldo.

Most of the audience knew Bernie well enough to dislike him. Fame and fortune hadn't changed him a jot. He had been a shit and a bully before making it, and those qualities had not in any way diminished. In fact, he was worse than ever. The group that waited for him to speak also knew that he had hated Fran Marcum. People had speculated all day on what he would say about her tonight. Would he try to mask his animosity with treacly words, or would his true nature reveal itself? Most of them had bet on Willis being Willis. They were wrong.

"Fellow toilers in the vineyard we call journalism, I stand here tonight with a heart heavy with grief and loss. As you all know, my colleague and collaborator, my friend and ally, sharer of secrets and visions, Fran Marcum, died violently and horribly. Sadly, it is an all-too-common death in these bloody days in the U.S. of A. as we approach the millennium. The brutality and terror she faced in the last moments of her life go beyond tragedy.

"We have all lost a fighter for justice, a clear voice that spoke truths that others didn't have the courage to state, a tireless champion for people and causes that had no champion. . . ."

He went on for another ten minutes, stopping twice to dry his eyes, until he ended his speech by looking up at the ceiling. "I know Frannie is up there now, ready to tell all of us not to let anything get in the way of reporting the truth."

When Willis got back to his table, the others there told him they had been moved by what he said, though none of them believed he'd meant a word of it. The guests in the large room were still scribbling furiously to capture choice phrases, the better to regale friends with the next day.

Though he wore a mournful expression, Bernie Willis felt great. He thought the tone and shape of what he had said about his rival were absolutely on target. After a suitable period of mourning he could begin to drop hints here and there that much of the writing of the book had been done by him. With a knowing shrug, he would tell other writers, "You know how it is when you work with someone who has a fragile ego and is primarily a reporter, *not* a writer. You have to let them take more credit than they deserve. It's sad but true."

Bernie Willis reached toward the center of the table for the bottle of red wine that sat there. Damn, it hadn't been uncorked! The bottle of white was open, but he abhorred white. Always gave him a headache. And right now he had a real thirst. He looked around for a waiter. Finally he spotted a young, blond-haired one a few yards away, leaning against the wall. Probably an out-of-work actor. He was staring at Willis oddly. Willis signaled to the waiter, who ambled over. Taking his time. Typical of young people today. No real work ethic.

"Yes, sir?" the waiter asked.

"I think you've forgotten something, my young actor friend," Willis said, pointing to the cork still in the bottle.

"Oh, you mean the cork.

"That's exactly what I mean."

"Would you like me to remove it?"

"What a good idea," Willis answered sarcastically.

The waiter produced a corkscrew from his pocket and deftly pulled out the cork. He handed it to Willis, who gave it an authorative sniff, then tossed it on the table. The waiter poured the wine into his glass and then turned and started to walk away with the bottle.

"Young man," Willis called out. "Where are you going with that?"

"To decant it, sir. It will breathe better."

Quite true, Willis thought. *The young pup is brighter than he looks.* Willis swirled the deep-purple liquid in the glass, and smelled the bouquet. *Nice, full pinot noir. Lots of berries.*

He took a swallow, and was about to take another, when an incredible tightness gripped him around his throat like a steel clamp. He tried to say something to the woman next to him, but he couldn't. The glass fell from his hand. All eyes turned to him. His mouth gaped open wide, like a fish gasping at the bottom of a boat. He tried to breathe, but he couldn't get any air into his lungs, which had been paralyzed by a massive dose of pulmonary narcotic injected through the cork into the wine. And before Bernie Willis even had a chance to be frightened, he pitched forward, clinically dead before he hit the floor.

part five

"And now
she would be
back with them."

1 "Hello?"

"Laurie? It's Nick."

Finally. For days, he had been trying to reach Laurie Abbott, his longtime friend in Alcohol, Tobacco and Firearms. Like most people with high-level government jobs, she was not easy to contact, and this wasn't going to be an easy telephone conversation. Bernie Willis's death had underlined for Nick again how calculating—and unrelenting—the Hummock kids were. Unless they were stopped, he knew there would be more deaths. Someone in the government had to believe him about the danger. He should have thought of Laurie right away, when Clayton Bosworth had been murdered.

"Ah, it's my one-time old friend, Nick Barrows," said Laurie, with more than a touch of sarcasm.

"Hey, it's good to hear your voice, but I detect a certain tone. Anything wrong?" he asked, thinking he might as well get this over with.

"What do *you* think's wrong?" said Laurie. "I've called you and written you, I don't how many times since Mesa Blanca, and from you, not a word. Is that the way to treat a friend? An old, old friend? I finally gave up on you."

"If you knew what I was going through—"

"I can guess, and we could have talked about it. That's what friends are for."

"I tried you recently, but you were at a conference in London."

"Big deal. That was two weeks ago. What about the four years before that?"

"Okay, I apologize." He waited for a murmur of understanding from Laurie, but there was none. "I'm living in Washington now," he said, taking another tack, "for a while, anyway, and I need to see you. Can we get together—and repair some of the damage I've wrought?" He allowed himself a small laugh at his own lame wit.

There was a long silence on the other end of the line.

"I can't see you now," said Laurie finally. Her voice had tightened. "Kitty's sick. She just had a mastectomy. A lump showed up on her mammogram and since then there've been tests, then waiting, then surgery, then more tests, and now chemo and radiation. I'm working as hard as I can here to keep my mind off it and when I get home, I stay put. She needs me, Nick."

Even though Nick understood how anxious Laurie must be, he still wanted to say, *I need you, too,* but instead he told her how sorry he was about Kitty. Before Nick could say another word, he heard Laurie saying she'd try to be in touch with him soon, and then the phone went silent.

Nick could not afford to wait for her to call and so, a few days after their conversation, gritting his teeth and hoping for the best, he telephoned Laurie again. He had been a real shit to her. She was right. Feeling sorry for himself, he had dropped out of her life totally.

This time he was in luck. Kitty had had a couple of good days, and more seemed in the offing. She had turned the corner. Laurie agreed to meet for a drink that evening at a bar near her house in Cleveland Park.

They had been classmates together at Duke Law. They had met

in their second year, in a litigation course taught by a professor who was the scourge of the school, a sharp-tongued, unforgiving tyrant, and to get through it they had leaned on each other for protective coloring. They became close friends, and then lovers. Six months later, Laurie left him for a woman she'd attended a yoga class with—just dabbling in the same-sex world, as so many women do, Nick had figured—but soon afterward Kitty had come on the scene.

Laurie and Kitty had now been together for twelve years, almost as long as Laurie had been with the ATF, "you know, short for Alice, Theresa, and Felicity," she had told Nick when she joined up. The only time their professional paths had crossed had been four years ago when she flew into Mesa Blanca with Ed Trainor, and that was for less than twenty-four hours.

When their drinks arrived, they toasted each other. "To friendship," said Nick, leaning toward Laurie to give her a light kiss on the lips.

"Despite your efforts to the contrary," answered Laurie, smiling. She was tall and elegant, with wavy blond hair and a husky voice. "I've been keeping track of you, you know," she continued. "I really felt sorry about what happened. Tulsa! I know it's been lousy."

"Lousy? If it only had been just lousy!" he said with an ironic laugh. "My marriage, which was never great, sank like the *Merrimac*. Or was it the *Monitor*? And then I became overly fond of an extra drink or two. I guess this is beginning to sound like a soap, but at least I'm over my drinking problem. I'm straight and fairly pure these days, but that doesn't score points with Phil LaChance. He ordered me put on medical leave. He thinks I'm nuts—literally."

"Come on!"

"Yes. Lunatic, deranged. Certifiably crazy. Take your pick."

"What's going on?"

"Well, you were in at the beginning of the Hummock story, but the story isn't over. Something incredible—terrifying—has been happening. I'm sure you remember, Hummock released twelve children from Mesa Blanca before he blew up himself and everybody else to kingdom come. Now, four years later, these kids, who range in age from about nine to twenty-one, have banded together and started . . . killing people."

Laurie's eyes widened.

"Yes, *killing*. That's what I said. All their targets have had something to do with the siege. I know it sounds unbelievable, but Sandy Price—she's the child psychologist who administered to the kids there—and I are convinced that that's what's happening. The Bureau thinks I'm—we're—off our rockers. They don't see any connections. But we do. Do we ever. Listen to some of these so-called coincidences. . . ."

When Nick had taken Laurie through the tale, from Ed Trainor's last ride in his boat to Bernie Willis's final glass of wine, he looked at her closely. "Laurie, this is real. Is there any way you can help?"

"Well, I could certainly check out our own database."

"Great, but be discreet," said Nick.

"Discreet!" she hooted. "Circumspection is my middle name. Being a dyke hones one's skills in that area. I didn't get where I am by coming out like a certain TV star. Seriously, I'll take care, and I have another suggestion, a friend of mine named Andy Backus, who's with the Secret Service. If there's a potential threat to the president or vice president, and from what you're telling me there may be, they have to know. I'll set up a meeting for you with him."

"Terrific, Laurie. Speak to him."

"Don't get too excited, Nick. Andy's reaction might be the same as mine. Real skepticism. I have to tell you I have problems with your whole scenario. It seems so unlikely, so improbable, that I can't imagine who'll rationally buy into it. Think about what you're describing: a bunch of kids, eleven to twenty-one, or whatever ages you said, who are totally organized and completely dedicated to avenging a mad prophet; who have millions of dollars at their disposal and know the intricacies of explosives, poison, and God knows what else; who have melded themselves into a vicious gang of skilled killers more adept than any insurgent group I've ever heard of. Why should anyone believe this?"

Nick shook his head and didn't answer. He stared at the floor, frowning.

"Yet maybe, just maybe," Laurie continued, perhaps only to cheer him up, "if you put down on paper everything you've just told me, where it began and where it is now, all the things you think have happened and why—especially anything that can be verified—well, maybe it'll look a little different. I can tell you that if I send you to see Andy Backus and you try to talk it out like you just did with me, it won't work. A report just might put it on another footing."

"You make your friend sound like a tight-assed bureaucrat."

Laurie laughed. "You of all people know the government's love affair with rules and regulations."

"True, but backtrack a second. These children left their homes at essentially the same time, as if by signal—and then just disappeared. All of them at once. It's got to mean something."

"Children disappear all the time. By the thousands. You remember the photos of missing children that used to be printed on milk cartons? Every morning at breakfast I would look at their faces and think of their families' sorrows, when all I wanted was my cappuccino and a little early-morning peace."

"This report may turn out to be a very long one," said Nick.

"With the allegations you're making, it should be long. When you've finished it, send it to me and I'll pass it along fast. And one more thing."

"What?"

"Don't ever drop off my friendship radar like a UFO again. Is that a deal?"

"Deal."

2 "Nick Barrows?"

"Speaking."

"It's Woody Pender. I got some news for you. I believe your boy is our boy."

Nick reached across the desk to get a pad and pen. His training made him automatically take notes of conversations.

"Two neighbors on the street made his picture. They saw him hanging around the day before. Avis also rented a car to an Alan Stone. New Mexico driver's license."

"Any other leads?"

"Nothing yet. But maybe you can give me a little more help."

"Like how?"

"You said you thought these kids who ran away might be living together."

"I'm pretty sure of it."

"Do you have any pictures of the others?"

"I can get photos of all of them. But remember, like the one I gave you, they'll be four years old."

"That's okay. I'm going to put all of them out on the wire as wanted as material witnesses in the homicide of Frances Marcum. There's a lot better chance of someone making an ID when you exponentially increase the number of suspects."

"You're telling me what I wanted to hear, Woody. Thanks a lot."

"Hey, you're the guy who should be thanked. By the way, would you and your lady happen to be free tomorrow night?"

"I'll have to check with Sandy, but I think so."

"Then how about the two of you coming over to our place for dinner. Say, eight o'clock. You'll see for yourself how some innocent home cooking can take the sharp edges off a man's body."

3

"I don't have any homework, Gina."

"Honest Injun?"

"Cross my heart," said Sarah, as Gina eased the station wagon into the driveway. Gina picked her up at school every day. Today Sarah was in a special hurry to get home because Nick had promised he would take her out to the park and teach her to head a soccer ball. From the moment Nick had started living at the house, Sarah had fallen in love with him. Sandy felt it was her need for a father figure. Gina, in a more down-to-earth way, believed it was because Nick was the "fun guy" and not the dispenser of the orders and bromides she and Sandy dealt out on a daily basis.

As soon as Gina unlocked the door, Sarah shouted out Nick's name. She ran to the back of the house, through the dining and living rooms, and when that yielded nothing, she ran up the stairs.

"Nick! Nick! We're home."

Gina went to the answering machine and hit the replay button. One message. It was for Nick from a Detective Pender. By the time Gina finished writing a note to Nick, Sarah, disconsolate, came slowly down the staircase.

"He's not here. I searched everywhere."

"Under the beds?"

"Don't be silly, Gina. Nick wouldn't be there."

"I guess you're right. Why don't you go up and change? I'm sure he'll be here in a few minutes. He probably just had to run an errand."

Sarah raced back up the stairs. Within minutes she was downstairs, dressed in jeans, sweatshirt, and sneakers.

"Nick! I'm ready," she yelled out.

"Knock off the shouting, Sarah. You're as loud as a heavy-metal band. Nick's still out."

"When's he coming home?"

"Any minute."

"Well, tell him I'm in my playhouse," Sarah said, sulking.

"Will do. How 'bout some cookies and a glass of milk before you start your redecorating?"

"I'm not going to redecorate, Gina. I have something else to do."

"And the milk and cookies?"

"Could you bring them to me in my house, pretty please?"

"I've told you a thousand times, I hate that 'pretty please' business. If you promise to stop saying that, I'll bring them out to you."

"I promise. I'll never say 'pretty please' ever again. But you do want me to still say 'please,' don't you?"

"Yes," Gina said, laughing, "please continue to say 'please.'"

Gina went into the kitchen as Sarah skipped away through the house to the back door leading to the garden. She poured a glass of milk, then arranged a few cookies on a tray and put the milk in the middle on top of a napkin. The napkin was a constant since Sarah liked nothing better than to wipe her mouth on her sleeve. Just as she was about to pick up the tray she heard the doorbell ring. It was probably Nick. He was always forgetting his keys.

Gina never opened the door without checking through the peephole first. It was Sandy's rule. She saw two young men in dark blue coveralls. Behind them she could see a piece of furniture.

With the chain still in place she opened the front door. "Yes?" she asked.

"Ms. Price?"

"She's not in right now."

"We have a delivery for her."

The one nearest to the door held up an invoice. "It's a desk."

"Could I see that, please?"

The young man had long hair and a nice smile. He slipped the paper to her. The invoice had Sandy's name and address on top. Apparently she had paid $615 for the desk. Sandy hadn't told her about it. Where was it supposed to go? It was probably for Sarah. She'd need a desk soon enough.

Gina unhooked the chain and opened the door. The two men picked up the desk and carried it into the hallway.

"This way, fellows. I think it should go up—"

Matthew brought a length of pipe wrapped in duct tape down on Gina's head. She fell to her knees and toppled sideways to the floor. Jebediah went to the door and snapped the top lock. As Matthew started to pull Gina's body away, one of her eyes squinted open and she stared up at Matthew.

"We're taking Sarah with us," he screamed. "She's the seed of our Lord. His blood child." He hit Gina again harder and dragged her into the dining room.

"Sarah, Sarah," Matthew softly called out then. "Where are you? It's Matthew. We've come for you."

With Jebediah behind him, he moved through the kitchen, into the dining room, and then to the living room. There, through the tall windows that looked down into the garden, he saw Sarah standing inside her playhouse. He smiled. It had been so long since they had seen her. And now she would be back with them.

"Matthew. What are you waiting for? Let's get her."

They pushed opened the door and walked down the steps to a brick path leading to the little house.

"Hello, Sarah," Matthew said, leaning inside.

"Who are you?" she asked warily, as she stepped outside.

"I'm Matthew. Matthew Hummock. I'm your brother."

"I don't have a brother."

"Yes, you do. And this is Jebediah. His last name is Hummock, too. He's also your brother."

"Where's Gina?"

"She went away."

Sarah looked closely at them. She was frightened, but instinctively she knew she shouldn't show it.

"Gina! Gina!" she yelled.

"Don't do that, Sarah," said Matthew, as he reached down and took her hand. "Yelling scares people."

"I'll yell as much as I want to. This is my house," she answered defiantly. "Go get Gina. Right now."

"Matthew's already told you, she's not here," Jebediah said irritably. "She had to go away. Now, come along with us."

Sarah pulled her hand away from Matthew's and dashed back inside the playhouse. She banged the small door shut. They heard the click of an inside bolt.

"Go away!" she shouted. "Go away right now."

"Come on, Matthew. Get her out of there. We have to get going."

"Sarah, listen to me," Matthew pleaded. "We are your brothers. You have to believe me. We're going to take you back to your family. Your *real* family. That's where you belong. Now, come out. Please."

Matthew stood outside the tiny house, the peak of the roof just reaching his chin.

"Come out, Sarah," Matthew entreated again.

"No. I won't come out until you bring Gina here."

Her little-girl's voice sounded as if it were coming from far away.

"Come on. We don't have all day," said Jebediah. "Just pull on the door."

"Give me another minute. I know I can talk her out. She's just scared, that's all."

Nick had to park at the curb because of the van in the driveway behind Gina's car. *Must be a delivery,* he thought. Then he had trouble getting into the house since the bottom lock was not locked, just the top. Gina generally locked both of them. A desk was blocking the passage into the hallway, so Nick pushed it to the side. He was about to call out Gina's name, but something made him stop. It was silly, but he almost felt like going upstairs to his room and getting his gun. He stood still and listened. The ticking of the hall clock seemed almost as loud as Big Ben. Then he heard something from the back of the house. It was faint. He moved quietly into the living room and it was there that he could make out the sound from the yard. It was a male voice. Then another joined in.

"Kick in the door, Matthew. We can't just stand around here waiting for her to walk out."

Nick edged toward the window and saw them. Their faces had changed from the photographs of four years ago, but not enough to prevent him from recognizing them instantly. His body coiled with tension and suddenly his shirt was plastered to his back. Where was Gina? What had they done to her?

Nick couldn't think about that now. He had to get a gun—but as he turned away from the window, he brushed a table lamp with his hip and it fell to the floor. It didn't break, but the noise caused Matthew and Jebediah to spin around and spot him. They would grab Sarah and get over the fence with her unless he acted fast, without a weapon.

"Good afternoon, boys," he said, in as neutral a tone as he could muster, stepping out of the house. The two stared at him. They might be shocked, but they didn't appear to be scared. "It's been quite a while, hasn't it? You two have been real busy fellows. Hope all the murdering hasn't cut into your praying time."

Without a word exchanged, Matthew and Jebediah moved apart and began to circle Nick. Matthew took the length of pipe out of his pocket and tapped it against his palm with the steadiness of a metronome.

"The smart thing would be for both of you to stop right where you are and sit down on the ground."

"You don't have a gun, do you, Mr. Barrows?" said Matthew. "Did the FBI take it away?"

"I don't need a gun."

They were moving slowly toward him, separate enough to force Nick to turn his head from side to side to keep both in view.

"We should thank you for interrupting us, Mr. Barrows," said

Jebediah, as he edged closer. "Now we can finish our business with you."

Out of the corner of his eye Nick spotted a rake leaning against the wall. He had to get it, even though it was closer to Matthew than to him.

At just that moment, the door to the playhouse sprung open and Sarah ran out. Matthew tried to grab her but missed, giving Nick the instant he needed to grab the rake. Sarah dashed up the steps into the house. Matthew tried to follow her but Nick swung the rake and caught him across the legs. Matthew fell into a flower bed but then jumped back up, rubbing his legs. He had dropped the length of pipe and now couldn't find it. Matthew hesitated for a moment and then lunged at Nick. Nick jumped to the side and swung again. The rake's tines glanced off the side of his head, but Nick caught him with enough force to drop him.

"You can't stop us from getting our sister back," Matthew snarled, blood streaming down his face. He stood up and rushed at Nick again, but this time Jebediah moved together with him, and they both landed on Nick before he could swing at them. The three rolled on the ground, fists pounding, legs kicking wildly, the only sound the gasps and snorts of determined, furious combat. Jebediah had Nick around the neck, while Matthew clawed at his face. Nick was having trouble breathing and the thought that maybe this was it, that Hummock would win—for his enemy was as much these two he was thrashing with in the dirt, as it was the dead Josiah Hummock—gave Nick a burst of energy. He kicked Matthew off, then clamped his teeth into Jebediah's arm, loosening his grip on him enough for him to slide out. He stood there panting, as Matthew and Jebediah circled him again.

"Jebediah, run inside and get Sarah," Matthew shouted, as he feinted a lunge.

"No, Matthew," Jebediah gasped, backing away from Nick toward the fence. "We have to get out of here."

"We can't leave without Sarah. We just can't."

"Listen to me. It's too dangerous. We can't stay here any longer," said Jebediah, who now stood next to the fence.

"Sarah, I'm coming," screamed Matthew, as he put his head down and rushed Nick. Nick jumped to the side and slammed the rake against the back of Matthew's head. Matthew fell and tried to get up again, but this time Nick was on him, landing blow after blow until Matthew sagged to the ground like an inflatable toy that had been punctured. Nick wheeled around, expecting Jebediah's charge, but he saw he was alone in the backyard. Jebediah was gone. When he finally was able to drag himself to the steps and sit down, he heard the sound which had never been so welcome, the sound of police sirens heading right to the house.

4 Sandy pulled aside a curtain in the living room and looked out. There, parked in front of the house, was the patrol car Woody Pender had sent over. Pender had promised one would be there twenty-four hours a day until all the Hummock children were found.

"You don't have to keep checking on it," said Nick. "It's not going away."

"I know, but it comforts me," said Sandy. "I'm still shaking. They'll stop at nothing. They want Sarah and they're not going to stop until they get her."

"They won't get her!" said Nick sharply. "I won't let them."

"I haven't told you yet, but she asked some questions when I put her to bed."

"What questions?" asked Nick, who was lying on the couch with a heating pad under his back.

" 'Who are they?' 'How do they know my name?' 'What do they want with me?' She also remembered Matthew from that attempt at the school. She's very upset."

"Jesus, I'd be surprised if she wasn't. What did you say?"

"Well, not too much. She's still so young. Basically I just said there are people in the world who are bad and don't act the way they should, but she mustn't worry—she'll be safe because we'll be with her all the time."

Nick nodded. "We can't let her out of our sight. Not for now. Come over here, Sandy, next to me," he said.

When Sandy sat down on the couch, he reached up, wincing with pain, and held her arms in his hands. "We have to institute one major new rule here. One of us is always—but always—going to be with Sarah until this business is settled. Okay?"

"Yes."

"We'll drop her off and pick her up at school ourselves. She'll be all right there. They know the score."

"I hope Gina doesn't blame herself," said Sandy.

"She won't. She's too smart."

Sandy nodded and stood up. "I'm going to check on Sarah. I started reading her *Charlotte's Web* after we talked, and she fell right to sleep."

In a few minutes Sandy returned. "She's sound asleep. God, I hope we get lucky here—that what happened today will just drift off out of her consciousness. No more questions, no anxiety, no nightmares. For a long, long time."

"Maybe even never?" asked Nick.

"That's probably asking too much, but we'll deal with it when we have to. I'm going to get myself a glass of wine. You want something?"

"Yeah, a Coke. Lots of ice."

A few minutes later, Sandy returned with the drinks and sat down again. "Has the heat helped?"

"I'll show you how much," said Nick, pulling the heating pad out from under him and throwing it on the floor. "That's how much it helped. Zero."

Sandy laughed.

"Or, to put it another way, I feel like a semi ran me down and parked on my rib cage."

"Oh, Nick, I'm sorry," said Sandy, leaning down and stroking his hair.

"Raise your glass up, Sandy, and let's drink to the end of this thing. We're close to it, I know we are, and this isn't a pep rally," said Nick. "Woody believes us. He'll do everything he can, and now they've got Matthew in custody. That's got to lead some-where."

"Absolutely."

Nick took Sandy into his arms again.

"No matter what happens, Sandy, I'm not leaving you. I hope you're ready for a full-time boarder. No more Tulsa, Oklahoma. Ever. I can't think of being anywhere else than with you and Sarah."

 "How are you feeling?" Sandy asked Gina. Nick was downstairs in the hospital lobby with Sarah, waiting for his turn to come up.

"If I look up to watch TV, I feel like throwing up. If I turn my head too quickly I feel the same way. Actually, almost all the time I feel like barfing. And quite a few times I do. But Dr. Weld says that in a week I'll feel fine. Football players get concussions all the time. I just have to take it easy."

Gina sat propped up in the hospital bed, her head encased in gauze and tape. She had described herself to Sarah as looking like a giant Q-Tip.

"We'll be able to check you out of here tomorrow morning. And when we get you home you're going to do exactly what you're doing here: Rest. Understood?"

"Yes, Mommy," Gina answered, smiling.

"The doctor told us you're very lucky. If you had been hit a half-inch lower you might not have woken up."

"My family has a lot of miserable qualities, but one thing we share is a hard head."

"Do you remember anything?" Sandy asked.

"*Nada.* I dimly recall that I was going to take a tray of cookies and milk out to Sarah, and that's where the tape stops. Have the police learned anything from the one you caught?"

"That's also a *nada.* Later this afternoon Detective Pender is taking us over to see Matthew and maybe we'll get something out of him."

"What about the other one?"

"Not a trace of Jebediah. He just vanished. He rented the van with a false driver's license. One he hadn't used before. He probably has quite a few phony ones. And all the money he needs. Wherever the group is hiding, I bet he's back with them now."

"How's Sarah taking it?"

"She loves it. She's ready to go on Oprah. I heard her talking on the phone to her best friend last night. She was flying high. Who else can tell a story about two crazy guys who tried to kidnap her before they were beaten up by her hero, Nick?"

"What should I tell Sarah if she asks me any questions?"

"She knows her parents died in an accident. I told her that as soon as she was old enough to take it in. But on this other stuff, I think we should fudge it for now. As a therapist, I know I shouldn't be saying this, but sometimes it's best to equivocate."

"Meaning?" asked Gina.

"Lie," Sandy answered.

6 Matthew Hummock knelt in his cell. He had been praying for over an hour. His lips moved but made no sound. After the police had arrested him and taken him to a hospital, where he was given forty-seven stitches in his scalp, he had been placed in this cell. A guard checked on him every forty minutes. Detectives had attempted to interrogate him twice, but he wouldn't even give them his name. In frustration they yelled at him, threatened him, shouted obscenities, but he remained silent. He just looked at them and smiled. He was not frightened. Not a bit. Yes, he was sad that he had failed to get Sarah back, but he knew that it was meant to be that way. There was a reason for it and he accepted it. He was now ready for his next mission. His last.

Matthew finished his prayers and sat down on the cot. He looked up to make sure the guard was not at the peephole in the door, and then rolled up the right-hand cuff of his pants. He carefully pulled a coarsely sewn thread on the underside. A small flap opened and he extracted from it four blue capsules. He knew that the four would do the work, but to make sure, he undid the other cuff and removed another four capsules.

He went to the sink and filled a glass with water. He swallowed all eight capsules, two at a time, as easily and quickly as if he were taking his morning vitamins.

He removed his sneakers and stretched out on the cot. He was about to take a beautiful journey, and at the end of it was Josiah Hummock, waiting to embrace him. He was happy, happier than he had ever been before. He kept repeating the name "Josiah" until a force stronger than anything he had ever known squeezed the life out of him.

7 "You're late," said Woody Pender, without looking up, as Sandy and Nick came into his office.

"It's my fault," Sandy answered. "I wanted to go to the hospital first, to visit Gina—"

"I mean, you're real late," Pender interrupted, finally looking up at them. His usual smile had been replaced by an expression of deep sadness. "I can't spend much time with you now. I have a press conference in a half hour."

"What's going on, Woody?" asked Nick.

"A whole potful of trouble. Your boy, Matthew Hummock, or whatever his name was, was found dead in his cell."

"No!" said Sandy.

"I'm afraid so. Suicide. He was found about an hour ago. He took something and whatever it was, it sure did the job. He was in complete cardiac arrest when the guard walked into his cell."

"Are you sure it was suicide?" asked Sandy.

"Maybe not. I guess nineteen-year-old boys die of heart attacks all the time, Dr. Price," he snapped. "It's a regular occurrence, like puberty." Woody Pender stopped to take a sip from a container of coffee, and then looked directly at Sandy. "Excuse me. That was uncalled-for. I was just barking at myself. We had removed the kid's shoelaces and belt, but, damn it, we let him keep his own clothes. He apparently had the poison hidden in the cuffs of his trousers. The press and the TV people are going to chew our asses real good on this one."

"Did he leave a note?" asked Nick.

"Nothing. I've seen a lot of suicides, but this is the first time I've seen a smile on the victim's face. He looked like he was getting ready to open his Christmas presents."

"I was hoping he might have led us to the others," said Sandy.

"Don't feel bad about that. I doubt there was anything he'd tell us, short of our giving him an injection of sodium pentathol. My guys worked him pretty hard for a couple of sessions and he wouldn't even give them his name. But I might have something else for you."

"What's that?" Nick asked.

"We've been using those photos you sent. Yesterday our guys canvassed the neighborhood where Clayton Bosworth lived. They showed the pictures to everyone. A housekeeper up the street from his house recognized Jebediah. She's sure she saw him hanging around the day before the explosion."

"Any makes on Matthew?"

"Not there, but we got a positive on him from a guy in the catering firm that did the banquet where Willis was killed."

"You've done good, Woody," said Nick.

"Real good," Pender answered, looking as if he had just sucked on a lemon. "One suspect will now only answer questions from God, and the other will be as easy to find as a winning lottery ticket."

8 "Nick, are you there?" shouted Sandy. She put two large bags of groceries on the kitchen counter and cocked her ear for sounds. Sarah was at her ballet lesson with Gina, home three days from the hospital. Nick must be upstairs. She headed for the staircase, almost bumping into him coming around a corner.

"Sandy, darling! I wanted to surprise you by suddenly materializing next to you," said Nick, wrapping his arms around her and kissing her.

"Give me a hand with the bags in the car. There are another seven or eight out there."

"What army did you invite for dinner tonight?" asked Nick.

"You laugh, but that's just our usual ration for a normal week of meals. We're sort of the Partridge Family under siege."

They were in the kitchen, putting the last of the groceries away, when the front doorbell rang.

"That must be one of your guests," said Nick. "A tad bit early, wouldn't you say?"

"Wise guy," said Sandy, as she went to the door. There, standing on the step in front of her, was a pretty woman she had never seen before.

"You must be Sandy," said the woman. "I'm Laurie Abbott. Nick's friend. He probably told you about me. I'm with the ATF."

"Of course. Come on in, Laurie."

She stepped into the living room, just as Nick came in. "Hi there, Laurie," said Nick, kissing her on the cheek. "Always a pleasure to see you, but—"

"I just flew in from Atlanta. You're on my route to my house, so I thought I'd give you some good news in person. Andy Backus at Secret Service reached me today. You've pressed a button with them, Nick. A big red one. They're taking your report very, very seriously. They've done a lot of digging and they want to see you and Sandy tomorrow morning. At eight. Can you make it?"

"Are you kidding!" said Nick, almost shouting.

"That's great," said Sandy. "How about a glass of wine? This calls for a celebration."

"I'll have to take a rain check. I'm pretty wiped out. But I'll be at the meeting tomorrow. Oh, and it's in Andy's office. Fourteenth floor."

As soon as they closed the door, Nick and Sandy fell into each other's arms. "I have a feeling that this time we're going to get somewhere," said Nick.

"Finally . . . *finally*. I don't know what else to say."

"Don't try. You've said it."

The next morning, as prompt as kids on the first day of school, Sandy and Nick walked up the steps of the Secret Service building on G Street, and rode the elevator to the fourteenth floor. Nick wore a jacket and tie, dug out from the back of his closet, and Sandy, a dress, which made her feel terribly proper but not too demure. This meeting, after all, was a serious occasion, the first governmental acknowledgment of what they had been trying to accomplish for so long.

They were immediately led into Andy Backus's office, and after introductions—to Backus, a friendly-looking man in shirtsleeves who headed field operations; to Ted Vargas, tall with heavy-rimmed glasses, who headed presidential security; and to Andy's chief assistant, Fred Crockett—they sat down at a conference table next to Laurie Abbott.

"I appreciate you two coming in on such short notice. I know it's been pretty rocky for you lately," said Backus. "Before we get to your report, Nick, I have to ask you a couple of questions. I hope you'll take them in the right spirit. You're on medical leave from the Bureau, right?"

"Yes."

"Drinking problem?"

"I had one, but I'm over it."

"AA?"

"No, it wasn't that bad. I took care of it myself. Haven't had a drink now for over two months."

"There are also references in your file to mental instability, but I dismissed that. I couldn't find any evidence for it."

"I'd be surprised if you had," said Nick, with a short, nervous laugh.

Backus smiled apologetically. "You understand, I hope, that I have to ask these things. Your charges are very serious. They astonished me when I first read your report, but no longer. My staff has put in a lot of time already and confirmed enough for us to believe these Hummock children are a real threat.

"What puzzles me, Nick, is why the Bureau didn't take your charges seriously. In fact, it appears they didn't even look into them superficially," said Ted Vargas, interrupting. "We intend to follow up on this with them and also with the attorney general. Thanks to LaChance, the AG may not even be aware of the situation."

"Right," said Backus. "It's really been obstruction on LaChance's part, and it may well result in negative consequences for him. But that's for later. First off, let me tell you about our approach. We decided to start this as a fresh investigation. I've put ten agents on it full-time and, to date, they haven't found anything that contradicts what you stated in your report. We've discovered that a D.C. Homicide detective that you know—"

"Woody Pender. He's a very good man."

"Woodrow Pender," Backus said, looking down at a paper on his desk. "Exactly. He's made significant progress on this matter. He's smart and thorough and once again demonstrates that good detective work, knowing who to question, and then following the chain of answers from one person to the next, is how cases are solved. But this one's a little too complex and widespread for metro police to handle. So far, we've verified Pender's findings and added some important details. For instance, the explosive that killed Clayton Bosworth is the same as was stolen from a military base in Arizona a year ago."

"I'll be damned," said Nick.

"Now, to business. We'll run over all the issues you've raised and we'll tell you what we've learned. Maybe some of it will trigger more from you than what's in the report. Things you may have forgotten, thought unimportant, and so on. And Sandy," he said, turning to her, "we want your input also."

"Try and stop me," she said.

"And specifically I want to go over each of the children with you, one by one, to see if there's anything more you can add. Particularly about the older two."

Sandy nodded.

"Then let's begin," said Andy Backus.

It wasn't until two hours later that they wound up their discussion. As if on signal, the five people in the room took long swallows of water and stretched in their chairs.

Laurie yawned loudly, making the others laugh. "Sorry. I didn't mean it. Those damn USAir seats," she said. "Can't even nap in them."

"Okay," said Andy Backus, looking at Nick and Sandy and clearing his throat as if to announce that recess was over. "Thanks to you two, we now know more—a hell of a lot more—than we did when we started. But there's one mighty big item that remains open. Where are these children? We have to locate them. And where is brother Bascombe? Hummock did, in fact, have a half-brother—that we know for sure. The mother, old Elvira, was a recluse, and she did things her own way. She never bothered to register either one of the boys, but everyone in town knows there were two of them. Apart from those sixty-four-thousand-dollar questions, what I'd like to do now is get clearance from LaChance for you to work on a temporary basis with me."

"When are you calling?"

"Right after this meeting."

"Do you think he'll agree?"

"He's going to be agreeing to a lot of things. He has a lot to answer for."

Later that day, Andy Backus reached Phil LaChance.

"You can have him," said LaChance. "He's damaged goods. A real conspiracy nut. He also got blown away at Mesa Blanca, except the fool doesn't know it."

"I want to set up a meeting with you about him."

"Look up the word *fabulist*," said LaChance, his voice rising. "Describes him to a tee."

"Did you hear me?" asked Backus, growing angry.

"I'm going to an Interpol conference in Brussels tomorrow.

Then I'm doing my annual tour of our main field offices. After that I take the family to St. Bart's. First vacation in over a year. I'll call you when I get back."

"See that you do."

"Did you tell your mother about our tennis game?"

"Of course I did, but don't boast, Dad. You know I hurt my knee last week."

"Rob told me next time he's going to win," said the heavily made-up middle-aged woman sitting next to her older son at the dinner table.

"And I will, Dad. That's a promise. You can take it to the bank."

"You got your old man quaking in his Nikes, Rob. And if you beat me, it's going to take your best game," said Ben Harpswell, winking at his son, who was a ringer for him.

"Yeah, but I got a plan. While you're at the economic summit, I'm going to play every day. And I'm going to concentrate on my serve. Just wait and see."

Benjamin Wesley Harpswell was tall and lean—and president of the United States. A two-term senator from New Hampshire, he was a Republican and a Yankee WASP, who had been swept into office for a second time a year earlier with fifty-four percent of the vote. Harpswell had his fans, as well as his share of detractors: he was smart and, when it came to politics, totally ruthless. He also possessed a legendary impatience that came with sudden and unexpected fury, like a tropical downpour. He tried hard to hold himself in check with his family, but he could never quite make it. He was mightily ambitious, or he wouldn't be where he was, and he worked and traveled almost nonstop. In theory, he looked forward to spending time alone with his family: his wife, Emily, his son Rob, a sophomore at Brown, and his younger son, Tony. This evening, the first in almost two months, it was dinner in the family quarters of the White House, all family present, with a movie to follow.

From his vantage point at the antique gaming table the family used when they ate alone in the dining room, Ben Harpswell looked directly at a large Bierstadt painting of a spectacular view of the Rockies on the far wall. The choice of the painting had been his wife's. The living room and hallways were lined with Peales and Whistlers, also selected by Emily. *In her sharper days,* thought Harpswell, as he watched his wife refill her martini glass. By six o'clock—"when the sun was over the yardarm," she repeated every evening, as if he had never heard that ridiculous, outdated expression before—the cocktail shaker was in her hands, and soon afterward her speech would start to slur.

During the time they lived in New Hampshire, she had earned an MFA in nineteenth-century American art, and curated shows on the Hudson River School at the Fogg and on luminism at the Boston Museum of Fine Arts. She had tried to steer Rob toward art history at Brown, but he had gravitated to film. These days the prospect of being a museum curator couldn't hold a candle to being a Spielberg or a Scorsese. Next week, which he couldn't wait for, Rob would be interning for three weeks at a movie studio in Los Angeles, and then, begrudgingly agreeing to his father's wishes, taking a monthlong survival course that went beyond Outward Bound in its rigor and toughness, on Kestrel Island, off the coast of Maine.

Emily signaled the butler, in his long white chef's apron, to pass second helpings of the chicken curry. Ben, Rob, and Tony, as well as sharing a love for sports, had voracious appetites. To Emily's annoyance, none of the three ever gained an ounce of weight.

"What are we screening tonight?" Ben asked Rob. Rob, when he was in from school, was in charge of picking the films they watched.

"We have a choice of *Sunset Boulevard*, *Fort Apache*, or *Les Enfants du Paradis*," Rob announced.

"Ooh-la-la—fancy French," said Tony, smirking. "Can't we see something that's less than fifty years old? How about something with a little action in it?"

"Be quiet, Tony," said Rob. "Don't underline what a yahoo you are."

"Then at least let's watch the western. I vote for *Fort Apache*."

"How're you doing studying for your exams, Tony? Particularly your French," asked his father.

Tony looked at his plate and hummed a rap tune.

"I asked you a question, young man," said Ben.

"Comme ci, comme ça, mon cher père."

"Is that the best French you can muster after the thousands of dollars I've spent on your education? You'd better go upstairs after dinner and spend a couple of hours hitting the books."

"D'accord, mon président," said Tony unhappily.

"Don't hang your head, Antonio. Exams will be over pretty soon, and then you've got a great two-week trip with your mother to the Far East. And Rob will be on Kestrel Island. I like the sound of that," said his father. "An island named after a fierce bird."

"I'm not sure I do," said Emily.

"Now's not the time to raise questions, Em. You agreed with me months ago that it would be fine. And," he added nastily, "take it easy with those drinks. I can handle them, but you can't."

Emily, still looking a little worried, glared at her husband and defiantly drank the remainder of her martini.

"Any chance I can skip Kestrel, Dad? You know I can't stand camping out. I'd much rather be at the studio all summer."

"You're going to Kestrel. I'm tired of discussing this. One of the networks is going to do a segment on our vacation plans, and Kestrel is the kind of thing a boy like you should be doing. *And* it looks good."

"Could you at least do me one favor?" Rob asked.

"What now?"

"I know I've got to have some Secret Service babysitters, so could you see if Jim and Sid could be two of them? They're pretty cool."

"I'll do my best. In fact, consider it done," Ben Harpswell said, smiling for the first time that evening. "You know," he paused and then continued as they dug into their dessert, "I was told the strangest thing today at a Secret Service briefing. You remember the terrible explosion in Arizona where a nut named Josiah Hummock and his followers died?"

"Hey, Dad, the only people who don't remember that were in a coma. It was bigger than Madonna's baby," said Tony, laughing.

"I guess you're right, but the thing you might not remember is that some of the children had been released by Hummock before the explosion. A dozen or so. Now, the Secret Service thinks maybe these kids have banded together to avenge Hummock."

As Ben Harpswell spelled out the story to them, Rob and Tony stared at him in fascination. As soon as he stopped talking, they pummeled him with questions. "I've told you all I know, guys. It's probably a lot of hogwash, but it's still a hell of a story. Perfect for Matt Drudge."

When dinner was finished and the family rose from the table, Ben Harpswell put his arm around Tony, whose shoulders drooped in anticipation of the studying ahead of him. "Cheer up. I'm feeling generous tonight. I'm going to give you a presidential pardon. We'll all watch *Fort Apache* together."

 The FedEx package arrived just after nine in the morning. Nick, who was alone in the house, hurriedly opened it when he saw it was from Duane Bascombe. Stapled to a thick folder was a handwritten note:

Mr. Agent Man—

Seems that little check of yours motivated me a bit. I think I got what you want. The old silver mine that I bought for Josiah is near Stovepipe Wells, CA. Enclosed is a copy of the deed and a BLM survey map. If you want me to keep digging, some more $$$ would sure give me some extra motivation. Get my drift?

Duane

Nick rushed to the phone and called Andy Backus. He told his assistant that it was urgent.

"What's up, Nick?" he asked when he came on the line.

"We're in business. I know where the children are."

11 The U.S. GeoSurvey maps of the quadrant that included Stovepipe Wells, California, covered half of the large conference table in Andy Backus's office. The other half was papered with aerial photographs of the area immediately surrounding the mine. The photos, taken by a Zeiss Beta infrared camera from an altitude of 2,000 feet, had been shot at night from a special Bell 407 helicopter with noise suppressors, flown out of Nellis Air Force Base.

The maps were topological, showing the contours of the land surrounding the mine. A line that snaked behind the mine indicated a ridge that rose steeply to almost eight hundred feet above the back entrance.

"Photo interp says the road to the mine is definitely in use," said Andy to the small group of Secret Service and ATF people gathered around the table. "The three night runs we've made have not picked up any of the kids or their vehicles, but that's not a surprise. The road, if it can be called that, is visible from the mine entrance, up to half a mile, so we'll have to leave our vehicles here," he pointed to a spot on a map that was taped to the blackboard behind him, "near this wash, which is about a mile from the mine. Nick and I have decided that the best time to stage the raid is just before dawn, which is at five-eighteen Pacific daylight time.

"There'll be fourteen of us involved in the assault itself. An additional four will come from the west. They will position themselves a half hour before then on this ridge here. Because of the vertical rise, we don't believe escape is possible this way, but our people will be able to monitor any activities hidden from our view. There is a garage here"—he motioned again toward the blackboard—"facing in the same direction, which looks large enough to hold up to six vehicles. Any questions so far?"

"Andy, where are you planning to assemble the team from?" asked the head of presidential security.

"We'll be joined by ATF, who will be supplying personnel from their Vegas office. I know most of them. They've done this kind of op before."

"No FBI involvement?"

"Since there's potentially a weapons cache involved and a threat to the security of the executive branch, we felt we should do this op without the help of Mr. LaChance," he answered, smiling.

"Why are you so sure the kids are in this place?" asked Laurie Abbott.

"For a couple of reasons. One is that there was a pattern of calls from the general area to Sandy Price's house preceding and following the attempt to kidnap her daughter. Also, Josiah Hummock bought this property a year before the events at Mesa Blanca. We believe he was thinking of using it as some kind of hideout."

"But didn't he buy several other properties in California at the same time? At least that's in Nick's report."

"Correct," Nick answered. "But this is the property that makes the most sense. We all think it's worth a shot."

"When are you planning to go in, Andy?" asked Laurie.

"We leave tomorrow. We'll do run-throughs for one day at Nellis. The mine isn't that far away from the base. We're aiming to pay our visit in three days."

"That would make it Sunday," Laurie said, after a moment.

"That's right," said Nick, almost to himself. "The Lord's day. Sort of fitting, isn't it?"

12 Jebediah was at the wheel of the Land Rover. Mary sat next to him. In the back seat were Hannah and Seth, the two kids they'd brought with them to help Mary shop for supplies later. Hannah, now that she was living with her older sister again, had picked up many of Mary's mannerisms, like tossing her hair and running her fingers through it to pull it away from her face.

They drove at the speed limit southeast through high desert toward Las Vegas, which had the nearest airport. It was a five-hour drive, so they'd started out before sunrise. There was no conversation between Mary and Jebediah. There was no need. They had made their plans days before and they both knew what they had to do. The younger children with them also were quiet, as long ago they had learned to be in their elders' presence.

As the sun started to edge above the horizon, Mary looked away from the highway for a moment and bowed her head briefly, signaling the two children to begin the first prayer they always recited at this time. Chanting softly, they began.

> "Our father, Josiah,
> Who is always with us,
> Honored is your name.
> Your path we follow,
> Your enemies are ours,

For vengeance is our joy,
In this world and forever more."

When they finished their prayers, silence again filled the car as the sun rose higher and flooded the highway stretching out before them. Nearing Las Vegas, they dropped farther south, skirting the city and heading toward the airport. When Jebediah got out, Mary slid into the driver's seat. She squeezed his hand as he stood outside the car.

"I'll be back with you soon," he said, then waved to the children and disappeared into the terminal.

When Mary and her helpers arrived at the supermarket, she handed Seth and Hannah a long shopping list and sent them off with their carts. When they were no longer in sight, she quickly wheeled her cart to the front of the store where there was a pay phone.

"It's me," she said, as soon as the phone at the other end was picked up.

She waited a long time before there was a response.

"Time for a trip," said the voice on the other end. "Do you understand?"

"Yes."

"You know what to do?"

"Yes," she said, and a moment later there was a click and the line went dead.

As she hung up, Seth and Hannah appeared in front of her. "Who were you calling?" asked Hannah.

"The weather. I wanted to see how hot it will be today. The car's been overheating."

"I couldn't read your writing," said Seth, pointing to a word on the list.

"Well, move your finger so I can see what it is. Canned tomatoes. Seems pretty clear to me. What's the problem?"

"I thought it said canned potatoes," the boy said sheepishly.

"I told him that was silly, but he had to check with you," said Hannah, with a smug smile.

"That's all right," answered Mary, as she tousled Seth's hair. "Now run along, and step on it. We have a job to get done."

13 When they set out, there was enough moonlight for them not to need their night goggles. The men were dressed in black fatigues topped by lightweight plastic-resin helmets. Their bulky Kevlar body armor made them look like bodybuilders.

The first half mile up the rutted, rocky trail was steeply pitched, and their labored breathing was the only sound in the vast stillness of the valley floor. Del Massey, a senior ATF agent whom Andy Backus had selected to head the team, was on point ten yards ahead. As they approached a sharp bend Massey signaled them to stop.

"Once we make that turn," he whispered, "we're visible from the mine entrance. So, extra quiet from now on. Okay?"

They nodded and crouched lower as they followed Massey around the bend. A line of red now outlined the peaks of the Grapevine Mountains to the east. The immensity of the sky that capped the valley was beginning to go from black to blue-gray. It would be light in less than thirty minutes. Nick realized that his hands were shaking. Not a whole lot, but too much. *Come on, Barrows. Pull it together. You're off the sauce. Your hands don't shake anymore. That was another guy.* He tightened his grip on the stock of his AR-15. *That's it. Now you've got the hands of a brain surgeon. Rocksteady. This is going to be a piece of cake. The kids'll all be sleeping in their beds. Clutching their stuffed animals. We'll just wake them up and then lead them out. Maybe we'll all have breakfast together at the House of Pancakes. What we're going to have here, Mr. Barrows, is a G-rated operation. No one hurt. Everybody happy. Just like in the movies.*

When they reached the mine entrance, Massey motioned to the men who would enter there, to move to the side and wait. They would stay there until contacted by two-way radio. Massey, Andy, Nick, and two other ATF agents moved around to the back. They walked slowly, carefully placing each step down. Massey stopped and knelt to pick up something. He turned and grinned. He was holding a Coke can. He tipped it upside down. A few drops of brown liquid dribbled out. Nick turned to Andy. They nodded to each other. The children must be inside.

The men spread out as they approached the garage. The aluminum door gleamed in the early light. There was no handle to pull it up. It worked on a solenoid. A door was set at the side. Something large was on the ground in front it. Massey moved near it and prodded it with his gun. He shined his flashlight down. It was a dead lamb. Massey rolled it over with the gun barrel. The animal's eyes, as lifeless as buttons, stared up. A deep, dark half-circle showed where its throat had been cut.

Andy motioned to Massey to try the door. Before he could open it, Nick stopped him. There was a mark drawn on it. Nick turned his flash on it and saw a large X scrawled from top to bottom.

"What the fuck?" Andy said under his breath.

"Jesus," muttered Massey. "What the hell is this?"

Nick reached out and with his gloved hand touched the mark. A few flakes parasoled to the ground. He flicked another bit onto his palm. The rusty chip disintegrated as he pressed down on it.

"It's blood," Nick said, looking at the others.

"Blood?" Andy whispered back. "You sure?"

Nick nodded. Massey stepped in front of him and turned the knob. The door opened easily. They entered the garage in single file. There was the smell of oil but nothing else. Whatever vehicles had been here, were now gone.

"Falcon. Falcon. This is Raven. Come in, Falcon," Massey said into his radio.

The radio crackled for a moment before they heard the response.

"Yes, Raven. Falcon here."

"We're inside site B. Proceeding beyond. Initiate your sweep. Read me?"

"Read you clear. We're moving."

They walked toward another door set into the back wall. It led into the main tunnel. The passageway was as dark as a pocket. They all turned on their flashlights. The air smelled wet and musty like leaves after a rain. A faint breeze blew at them from the mine entrance. A hundred feet beyond they came to a large metal door. They stood outside the door for a full minute, listening intently for any sound from the other side. Nothing. Then they heard a noise. They instinctively gripped their weapons. A shaft of light danced along the wall in front of them. It was the team who had entered from the front.

"Anything?" asked Massey.

The agent in the head shook his head.

"Well," said Massey softly, "let's do it."

He leaned in against the door and with all his might slid the heavy door to one side. A flood of white light poured out of the room as they rushed in. All the lights were on, but the room was empty. Absolutely empty. The only thing that broke the starkness of the place were some words that had been painted in black on the opposite wall. The lettering was precise and the words were poster-size. Whoever did it had spent a lot of time at it.

I AM HE THAT LIVETH, AND WAS DEAD;
AND, BEHOLD, I AM ALIVE FOREVER MORE, AMEN;
AND HAVE THE KEYS OF HELL AND OF DEATH.

"What the hell does that mean?" asked Andy loudly.

"It must be from the Bible," answered Nick.

Four men came back from searching the other rooms.

"Anything?"

"Same as here, Andy. They're as empty as a nun's fridge."

"Massey, tell the guys on the ridge to come on down. As soon as we have full light we'll do a complete search of the surrounding area. Also, call the lab people. I want every fucking surface here dusted. Got it?"

"Right, Andy."

"Hey"—he turned after Massey had left, and looked at Nick—"let's get out of here. I need a cigarette."

The sun was peeking over the mountains and the first intimation of the intense heat that would come later was in the air. Nick and Andy walked down the rocky trail in silence.

"This is not going to look great when I file my report," Andy said finally, as he tossed his cigarette to the ground.

"What do you mean?"

"The cost of this op wasn't chicken feed, Nick. The people in D.C., they like results. But what'd we turn up? A dead lamb and some Biblical graffiti? Not much of a payoff for the expense and effort."

"But we showed that they had been here," said Nick, his voice rising.

"I believe that and so do you, but will we be able to prove it? All we know positively was that *somebody* was living here."

"Who else would leave a quote like that on the wall?"

"You're preaching to the converted, Nick. You know what I think? The real question here is not that the children were or were not living here, because you and I know that they were. No, what we have to find out is who tipped them off." Andy turned and looked at Nick.

"Bascombe!" Nick said.

"We have to locate him. We both have a lot of work to do. And we don't have much time. I think these kids are using Bascombe.

They're very smart and very dangerous. And if we don't find them soon they're going to kill again. And again. Until they reach the top."

"The top?"

"You know where they're aiming. They want POTUS."

"Yes," Nick agreed as he looked up at the sun that was now arching into the cloudless sky. "Everything so far has just been small change. Curtain raisers. . . . That's their goal. Jesus! The president of the United States."

part six

"The children
are back."

1 The houses were large and luxurious, eight-thousand-square-foot statements of their owners' status in the world. They were designed in a number of styles, mostly Spanish, but their sheer bulk and expensiveness made them compatible. Each occupied a four-acre site and was landscaped with desert flora that shielded one from the other, creating private domains. None were visible from the road that coiled around them.

Saguaro Vista was east of Phoenix, tucked beneath the Superstition Mountains, and a winter retreat for most of its older, retired residents. At this time of the year, only a handful of the thirty-five houses surrounding either the golf course or the artfully designed lake next to it were inhabited. The only people the Hummock clan had seen so far were half a dozen Mexican gardeners who were clipping, mowing, and raking.

The emptiness of the enclave was perfect for them. They had arrived several days before, in two Land Rovers, late in the evening in order not to attract attention. The guard at the front gate was expecting them and turned over the keys at once, no questions asked. Mary marveled at how smoothly everything ran, just as it had in the mine, and she knew she could count on it.

On the second morning after they had arrived, following prayers and breakfast, she called the young ones into the living room to go over the new rules once again. They avoided the chairs and sofas, as if they were artifacts of another tribe, and sat on the floor. Jebediah leaned against a door frame behind Mary, observing the proceedings.

"I told you yesterday," she said to the group, "that the owners of this house are named Hutchinson. If anyone asks who you are, tell them you're their grandchildren. They're traveling in Greece. Your two older cousins, that's Jebediah and me, are taking care of you. Understand?"

The children nodded. Mary looked at their faces for confirmation and then continued.

"Always carry the IDs I gave you. They have private security here and they don't know you. They might stop and question you, but with your IDs, there's nothing to worry about. You can walk or bicycle, but don't go out in the middle of the day, you'll stand out too much. Don't poke around anyone else's property, and don't go out in groups of more than two. Adults don't notice kids too much, but if they see too many kids it makes them nervous and they get suspicious."

"When is Matthew coming back with Sarah?" asked Seth.

Jebediah jumped in. "They'll be here very soon."

"They should have been back by now. Matthew went away weeks and weeks ago. He said it wouldn't take long."

"You have no sense of time," said Jebediah curtly. "Take my word for it, we'll see them soon."

"Something's happened," said Seth. "Something bad."

"What do you know, Seth? You talk way more than you know. Keep quiet and listen for a change," shouted Jebediah.

"I know plenty," said Seth, in a nasty voice.

"I've had enough of you," said Jebediah, his face flushed with anger. He strode over to the boy and slapped him. Blood immediately spurted from Seth's nose.

Mary ran to his side, pulling a handkerchief from her pocket and holding it to his nose. The blood ate hungrily at the cloth, soaking through it.

"Go outside," said Mary to Jebediah. "I'll be right out."

A few minutes later, Mary joined him. "Seth is lying down. The bloody nose has stopped. It's nothing, you know. But we've got a problem. We can't answer his question about Matthew without making a bigger problem. And I think there'll be more questions from the kids. They're getting anxious and upset."

"So am I," said Jebediah.

"The main point is, we've got to push to finish our mission. Now. We can't wait any longer. For our sake and theirs."

"And for Josiah's."

"Amen."

2 "Boring!" said Sarah. She and Sandy were seated in front of the TV in the living room.

"Pipe down, Sarah."

"Change the channel, Mom. You promised I could see *The Simpsons*. This is capital *B*, capital *O*—"

"That's enough, young lady."

Sandy held the remote in her hand. She had just mistakenly hit the wrong button and instead of Sarah's show—her half-hour quota of television for the day—they were face-to-face with Katie Couric.

"Good evening and welcome to Dateline," said the host. "How are you going to spend your summer vacation? Tonight I'm going to show you what the nation's First Family will be doing. I'll be back in a moment."

"Nick! Oh, Nick! Come in here," Sandy called out, as the commercials rolled. She could hear him in the kitchen, opening and then shutting the refrigerator door. *After-dinner ice cream?* "Something's coming up on TV."

"Oh, Mom, you said you'd watch *The Simpsons* with me."

"I'm sorry, but not tonight, honey. Go upstairs and watch with Gina."

Sarah didn't move from her corner of the sofa. Her expression was a Kabuki mask of indignation. "But I wanted to see it with you."

"Get going. Quick, or you'll miss some of it."

Sarah reluctantly got off the sofa and walked to the staircase, just as Nick came in, holding a quart of ice cream with a spoon stuck in the center like the mast of a sailboat.

"Welcome to the White House living quarters," said Katie Couric, as the camera panned down a hallway to French doors that swung open to a large living room awash with chintz. ". . . and to its very special residents, President Harpswell, the First Lady, and the younger generation, Rob, nineteen, and Tony, fourteen. Boys," continued Couric, starting from the bottom up, "are you ready for vacation?"

"I'm amazingly ready," said Rob.

"Me, too," added Tony.

"Is that a beard I see you growing?" asked Couric, as the camera zoomed in on the older son's face.

"Yeah," he said, rubbing his chin to make sure the small swatch of hair was still there. "It's going to be a Vandyke, but without the point."

"I love it," said Couric, laughing as if Rob had said something terribly witty. She then turned to the president. "Sir, will you please tell us your plans?"

"Let me tell you first what I am *not* doing. I'm not doing any personal campaigning. I'm not courting any political groups. Fund-raising, any fund-raising, is strictly off-limits," the president paused to let his words sink in, beaming a deep smile at Couric and at the television audience. "And I'm not, positively not, growing a beard. What I *am* doing is making a major tour of Western states, discussing their interests and concerns, seeing some of our great national parks—and playing tennis. Hopefully, a lot of tennis."

"And didn't I hear something about a family vacation?"

"We'll all meet in Hawaii for a week at the end of August," said Emily Harpswell. "Before that, I'm leaving tomorrow on a good-will tour of Southeast Asia. Tony will be accompanying me, and I hope to give him a taste of that part of the world. We'll have a chance to see some of its wonderful art."

"It all sounds marvelous," said Couric. "Now, Rob, the last word is yours."

The camera once more focused on Rob's beard. "What I'm most excited about is my survival course in Maine. It's kind of like Outward Bound, only tougher. The finale is a two-day solo on a small island near Kestrel Island where the camp is located. And who knows what this"—he rubbed the hair on his chin—"will look like by then."

"What he's hoping for, Katie," the president interjected, "is that the young ladies will find him looking older and more dashing."

"And on that hairy note, let's say good-bye."

Sandy switched off the set. "What do you think?" asked Nick, a moment later.

"Well, POTUS is surrounded by an army of Secret Service. They certainly know how to protect their most important client."

"I just wish Harpswell wasn't going to be pressing the flesh so much," said Sandy.

"He'll still be protected up the gazoo," said Nick.

"Am I hearing a note of optimism, darling?"

"Maybe it's finally time for some of that, Sandy. God, I hope it is."

3 The time they had awaited so long was here.

At six-thirty A.M. one of the two Land Rovers drove past the gate for the last time and away from Saguaro Vista. Minutes earlier, when they had finished their prayers, Jebediah had supervised three of the kids into the first car and headed west toward the airport in San Diego and then north to Los Angeles.

Half an hour later Mary left the house they had stayed in for little more than a week, and turned toward Tucson. She dropped off two of the young ones at the bus depot in town with money for their fares and a ten-dollar lunch, then took the first exit onto the highway to the airport. Solomon sat beside her, and Seth in the backseat. Nobody talked.

Mary was excited, though nothing in her demeanor showed it, so adept was she at controlling her emotions. This was the moment she had anticipated for weeks, an ending and a beginning, a yin and yang of resolution. It had been difficult for her and Jebediah to restrain themselves, to proceed slowly step by step toward the final mission, fitting the earlier pieces together, always moving forward to the last, most critical act of expiation. Now that they were at the edge of the cliff, she was consumed by what they had to do, and could think of nothing else. In Saguaro, she and Jebediah had taken long night walks, out of earshot of the children, rehearsing precisely how they would accomplish what they had to do, how to deal with anything that went wrong, how to extricate themselves and, finally, how to cover their tracks. They were both lean and strong and could handle anything that came their way. They had chosen the place and the time when they would meet the following afternoon, prepared to begin.

When she turned onto the road leading to the airport, Solomon's face lit up with eagerness. He had a role to play, as did the other children, and he was more than ready. When she stopped at the gate, he slid from his seat without a word. Seth jumped out after him and the two of them ran into the terminal, not looking back or waving good-bye.

Once the two boys disappeared through the revolving door, Mary drove to the parking lot. She took a ticket from the machine and parked the car. She left the keys in the ignition and didn't stop to lock it. As she walked toward the gate, she ripped up the ticket and let the pieces flutter to the ground.

The car would not be claimed by her. Ever. She no longer had use for it. Mary had embarked on something larger and more important than any other event in her life, and nothing would bring her back here again.

4 Le Bateau Bleu was a ten-minute walk from Sandy's house. It was a simple and unassuming bistro, and although it was in the heart of residential Washington, to Nick and Sandy's pleasure it was not a hangout for the political crowd. Once or twice a month they would drop by for a quiet dinner. The proprietor, Jean-Luc Marigot, who doubled at the bar, was a native of Marseilles, whose nostalgia for the Mediterranean declared itself in the watercolors, big and small, of fishing ports, sailboats, and beaches, that covered every available inch of wall space. Tonight they were having an early dinner. Sandy could come directly there from her office, and even after a leisurely meal, enough of the evening remained for reading, a movie, playing with Sarah, or getting into bed together.

Nick arrived at seven, but there was no sign of Sandy. His first couple of Cokes, his standard bar drink now, tasted good, but the third was overkill—dull and cloying—and he pushed it aside after a swallow. He waited thirty minutes before he called her office. The line was busy. Ten minutes later it was still busy. She knew he was at the restaurant. Why hadn't she called? He was becoming more annoyed by the moment. And worried. Out of desperation to distract himself, he began picking the toothpicks out of the holder on the table and breaking them in half, then in quarters, then in eighths.

He sensed someone standing next to the table and looked up. Jean-Luc smiled down at him. "I don't blame you for not liking that stuff," he said, pointing to the Coke.

"It tastes too sweet after a while."

"How about a pastis? Very refreshing. Very calming. On the house, of course."

"I think I'll stay away from the hard stuff tonight, Jean-Luc," said Nick.

"Then how about a kir? Perfect for waiting for a lovely lady."

"I'll just have to take a rain check on that, too."

Jean-Luc turned to greet a new customer which gave Nick a chance to try Sandy again. Still busy.

He decided to call the house on the chance she had stopped there. Sarah picked up the phone.

"Hi, darling," he said, keeping his tone casual. "Is your mommy there?"

"No, but wait till you get home. We have a surprise for you and Mom. Gina and I are making it right now. It's in the oven baking."

After playing a short guessing game with her about the contents of the oven, Nick hung up and sat down again. Sandy was almost an hour late now. He would give her five minutes more and then go to her office.

A few minutes later, as he was about to head for the front door, Sandy came up from behind and hugged him. "Nick, thank God you're still here. I'm sorry to be so late. You won't believe what happened."

"Late? Oh, just a bit. One hour and five minutes' worth of late."

"I said I'm sorry, darling."

"You should be sorry. But since you're finally here, sit down." He pulled out a chair, not yet cracking a smile. When she was perched opposite him, he was still so annoyed he couldn't leave it alone. "What's wrong with you?" he demanded. "Why didn't you call me and tell me you'd be late?"

"I would have, but I couldn't get off the phone."

"Can't you come up with a better excuse than that?"

"I'm really sorry, Nick. You must have been worried."

"Damned right. You scared the hell out of me. I didn't know what to think."

"Nick, stop for a second. You're upset and you have a right to be. But what I have to tell you will . . . Well, you won't believe it."

"It'd better be good. Just don't ever, ever do that to me again."

"I won't," said Sandy. "I promise. But, Nick, listen to me. The children are back!"

"What are you talking about?"

"The Hummock children. Every single one of the younger children, with the exception of Caleb, has returned. They've all gone home."

"What? I don't understand."

"About six o'clock, Alma Johnson called me. She was thrilled. Solomon had walked in earlier in the afternoon, behaving as if he'd biked into town to run an errand and had been away an hour. He didn't say a word about where he'd been or why he was back. Nothing. He wasn't at all sullen, she said. Maybe a little preoccupied. As soon as I hung up, Seth's grandparents were on the phone. Seth was home. Then Rachel's stepmother called. The same. So I called the other families myself. Their stories about the children were identical. Most of all, no explanations from them."

"Amazing."

"Exactly what I thought," said Sandy. "I made plane reservations to go see some of them tomorrow. Then I decided to try talking to a couple of the kids on the phone to see if I could get anything out of them. Solomon has always been pretty forthcoming, so I called him first. He said he was happy to be home, he was sorry he'd just taken off the way he had. He was perfectly pleasant, but that was it.

He wouldn't say anything more. Not a word. So I gave up on him, and tried Rachel. Our conversation was even shorter. Then Mark. Ditto."

"What do you think?" asked Nick urgently. He noticed the other diners glancing at them and knew they were trying to listen in to this unexpected slice of soap opera. He leaned toward Sandy, almost whispering. "Maybe it's all over."

"You don't believe that, do you, Nick? I certainly don't."

"You're right, I don't, either. I'd like to, though." He sounded almost wistful. "It just doesn't stop, does it? Well, then, how do you read these tea leaves?"

"They want us to think it's over. Especially the Secret Service. I bet that's what Backus and his people will think."

"What are they going to do next?" Nick asked, hoping Sandy wouldn't say what he knew she would.

"They're getting ready for the endgame."

5 The hotel operator rang Sandy's room. She snatched up the phone at once.

"I just got your message," said Nick on the other end. "Area code 305? Where the hell are you?"

"Coral Gables. Seth's hometown. I've had it for now. I have a flight home tomorrow morning at seven."

"I want to hear what he said, but first I want to tell you Esther called. Can you meet her tomorrow in her office?"

"What time?"

"Two-thirty."

"Great, and tell her yes. It must be about the stuff I gave her from the mine. The quote from the Bible and the slaughtered lamb."

"Also, you were right about the Secret Service. I just got back from seeing Backus and Vargas. Laurie was there, too. As soon as I told them all the younger kids had returned home, they started smiling as if they'd won the lottery. It was almost high-fives time. 'That's great,' they said. 'They've given up. The whole thing's over. There's nothing to worry about any longer.'"

"They're crazy. What about Jebediah and Mary? And where's Caleb? He hasn't returned."

"Caleb, they said, will probably show up in a day or two. The key is the two oldest ones. They were the leaders and now it's just the two of them. Backus pointed out that they still have an APB out on them. They're convinced they'll be picked up any day now. They're obviously on the run which makes them more vulnerable and infinitely less dangerous. They have to be thinking most of all about how to avoid detection, not about knocking off someone else."

"Well, I see their point . . . but they're completely wrong."

"You're not kidding. They think their security operation can handle any threat. Backus says the Service has as large a protection detail as they've ever had on POTUS and the vice president. The First Lady and her younger son are out of the country. Rob, the older son, is on a wilderness trip on a remote island in Maine with Secret Service protection. So they asked, what's the problem? But tell me about Seth," said Nick.

"It was a perfectly pleasant meeting," said Sandy. "Norman Rockwell could have painted it. He came in for milk and cookies after seeing some old friends, and he was all smiles. We sat down in the living room and talked for over a half an hour. He admitted straight off that he and the others had been in touch all the time and had planned almost from the beginning to run away. They never saw Mary or Jebediah, he said, or even talked to them on the phone. They lived together in the streets, mostly in New York. If anyone looked at them suspiciously, they went to a new place— first Newark, then Albany. When I asked him why they wanted to live that way, he said they just wanted to be together again, that was the only reason. But it didn't work out. It was not the same as when they were together at Mesa Blanca, so they decided to come home. Period. End of story."

"It sounds familiar," said Nick. "A replay of what the others told you."

"Yes, and a total fabrication. But this is what gets me. They've all used the same—the very same—words to describe what happened."

 Esther Blum's office was located two floors below Sandy's. The Theology Department was a small one, tucked between Archaeology and Classical Literature. The department head was constantly fighting for more space, mostly without success. Esther was an unredeemed chain-smoker which had led her to put a large sign on her office door: IF YOU SMOKE THERE'S NO NEED TO KNOCK!

Sandy rapped twice on the door and walked in.

"Sorry. I thought you were alone," she said, seeing her friend with a student. She turned and started to close the door behind her.

"Come on in, Sandy. Arthur's just finished," Esther Blum called out. "Arthur Garvin, this is Dr. Sandy Price. She operates in an all-too-real world: abnormal psych." A tall student with hair as red as cayenne, stood up and formally shook Sandy's hand. "Arthur's doing a paper on the relevance of Sodom and Gomorrah to today's accepted views of sexual conduct. He has a great title: 'Sodom and Gomorrah—Cautionary Parable or Today's Theme Park?' Don't you love it?"

"Next Wednesday?" the student asked, as he walked to the door.

"Same time, same place, Arthur. Have a good week."

"You, too, Professor Blum," he said, smiling broadly as he left the office.

"We need a little air in here, Ess. Desperately," said Sandy, as she went to the window and opened it. "That's better. God, this place is murkier than London in the days when they burned coal."

"Do I have to hear this from a friend?" Esther asked, as she lighted an unfiltered Gitane. "Remember what Disraeli said? 'Tobacco is the tomb of love.'"

"What the hell does that mean?"

"I have no idea, but I adore it. Now sit down and relax. You look a bit out of sorts. Some coffee? Water? I have gas and nongas. Chiclets? Tums? You name it and Blum's got it."

"Nothing, Ess. Just blow the smoke toward the window." Sandy studied her friend. Today she was wearing a dress that a flamenco dancer would have felt comfortable in and orange medallion earrings the size of Ping-Pong balls.

"You like?" she asked Sandy, after exhaling contrails of smoke from her nostrils. "Got them at a flea market in Bethesda last weekend. Aren't they a scream?"

"What are they?"

"Pizzas made of Bakelite. I love them."

More smoke issued from Mount Esther, which Sandy tried to wave away from her face.

"Ess, you're gong to be the first individual in history to have a class-action suit brought against you for secondhand smoke pollution."

"Stop complaining. I'm the one with the two-pack habit."

"I guess you have something there."

"How's the FBI-agent hunk?"

"Nick's fine."

"Sarah?"

"Fine, too. That Hummock business seems far in the past now for her, and she never brings it up," said Sandy as she pushed the ashtray on the desk closer to Esther. "Did you get a chance to look at that material I sent you?"

"Of course. What are you and Nick doing? Thinking of reviving the *Twilight Zone*?"

"Stop joking. That was just a recap of what Nick and the others found when they raided the mine in Death Valley."

"Pretty creepy, I'd say."

"I don't need you to tell me that. That's not why I had you look at it. I want your opinion as a theologist."

"Unfortunately, a very single theologist."

"Very funny, Ess. Did you see anything that might help us?"

"The passage is from Revelation, which, of course, I'm sure you already know."

"That's about all we know."

"It's from a section called The Revelation to John. This is the part that has all the 'sevens': seven golden lampstands, seven churches, and, most importantly, the Seven Seals. Fringe religious groups are gaga for the Seven Seals. They love 'em to death. David Koresh was obsessed with them. And maybe the Seals were the touchstone of what Hummock's teachings were all about." She took a book out of the bookcase. "Listen to this: 'The second is blood-red. A gleaming sword swings in deadly arcs. Where it passes slaughter follows. Men slay one another, brother against brother in deadly combat. Peace is removed from the earth.' And the Seventh Seal is the capper: 'Then, an eerie silence covers the devastated landscape, with corpses for company. Even the wind is dead.' That's it. The end of the world."

"And that's where Josiah Hummock led them. But what do the slaughtered lamb and the blood on the door mean?"

"I know you're a shiksa, my favorite shiksa by the way, but don't you remember anything from my folks' seder last year? I know that my mother's lighter-than-air matzoh balls are memorable, but the lamb and the blood were certainly discussed. It's an integral part of the story."

"Remind me."

"I guess you need a little touch-up on the meaning of Passover. Do you remember who Moses was?"

"Cut to the chase, Ess. And please don't light up another cigarette."

"You're such a nag, Sandy. Now, where was I? Yes, Moses. I'll skip the whole business of Moses being found in the bullrushes, and being saved and adopted by the Pharoah's daughter. Jump-cut to years later, when the Pharaoh resisted Moses' pleas to free all the Hebrews. This pissed God off, so he sent ten plagues to Egypt. The last was particularly devastating: the firstborn son of every Egyptian family, including the Pharaoh's, would die. So, before the killing began, Moses instructed the Israelites to kill a lamb and to put its blood on their doorposts. That would signal to the Angel of Death that the house was occupied by an Israelite. The Angel would then *pass over* it when he came to kill the firstborn. End of story."

Sandy Price stared at Esther.

"I know I tell a pretty good story, but I generally don't leave my audience catatonic. Are you still with me, Dr. Price?"

"Firstborn," Sandy said, almost to herself. "It's not the president they're going after."

"What are you talking about?"

"The blood on the door of the mine must refer to the president's son."

"I still don't get what you're talking about. Clue me in, will you, Sandy?"

Sandy Price stood up quickly and walked to the door.

"Where you going? I thought you'd stay and we'd have a good old-fashioned schmooze."

"I have to call Nick. Right away," Sandy said over her shoulder.

"Hey, Sandy. At least you can close the frigging door. Do you hear me?"

But by then she was gone and the only response Esther Blum

received was the sound of Sandy's heels clicking as she ran down the hallway.

7   When Nick was finally patched through to Andy Backus, he was flying with the First Lady and her younger son from Manila to Jakarta. He sounded tired. As soon as Nick started to tell him whom they believed was Jebediah and Mary's ultimate target, he snapped at him.

"Damn it, Nick, you know better than to say anything like that on an unsecured line. Get your ass down to my office and we can talk from there. I have another hour and a half left to go on this leg, so if you get going now, you'll still be able to reach me."

Andy had called ahead to Secret Service headquarters on G Street, and within minutes of arriving at the building, Nick and Sandy were on the line to Andy. After Sandy went through everything Esther Blum had told her, Nick jumped in.

"It all adds up, Andy. These kids have been following step by step a plan that Hummock laid out for them four years ago. All the earlier killings have been a rehearsal for the final set piece. They're going to try to kill Rob Harpswell, the president's older son—his firstborn. They're so confident they've even given us clues."

At first Nick and Sandy thought the connection had been broken because it took Backus so long to respond.

"This is so bizarre, Nick, I don't know what to say. What do you want me to do?"

"I want you to double—no, triple—the detail protecting Rob. He's at that camp in Maine now, isn't he?"

"That's right. Look, Nick, after our mine caper, a lot of people—and I mean a lot, in my agency *and* in Treasury—decided I wasn't wrapped very tight. When you told me about the Hummock business, and after we investigated the hell out of it, I went along with you. What you were saying made sense. Terrible sense. But we struck out at the mine, and since then nothing, but nothing, has happened. And all of the younger children have returned home. I can't just increase the detail on Rob Harpswell now because you have a new theory. The slaughtered lamb at the mine signifies the Angel of Death—oh, excuse me, I mean the two older Hummock kids, who are now going to assassinate the president's son, instead of the president. Give me a break. By the way, I called Kestrel Island after you called me the first time and my people assured me everything is fine there. Totally under control."

"Well, at least let us go up there and and see if there's anything they haven't picked up on. That's all I'm asking for, Andy," Nick pleaded.

"Jesus, Nick, you never give up, do you? Okay, this is what I'll do. You know Fred Crockett, right? You met him in my office when we were planning the raid on the mine. He's chief assistant. I'll have him line up a plane tomorrow and he'll go with the two of—"

"It has to be today!"

"All right. Today. I'll call him as soon as you hang up. Just stay where you are. He'll pick you up."

"You're doing the right thing, Andy."

"I hope so. Just don't tell anyone what the reason for your going up there is. If you do I could wind up in Garry Trudeau's strip on a regular basis," said Andy Backus, sighing.

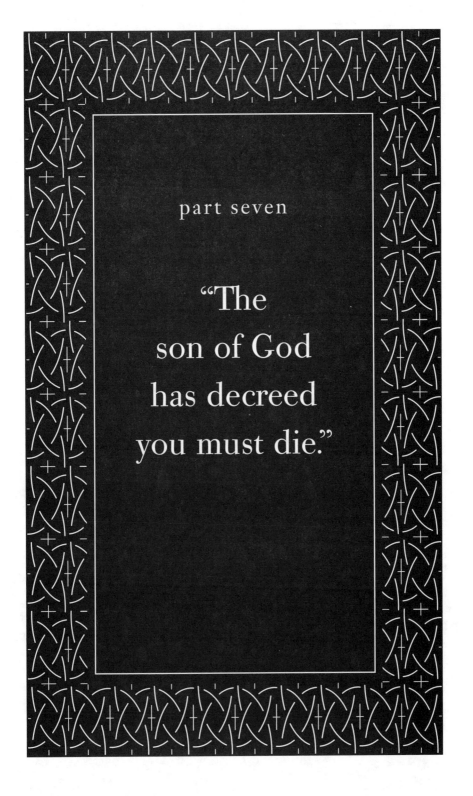

part seven

"The
son of God
has decreed
you must die."

1 Fred Crockett wasn't built for small jets. When he emerged from the flight deck of the agency's Citation IV after consulting with the pilot, he had to bow his head so low it looked as if he were inspecting his shoes for scuff marks. Fred was six-three, with skin so pale that the veins in his temple and forehead stood out in their blueness like rivers on a map.

"Well, we can't land in Bar Harbor," he said, as he fitted himself into the seat opposite Nick and Sandy. "It's totally fogged in."

"Oh no," said Nick, who was increasingly anxious to reach the camp.

"They don't have the right navigational equipment. The pilot's going to try for Bangor instead. The weather's not much better, but he thinks we can make an instrument approach."

"How much farther away is it?"

"Not far. It'll add about an hour to our trip."

Nick realized his foot was tapping like a metronome. *Come on,* he told himself. *Relax. We're going to get there in time to stop anything Jebediah and Mary might try. They'd been stopped before. They didn't get Sarah and they didn't get me, either. And they can be stopped now. Switch your attention to something a little lighter. Like some normal conversation. It's called "small talk." Remember?*

"Didn't Andy tell me you're from Maine?"

"Wiscasset. Born and raised there. Fifth generation. My mom and dad live in Brunswick now. Just south of Wiscasset."

"Guess you're used to fog," said Sandy.

"You bet. My dad's a lawyer but he and I used to pull traps to-gether—"

"Pull traps?"

"Oh, excuse me. My dad had a lobster boat. As a hobby. I used to go out with him whenever I could. At least half the time, we were operating in fog. Sometimes it was so thick we could barely see twenty feet in front of us."

The FASTEN SEAT BELT sign flashed on, accompanied by a soft sound of chimes.

"We'd better buckle up," said Fred, as he looked out the small window at the dense futon of fog below them. "Boy, look at that stuff. We'll be lucky if we can find the luggage carousel when we get on the ground."

The *Marambo,* the converted lobster boat the camp used as its util-ity craft, slowly pushed through the fog and small swells toward Kestrel Island. Kestrel was four miles out to sea from Bar Harbor. The captain of the boat only occasionally looked through the windshield, preferring to direct his gaze at the dark green radar screen mounted in front of the steering wheel. Every few seconds a light swept the circle of the screen, highlighting whatever was in their path.

"Is that Kestrel?" Sandy asked the captain, pointing to a round blot off to their right.

"No, ma'am, that's Badger Island. Kestrel's up here," he replied, placing his finger on a small fanlike shape.

"When will we see it?" Nick asked, as he moved next to Sandy.

"When we're alongside the dock," said the captain, laughing. "Kestrel's about the prettiest island around here, but you're not going to see much of her today, or tomorrow according to the latest weather bulletin."

As soon as they arrived on the island, they were directed to the camp's office where they met Hector Vidal and Wendy Sluman, the two Secret Service agents based there. Andy Backus had instructed Fred not to tell the agents about Nick's belief that there could be an attempt on the life of Rob Harpswell. The reason they were there, Fred told the agents, was that Andy wanted Nick, who was doing liaison work between the Agency and the FBI, to see how a small security operation was set up. Sandy was introduced as a research psychologist working with Nick. Vidal and Sluman didn't seem a bit suspicious, in fact they appeared happy to have them there. It was a welcome break from their routine and a chance to have some fresh conversation after being on the island for almost three weeks.

"We've always been told that the most boring assignment in the history of the service was guarding Mrs. Truman in Independence, Missouri, after President Truman's death," said Hector, "but being stuck here sure comes close."

"It hasn't been like this all the time, has it?" Nick asked.

"You got to understand Hector," said Wendy Sluman, smiling at her partner. "He's a city boy."

"*Barrio* boy, Wendy—there's a big difference."

"You see, he feels distinctly uncomfortable if he isn't surrounded by the gentle sounds of boom boxes and police sirens. For Hector, Kestrel Island is like being on the dark side of the moon."

"Give me a police siren over a foghorn any day."

"Who's out with Rob now?" Fred asked.

"Jim Rinker and Sid Blau. We're running an eight-agent detail. The two of us here, two at the Coast Guard station in Bar Harbor, two swing men, and Rinker and Blau, who are on a boat moored just off the island where Rob is. We radio them every two hours. They're going stir-crazy a little faster than we are. Imagine," said Hector, "being trapped on a boat the size of a holding cell for two days. We were supposed to relieve them, but with the fog we decided it would be more efficient if they just stayed out there."

"Why're they on a boat?" Sandy asked. "Shouldn't they be on-shore with Rob?"

"Against the camp's rules, Dr. Price," answered Agent Sluman. "He's doing a solo. He has to be alone. And that's what the president ordered, too. The island's called Little Bucket. It's about ten acres of forest, rocky shores, and mosquitoes. Lots of mosquitoes. Hector and I did the security survey. This place is the easiest setup we've ever had. We chose it for Rob's solo because it's the farthest island from the mainland.

"Our compromise was to have Rinker and Blau anchor just past the cove where he's camping. Rob also has a two-way radio we gave him. If he needs us, we're there in minutes. The whole purpose of the forty-eight-hour solitary is to be alone and self-sufficient. He was put on the island early this morning without—"

"Food, tent, bedding, extra clothes . . ." said an older man with a tanned, deeply creased face, from the doorway.

"Win, come on in," Hector called out. He quickly introduced them to Winthrop Blair, the founder and director of Camp Kestrel.

"Call me, Win," he said. "Everybody does."

A few minutes later they walked to his office, a square-timbered room with a large picture window, to sample his celebrated sassafras-bark tea, which even Hector had grown to appreciate.

"I wouldn't be surprised if Rob was drinking a cup himself right now," Win said, as he poured the tea into mugs. "There's sassafras on the island, he can get water from a small pond not far where he's soloing, and he has flint to start a fire with. Aside from the flint the only thing we allowed him to take was a pad and a pencil. All the campers are encouraged to keep a journal of their thoughts and feelings. The purpose of the experience is to dig deep into both your body and your soul."

"When will he finish?"

"He's been on Little Bucket almost eight hours," Win answered, looking at his watch. "That means he's got a little more than a day and a half to go. We'll be taking him off at sunup the day after to-morrow."

"Where are the other campers?" Nick asked.

"There are eight others, each alone on their own small islands. All of them are scattered around Kestrel," he said pointing to a large nautical chart hanging on the wall behind his desk. "None is more than a couple of miles from here."

"Nine campers. I'd say you run a pretty small camp," said Nick, jokingly.

"I'd agree with that assessment," Win answered. "But we run a pretty-normal-size camp the rest of the summer. It's only now that we do the wilderness survival course for a few qualified candidates. Culminating, of course, with the forty-eight-hour solo. We get over two hundred applicants for the nine slots each year. This year we started a Web site. You wouldn't believe the number of hits we've gotten."

"Everybody seems to have a Web site these days. What do you put up on it?"

"Funny you should ask that, Nick. As soon as you folks finish your tea I'm going to be posting what happened yesterday. I try to update it every day. I include things like how many kids are solo-ing, what islands we're using, sea temperature, the weather—"

"You don't mention Rob, do you?" Nick asked.

"Of course not. My Secret Service friends have given me strict guidelines on that," answered Win.

"Speaking of guidelines, Hector," said Wendy, "it's getting to be time for us to check with the guys watching Hitch. Why don't the three of you come along. We can have lunch afterward."

"Hitch?" asked Nick.

"Everyone in the First Family has a security handle. Rob, because he's into movies, particularly anything by Alfred Hitchcock, naturally became Hitch."

—Kestrel Base to Novelty. Come in, Novelty.

—Novelty here, Kestrel.

—How you doing, Sid?

—Rinkydink and I are having a fine old time here on the QE 3. Fog's so thick we didn't have to wash this morning.

—Any contact with Hitch?

—Jim took the dinghy in at thirteen-twenty and eyeballed him.

—Did Hitch spot him?

—Negative.

—Good. How's he doing?

—Better than we are, I'm sure. Jim said he was writing in his journal and looked as comfortable leaning against a rock as if he were at Club Med.

I've been here now on Little Bucket for almost six hours, I think. It feels more like sixty. Thanks a lot, Dad! The great El Presidente strikes again. My father's rule: As long as it looks good in the media, it's worth doing. God, I wish I was back in L.A. The studio was great. And the girls were greater. We're supposed to be keeping a journal, which I've already started. I'm sure my father will ask to see it when this thing is over. I'm loading it with lots of nature shit. Makes me sound sort of like Thoreau in Timberland boots. But what I'm writing here is my anti-journal. I really do like to camp out but this is ridiculous. Prisoners at the Hanoi Hilton had it better. Since I don't have a watch, I don't have a clue what time it is. The fog is so dense you can almost chew it. I've already cut branches for my "bed" and it looks like a torture device. I do have a nice fire going and I even made myself some tea. I had no problem finding the sassafras but when I brewed it up, it tasted nothing like the stuff

Win makes. In fact, it tasted like shit. The raspberries and blueber-
ries are a lot better, though. I'm waiting for low tide now. I spotted
some mussels in a tidal pool. Maybe I'll be able to cook some up.

An hour or so ago I thought I heard something rustling around
in the woods. There are no animals on this island (at least that's
what Win told us), and it made me a little nervous. I went and
checked, but found nothing. I guess it was either Jimmy or Sid. I
know my dad told them to let me do this on my own, to stay away,
but I wish they were right here with me. I know they're sitting in
their boat not far away but I still feel totally alone. It's actually
pretty scary. Yes, I do have the two-way radio but I still feel jumpy.
I've never been alone like this before. It really is strange. And the
fog makes it even stranger. This place would make a great setting
for a Wes Craven movie.

2 Nick awoke before first light. He tried to get back to sleep, but after fifteen minutes of tossing and turning, plumping his pillow, and pulling the blanket back over him from Sandy's side, he knew he couldn't. He got up, dressed quietly in the dark, and then went to his overnight bag and took out one of the two guns he had brought with him. He put the snub nose in his pocket and left the cabin. There was no reason for taking the gun, in fact, they'd probably be leaving Kestrel later in the day, but Nick felt better with the gun on him.

He made his way with the aid of a flashlight to the command post. He pushed the door open a fraction and saw Hector Vidal asleep on a cot, the amber and red lights of the radio phone glowing on the table next to his head. He closed the door and walked down to the dock. The *Marambo* sat in its slip, its rubber fenders compressing against the pilings from the light chop that tapped rhythmically against the boat. A chorus of foghorns rolled over the island. He left the dock and walked across a field and then through a stand of old pine trees to the water. The rocky shore that ringed the island, was made up of huge slabs of granite randomly piled atop each other as if a child had grown tired of playing with them and left them there. Nick sat down on a gray stone, flat as a bench. Though he was less than forty feet from the shoreline, he could not make out the water through the fog. He reached down and picked up a small, rounded rock. He tossed it into the water.

What's bothering you, Barrows? Stop worrying. They can't get to Rob Harpswell. He's on an island out at sea, for Christ's sake. And don't forget the fog. It's thicker than Schwarzenegger's biceps. Plus there are two agents with him. Okay, so technically they're not with *him. But they're on a boat that's only a few hundred yards away. And he has a two-way radio. Anything goes wrong and they'll be with him in moments.*

Then why the hell are you starting to panic again? The other Hummock kids are all back with their families. This crazy, murderous thing is over. That's what Backus thinks. And he's no dummy. And the rest of the Secret Service agree. But they don't know Jebediah and Mary, do they? Not the way you and Sandy do. That's why you're scared. As long as the two of them are out there, the threat exists.

After breakfast you'll play it real nonchalant and get Win to allow you, Fred, and Sandy to go out to Little Bucket in the Marambo. *Just a social visit to the agents in the boat. Won't disturb Rob a bit. Won't set foot on the island. Scout's honor. Maybe seeing that things are nice and secure will stop this feeling in your gut, this cold, steely feeling that keeps twisting your insides. Let's hope so.*

Nick stood up. The sky was beginning to lighten. It was time to wake Sandy, then Fred.

Last night sucked. My "comfortable" pine-bough bed felt like a bed of nails after a few minutes. When it wasn't pinching it was itching. I sat up most of the night, which is not my favorite way of sleeping. When I finally dozed off near daybreak, something woke me up that scared the crap out of me. I could have sworn that I heard voices. Just off the shore. Real close. I was so rattled I almost radioed Jimmy and Sid. But then, just like that, the voices were gone. I guess I was just dreaming. Now that it's light I'm going to get something to eat. More berries, I guess. (I'd give anything for a jelly doughnut right now!) Then I'll refill my canteen from the pond. After I eat I'm going to give this bed thing another shot. Don't want to spend tonight, my last night, sleeping sitting up! Maybe I didn't cut enough boughs. Oh, for a real bed and a pillow!

I just heard a voice again. It's coming from the water. And I'm not dreaming. It sounds like a guy's voice. Seems nearby. Maybe I should call Sid? But he'll think I'm just a scared kid. Well, I guess I am scared. I think I'll go see what's up. More later.

"Hello! Anyone there? Am I near land? Hello!"

The voice sounded close. Very close. Rob peered into the white blanket of fog, but couldn't make out a thing.

"Hello!" he yelled back, his hands megaphoned around his mouth. "Head this way. I think you're right offshore."

"Keep talking. I'll head toward you," the voice yelled back.

"Over here. This way."

And then he heard the splash of a paddle and a moment later the nose of a yellow kayak, bright as a crayon, slipped out of the fog. Rob reached and grabbed the bow line and pulled the kayak in.

"Hey, thanks a lot," said the young man, climbing out of the tight cockpit of the boat. "Where am I?" he asked, as he shook Rob's hand.

"Little Bucket Island."

"Wow! I'm way off course. I was going for Ram's Horn. This fog can sure throw you off."

"You must know your stuff to set out in weather like this."

"I've been kayaking for a long time. And it wasn't this bad on the mainland when we set out."

"We?"

"My friend and I. We must have been circling this island for the past hour. I'm glad you heard me. What's your name?"

"Rob."

"Hi, Rob. I'm Jebediah. Jebediah Hummock."

"I'm sorry, Nick. Obviously I have no problem with the three of you going out to Little Bucket, but there's no way for you to get there."

"I thought we'd take the *Marambo*."

"That's impossible. I had to take the captain off Kestrel last night. His wife had an appendicitis attack. She was operated on this morning. I'd take you myself, but I have to stay here. And no one else is qualified to pilot the boat in this kind of weather."

Nick stared at Win. He didn't know what to say. Fred had reluctantly okayed their going out to see Rinker and Blau after Nick had pleaded with him during breakfast. He would never agree to ask the agents in Bar Harbor to come to Kestrel to take them there. They were stymied. That icy, steely hand that had been lying dormant suddenly grabbed Nick's guts again.

"Win," said Sandy, "Fred comes from Maine. He knows how to handle a boat in this weather. Don't you, Fred?"

"Well, I guess I do," Fred said hesitantly.

Win Blair peered at the agent.

"We have a JMA-3810 radar on the *Marambo*. Can you operate that?"

"My dad has a Si-Tex T-150. I've used it a lot. They're pretty similar."

"How big is your father's boat?"

"Thirty-two feet."

"What kind of radio does he have?"

"Apelco 5160."

"That's what we have," said Win, rubbing the stubble on his

chin. "Know how to use a depth sounder? There's a lot of ledge around here."

"Sure. I'm used to the Interphase Probe, but I think I could handle any equipment you have. It's all more or less the same."

"I shouldn't be doing this, Fred, but I guess you can take out the *Marambo*. And do me a favor?"

"What's that?"

"Bring the boat back in one piece."

"You sure you don't want me to use my two-way radio?"

"That's okay. My friend will be here pretty soon," said Jebediah, as he stared out at the fog.

"I can get the Coast Guard on this. Maybe your friend is lost."

"I doubt it."

"I hope you don't mind me saying this, but I bet you get a lot of kidding about your last name."

"What do you mean?"

"Well, you did say your name was Hummock, didn't you?"

Jebediah, whose back was turned to Rob, nodded his head.

"I imagine people make a lot of jokes about you being related to that nut Josiah Hummock."

"He's my father," he answered.

"You got to be kidding," Rob said, with a laugh that had nothing to do with amusement. He suddenly felt very scared. Jebediah kept his back to Rob, continuing to search the wall of fog. Rob moved toward the radio.

"Don't touch that!" Jebediah said, as he wheeled around.

Rob put his finger on the call switch.

"I said leave it alone."

Before Rob could flip the switch, Jebediah was on him. Though Rob was strong, the surprise of the attack knocked him onto his back.

"I told you not to go for that radio," shouted Jebediah, as he brought down a fist-sized rock against the side of Rob Harpswell's head. The blow knocked the boy out cold. A finger of blood snaked down the side of his head, winding around his ear and dripping to the ground.

3 "We're going round the arm of the cove now," said Fred, as the *Marambo* slipped through the water. He stared at the radar screen mounted above the wheel. The island resembled a claw, with two arms of land extending out from the north end. "There's the boat." He touched a small green blot on the screen. "They can't be more than a couple of hundred yards away."

"Maybe we should contact them on the radio," said Sandy.

"What's the point?" said Fred. "We're almost there. Keep your eyes peeled, we should see them any moment now."

Nick took out the small snub-nosed .38 from the canvas bag he was carrying and put it into his pants pocket.

"I thought this was a social trip, Nick," Fred remarked.

"Force of habit, I guess," he answered. *I wonder,* Nick thought, *what he'd say if he knew I had another .38 in my ankle holster?*

Fred eased off the throttle and the boat inched forward. Nick leaned out of the pilot house, peering into the mist that bathed his face as if he had walked out of a steam room.

"There they are," said Nick.

The agents' boat, rocking gently at anchor, suddenly appeared in front of them. Fred threw the boat into reverse, turned the wheel hard to port, and the *Marambo* slid next to the other boat. He cut the engine.

"Not bad, if I say so myself."

"Sure you haven't handled this boat before?" asked Sandy, with a laugh.

"Hey, you guys," hollered Fred, "you got company."

"They're probably still asleep," said Sandy.

"Nick, tie this line to the bow cleat," Fred said, as he tossed the rope to Nick. "I'll do the stern."

After they secured the two boats together, Fred walked toward the bow and opened the hatch. "Rise and shine, boys," he called down. "Visitors from the main office on board."

There was no response.

"We didn't expect a band to greet us, but how about a hot cup of coffee," he yelled down. The only sound they heard was the soft slap of the water against the boat's side.

Fred knelt and looked into the cabin.

"They're not here," he said quietly over his shoulder. "The cabin's empty." He stood and walked over to Nick and Sandy, who were standing in the wheelhouse. "Guess they went onto the island to check on Rob."

"Both of them?" asked Nick.

"That's odd. You're right. One person should always be on board to man the radio."

They all looked at each other.

"And their dinghy is still here," said Nick, pointing toward the stern. "I don't like this."

"Sandy, you stay here. Nick and I are going to take the dinghy ashore. We won't be long." He reached down and pulled the gun out of his ankle holster. "Hold on to this. Just in case."

"I don't want it. I don't like guns."

"Now's not the time to be afraid. If you don't want to carry it, put it under those cushions there."

"Maybe I should come with you." She didn't have to tell Nick she was scared, it was etched in her voice and in the thin line of her mouth.

"No, it's better that you stay here."

Fred pulled the dinghy alongside.

"Where the hell are the oars?" he asked loudly, as he looked down at the small boat.

"And look at the oarlocks."

"What oarlocks?"

"That's what I mean. They're gone, too."

"We'll take a rubber dinghy from the *Marambo*."

"Good idea. Let's get going."

The two men took out a dinghy that was stored under a console in the bow. Fred pulled the pin on a cylinder that immediately inflated it.

"Nick! Fred!"

Sandy stood near the stern of the agents' boat. She screamed their names again.

The two scrambled back to the other boat and ran to Sandy. Nick grabbed her and pulled her close.

"What's wrong?"

Sandy didn't say a word, she just pointed down at a crumpled, bright blue tarp. Nick and Fred looked down and at first couldn't see why Sandy was screaming. Then they saw the fingers. With his foot, Fred pushed the tarp to the side.

"Jesus, God," Fred murmured.

Sandy continued to scream.

There were four severed hands under the thin blue covering. They were paired and arranged in a row, all with palms facing up. The hands had been so carefully severed they looked like grisly props, the kind that kids like to leave on the sofa on Halloween night to scare their parents. But these hands were all too real. There were wedding bands on the fingers of two of the hands. A bulky college ring was on the finger of a third. The ring was from Notre Dame. Sid Blau's alma mater. And on each palm there was a carefully drawn *H*. The *H* was faint because it had been put on with blood that was now dry.

"Sandy, it's going to be all right," Nick told her, as he held her tightly. "Fred and I have to get onto the island. Right now. We don't have time to show you how to use the radio, but try to raise the agents in Bar Harbor. Or the Coast Guard. Or anyone. Understand?"

She nodded her head as if she were asleep. There was no time to tend to her. They had to get to Rob Harpswell.

"'And I saw, and behold, a pale horse, and its rider's name was Death, and Hades . . .'"

Who was that talking? He was having a terrible dream. He had to wake up. The voice droned on. He couldn't understand the words. Where was the sound coming from?

His head ached. The pain swirled like a child's pinwheel, down the back of his head. And then he opened his eyes. He tried to focus, but he couldn't. Someone stood above him. That's who was talking! He could make him out now. It was the fellow in the kayak. What was his name again? Something strange. He tried, but he couldn't remember. Boy, did he feel lousy. He had to get up. There was something very wrong going on. He felt terrible. He had to call Sid and Jim. They would help him. Where was the radio? He tried to sit up but he couldn't. He tried to move his right arm. It wouldn't budge. The same for his other arm.

"Sid! Jim! Help me! Please!" Rob yelled out.

"No one can help you."

"Help! Help!"

"Your father, the Pharaoh, can't help you. Nobody can. The son of God has decreed you must die."

That was it. He remembered now. This guy had said his name was Hummock. And that nut Josiah Hummock was his father. Where were Sid and Jim? They had to come quickly. *This guy is crazy. Calm down, Rob. Maybe you can talk to him. He could be on some kind of drug and maybe it'll wear off soon. Try to reason with him.*

But what's that in his hand? Oh, no. He's got a knife!

They dug their oars fiercely into the water. They were only a hundred yards from shore, but the distance seemed to mock them and the rubber dinghy felt as if it was barely moving. Nick and Fred didn't speak, for there was nothing to say. They knew they had to find Rob Harpswell as fast as possible. What they would discover when they got to him, they kept out of their minds.

When they were ten feet from shore, their oars scraped bottom. They jumped out of the dinghy and waded to shore. With guns drawn they scrambled up the rocky beach and scanned a dense barrier of wild rugosa. Nick spotted a trampled path in the thick foliage.

"This way," he called out, and then plunged in. Whiplike branches studded with thorns raked Nick's face and arms, but he didn't feel a thing. He heard Fred running behind him. After a hundred feet Nick broke out onto an open area bordered by a stand of pine trees. The ground beneath the trees was covered with moss shaped like large pin cushions. Nick pushed himself harder, his breathing labored. He had to keep running. He couldn't stop. He remembered the map of the island. Rob Harpswell should be just on the other side of the trees.

"Nick!"

He turned to see Fred fall to the ground.

"There's something wrong—" Fred started to say. Nick could see at once that something indeed was terribly wrong. A silver arrowhead protruded from Fred's side. Nick pulled the agent behind a tree and propped him against the base.

"Take it easy. Don't try to speak. You're going to be okay."

Fred tried to smile but his mouth froze into a rictus of pain.

"You've been wounded but it's not bad. You're going to make it. No sweat."

As Nick looked down at the wounded agent, another arrow hit the ground near his leg. He saw someone duck down behind a bush forty yards away. He aimed his gun and waited for the person to move.

Stop it, you idiot! If you fire your gun, then whoever's on the other side of these trees will know you're here also. You don't want to warn them. Crawl into that brush behind you and then run like hell until you find Rob Harpswell.

"I need you to cover my ass, Fred. Don't fire until you have an absolutely clean shot. You're protected by this tree. I don't know if it's Jebediah or Mary out there, but they probably have a crossbow. I don't think they'll try anything for a while, but the more time you can give me without shooting, is important. You got it?"

The agent nodded and then clenched his teeth in pain.

"I'll be back real soon, Fred. Promise."

Now run, damn it. Pray you're in time. Run.

Jebediah was careful not to cut too deeply into Rob Harpswell's chest. The boy moaned but didn't move as the knife sliced his flesh. The blood flowed freely, tracing lines as straight as those on a chart. Rob began to stir, straining against the ropes holding him down. Jebediah had struck him again a few minutes earlier, to keep him quiet. He had been worried that he had hit him too hard. He wanted Rob awake when he killed him. Jebediah looked down at the scarlet *H* he had carved into the boy's chest. He would plunge the blade in just below the sternum. Jebediah smiled as Rob's eyes snapped open. His pupils were dilated with terror. He stared up at the knife that Jebediah held over him.

"What are you going to do?"

"God is back on Earth," Jebediah intoned, his voice strong and clear, as he raised the knife.

"No!"

"All who stand in his way will turn to dust."

"Please! Don't do it."

He remembered that Josiah wanted this boy to suffer. Suffer

mightily. There was no reason to hurry. He slashed at Rob's shoulder. Blood welled out of the wound. The boy screamed again. Then Jebediah laid the knife against his cheek. He was good-looking, and certainly vain. Vanity was a sin. He drew the blade against the skin, and blood washed down the boy's face. His scream this time was fainter. He was losing consciousness again. Jebediah grabbed the hilt of the knife with both hands. The blade was mirror-bright. He lifted it above his head.

"All who stand in his way will perish. Eternal darkness awaits this son of Pharaoh."

He straddled Rob's body. He tightened his grip on the handle. The time had finally come to deliver Rob Harpswell to the dark world that awaited him. In a moment Jebediah's work would be finished.

And then, as he was about to bring the knife flashing down, Jebediah saw a brilliant burst of light, brighter than a hundred suns. His head dropped against his chest, like that of a puppet whose strings had been cut. The knife fell from his hands and clanged against a rock. His body pitched to the side and hit the ground like a bundle of newspapers thrown from a truck.

The bullet Nick had fired, the only shot that could save Rob's life, had entered the back of Jebediah's head. Death came so swiftly he hadn't even heard the sound of the gun that ended his life.

 "You're going to be okay, Rob. He can't hurt you anymore. I'm going to get you help. It's all over. You're safe."

Who the hell are you talking to, Barrows? The kid is out cold. And you don't have to take his pulse again. It's weak, but it's steady. He's alive. Badly hurt but alive. You have to get him back to the boat. Back to Sandy. That's all you have to do. Then you'll get on the radio and call for help.

He needs a doctor. And fast. And stop whipping yourself about Fred. You'll come back for him later. He's got a serious wound but he'll make it. This kid has lost a lot of blood and he has a serious head wound. And he's the president's son! Your job is to protect him.

Nick stopped rowing and looked up. The boats were only fifty feet away. Rob Harpswell groaned, his right hand clenched, and then he passed out again.

"We're almost there, Rob. We'll have you good as new in no time." Nick looked up as he rowed, searching for Sandy. "Sandy!" he called out as he neared the *Marambo*. "Sandy, I need a hand."

"Here, Nick," she called back, standing at the bow.

"Take this line," he said, handing it up.

"I don't think I can lift Rob into the boat from here," he said, as he pulled himself out of the dinghy, onto the deck of the *Marambo*. "I'll bring it around to the stern. I think I can get him out from there."

"Why don't we just leave the Pharaoh's son where he is, Mr. Barrows?" said a voice from behind Sandy.

There, stepping out from the pilot house, holding a double-barreled shotgun pressed against Sandy's back, was Duane Bascombe. He was wearing fatigues and now had a short, thick beard.

"Your gun, Mr. Barrows. I know you have one on you. Take it out by the barrel and drop it over the side. Now. If you give me a hint of trying to do something, I'm going to blow a hole through Dr. Price big enough to put my boot through."

Nick took the .38 out of his waistband and tossed it over the side.

"That's good. Now move over there next to your lady friend."

"You're not going to get away with this, Bascombe," said Nick, as he moved next to Sandy. "The Secret Service will be here any minute. There was supposed to be a radio check within the past half hour. They'll know that something's wrong. They're probably on their way here now."

"I think the agents on Kestrel are not concerned at all," he said, fishing a miniature tape recorder out from his pocket. "Listen." After pushing the on switch, there was a moment of dead air, then Nick and Sandy heard the voice of Sid Blau:

"Novelty here, Kestrel."
"How's it going, Sid?"
"Foggy but fine."
"You sound a little hoarse, Sid. You okay?"

"He sounded that way because I had this shotgun at the back of his head. It always changes the timbre of a person's voice."

"Any news on Hitch?"
"Not a word. We checked him an hour ago. Everything's fine."
"Great. Call you at the usual. Be good."

"I guess I don't need this anymore," he said, and casually flipped the recorder into the water.

"What are you going to do, Bascombe?"

"What a silly question, Agent Barrows. And please stop calling me by that name," he said, as he opened his fatigues to reveal a tattoo that covered his chest. It was an exact depiction of the jewel-studded cross that had hung around the neck of Josiah Hummock.

"Josiah!" blurted Nick.

"No! You can't be Josiah," said Sandy.

"This son of God can be whoever he wants to be," he said.

"But the explosion—"

"I stayed in another underground shelter for six weeks after I sent my congregation to Paradise. It was snug and quite well-stocked. When my followers were building it, they asked why I needed it. After all, it could contain only one person and was over a half mile away from the main building. It was a shelter you knew nothing about. I told them that my Father wanted me to have a place where I could talk to him alone."

"But you don't—" began Sandy.

"I don't look like the man you knew as Josiah Hummock? Well, Dr. Price, that took some earthly intervention. I thought it wise to go through the necessary procedures out of the country. Face, voice, fingerprints, everything that had shaped my mortal flesh into Josiah Hummock I had transformed."

"But your height! You were much taller," said Nick.

"With Josiah Hummock's boots on, Mr. Barrows. I always knew a congregation wanted to look up at their leader so I always wore my 'special' boots."

"And your brother?"

"Duane? A little slow, but quite devoted actually. Yes, he really was my half brother. He was very helpful. He served his purpose. I borrowed his name—his whole life. He's now resting near the mine. He's been there for a long, long time. Resting for eternity."

"Whoever you are, you're not going to get away with this."

"It is destined that I will. And if I die on this earth like his first son, then my young disciples will continue my work."

"What work? Killing people?

"Until the world acknowledges me as the true son of God, all who stand in my way will perish."

"God with a shotgun!" Nick spat out, as he took a step forward. "You're even crazier than I thought, Hummock. You're a raving fucking psycho."

"Be quiet, Barrows."

Josiah Hummock pulled the trigger. The noise was deafening. The shell tore into Nick's left foot. Blood cascaded from the wound. He fell to his knees and rolled over on some cushions scattered on the deck.

"Christ had nails driven through both his feet. I don't think I'm finished with you yet."

Hummock fired again. This time the shell buried itself in Nick's right ankle. He screamed in pain.

Sandy knelt down and held Nick.

"It took Christ a long time to die. I'm just beginning with you, Mr. Barrows."

Sandy took Nick's hand and squeezed it, then placed it on one of the cushions and pressed down. She looked steadily into his eyes. He could see she wasn't frightened. She glanced down at his hand. Nick realized his hand was resting on something hard under the cushion. It was the gun he had given her.

"Help him stand up, Dr. Price. A man shouldn't die like a dog." Cradling the shotgun, he pulled a long-bladed knife from his pocket. "I think this will do fine on your hands. You're about to receive some very real stigmata."

Nick slipped his hand under the cushion and grabbed the gun. Nothing had ever felt so good.

Sandy helped him to his feet. He felt the warm blood fill his shoes. He knew he was going into shock. He had to hold out a little longer. Nick looped his arm around her back, hiding the gun from Hummock. "You're also a hell of a healer, Josiah. I'm beginning to feel better already. It doesn't hurt much at all."

He slid the revolver around Sandy's back until the muzzle pointed toward Hummock. And then Nick fired. Again and again. The bullets smashed into Hummock's chest. The shotgun clattered to the deck as Hummock fell backward to the deck. He moved his mouth as he tried to speak.

Nick stared down at Josiah Hummock. His wounds probably would end his life, but what if he survived? Neither Nick nor the country could chance that.

"I see it, Barrows. I'm going . . . going . . . to Paradise."

"Yes, you are, Josiah," said Nick, placing his gun against Hummock's forehead. "But why take the local when you can take the express?" And then Nick squeezed the trigger for the last time.

final business

"The
new Josiah!"

1 "Favor time?" asked Nick.

"I think I hear an invalid calling. What now, my wounded warrior?" said Sandy, putting down the newspaper she was reading.

"Would you please tilt the umbrella a little more this way? The sun's in my eyes."

Sandy stood up and twisted the large green umbrella sticking up from the middle of the table like a metal palm tree.

"That better?"

"Perfect."

Nick sat in his wheelchair, his legs straight out before him like a stick figure's. Both his feet were wrapped in thick casts.

"Anything else while I'm up? More coffee? Something to eat?"

"Nope. I'm fine."

The sounds of the neighborhood, normally quiet, were particularly so on this Sunday morning. Sarah was in her playhouse having a tea party with two friends from school. Occasionally a squeak of conspiratorial laughter came out of the little house. Two birds chattered deep within the canopy of a maple tree in the corner of the garden.

"You know what this is?" Nick asked.

"What?"

"Something very, very rare."

"You've got my attention."

"It's a quiet, peaceful Sunday morning. Nothing more, nothing less. And I love it." He was close enough to Sandy to reach out and touch the slope of her neck.

"It does seem a little hard to believe that all that—horror . . . that's the only word for it—is behind us. It is, isn't it?"

"I give you my guarantee."

"But Mary's still out there."

"So what? Hummock's dead. She's a fanatic without a Messiah, like Charlie Manson's family without Manson. They'll catch her soon, but until then she's totally harmless."

"It's really over, isn't it?"

"Yes, it really is."

Sarah shouted from the playhouse, "Mom, can we have some cookies?"

Sandy looked at Nick, then called back, "You can have anything you want."

 The parrot screeched. The boy standing next to it pulled his hand back and with a guilty smile scurried back to the table where his family was sitting.

"I told you not to go near that bird, Todd," said Phil LaChance.

"I'm sorry, Dad."

"You'll be sorrier when it bites you. The lady who owns the restaurant told us the bird doesn't like men—or boys, apparently. Remember?"

Todd giggled. "What's wrong with him? Is he jealous?" He turned his head and looked again at the parrot's bright turquoise-button eyes as it scuttled crablike from side to side on the bar. The owner, dressed in a tight white T-shirt and jeans, worked at a grill with two young men who helped prepare the food and wait on table. The restaurant, Tamarind, was named for the large tree that stood beside it. Several chairs were drawn up under the shade of the tree, and a swing hung from a thick lower branch. Noticing Todd still watching the bird, the owner smiled at him and winked. The boy, flushing, immediately turned back to his family.

"Behave yourself and stop gawking at that bird," barked La-Chance with a scowl. "And sit up straight. All of you. Hands in your laps. You know you're not supposed to lean all over the table. It's bad manners." Todd and his younger sister and brother squirmed and shifted under their father's scrutiny. They knew it was prudent to obey him.

"Listen to your father, children," his wife, Elizabeth, said mildly. The tone of her voice suggested she had long ago decided not to challenge the voice of authority in their family.

Sitting on the opposite side of the small, open-air restaurant were LaChance's three FBI security agents. Three was the bottom-line number that provided his protection, wherever he went, but on St. Bart's, the island where they were, there was no history of terrorism or violence. The usual way to lose your life on the island, so everyone said, was to veer off one of the narrow, steep, and winding roads that crisscrossed its volcanic terrain, and crash onto the rocks below.

"Look at him," said one of the agents in a low voice, nodding toward the LaChance table. "When no one else is around to boss, he bosses his kids. Once a shit, always a shit."

"This detail isn't bad, though," said another agent. "A reward."

"Of sorts," the first one said gloomily.

"Here comes lunch," announced LaChance.

"I'm starved," said his daughter.

"Me, too," added the boys.

The two waiters emerged from the galley-sized kitchen with hamburgers and fries for the children, and smoked salmon and salad for their parents. The table fell silent as everyone concentrated on their food, then on dessert.

"When are we going to the beach?" asked Todd, after a short while.

"When your mother and I finish our espresso."

"I don't see any."

"You're right, said LaChance. "We haven't ordered it yet. Learn to cool your heels, mister."

"Oh," said Todd, groaning.

"Phil, let the kids go out and use the swing," said Elizabeth, gesturing toward the tamarind tree.

"You're too lenient with them, Liz. But okay. This one time. You're excused, children," said LaChance.

The beach they went to, called Saline, was only a short drive away. It was long and wide, with beautiful, fine sand and lots of topless women lounging on the beach. The children by now were blasé about the undressed women, and Elizabeth, indifferent. The only thing that interested LaChance was an extensive underwater constellation of coral off to one end of the beach that attracted squadrons of bright-colored and patterned fish. He had a passion for snorkeling (pure pleasure, with little effort, and, thankfully, removed from the arguing and yelling of his children), and he never set off to the beach without his flippers, snorkel, and mask.

As soon as they arrived, the children ran into the water, with cautions from Elizabeth, who settled down under a large umbrella to watch them, before opening a novel. The agents sat twenty yards away, enough to give the family privacy yet keep them all in view, and LaChance immediately set off to snorkel. They followed him with their eyes to the spot they knew well by now, and watched him paddle out to it.

"I'll take that one," said one of the agents, nodding toward a young woman who walked down the beach carrying an air tank, flippers, and mask. A teenage boy carrying the same equipment walked beside her.

"Damn it! Why can't *she* be topless? Give those beautiful hooters a chance to breathe."

"I love the way her stomach swells out just a little bit."

"That's my selection of the day."

"That schmuck LaChance would rather look at a fish's bunghole than watch the greatest sights in the world."

"What do you expect from him? The only thing normal about our beloved director is his temperature."

Some days were better for snorkling than others, mostly because of the currents, LaChance had discovered. Today was one of the best. He swam contentedly along the surface, gazing down at a school of clown trigger fish that floated above some parrot fish that were feeding on the pink-and-gold coral filagreeing the bottom. Then his attention was caught by a fish he had never seen before, pancake-shaped with bold electric stripes like lightning bolts, and he began tracking it.

This was the perfect release from the pressures of the office, thought LaChance. Who would have known that that wino Nick Barrows had been right about the Hummock kids? But not even Barrows had believed Hummock had survived the explosion. And he had been in charge of the operation. After the explosion, he should have found the shelter where Hummock had been hiding. So what if it was a half mile away? Now Barrows was a fucking hero. LaChance knew that he would be attacked for not listening to Barrows and his girlfriend. But he was prepared. When the Senate hearings started, he would more than hold his own. When it came to infighting and survival he'd take on Barrows any day. Some people in Congress and the media were talking about giving his job to Barrows. Let them try!

Out of the corner of his eye, he saw another diver approaching. It was a young woman. He paddled to one side to let her pass. She wasn't snorkeling but instead had a tank on. Right behind her was another scuba diver. A boy. Then they were swimming toward him, side by side. As LaChance moved aside, so did the other two, following his movements the same way as he had been tracking the striped fish. The woman drew closer, bearing down on him like a hawk on its prey. LaChance now saw that the woman and the boy were pursuing him. Before he could swim away, they wrapped their arms around his neck and pulled him down deep into the water, holding him there. They ripped the snorkel out of his mouth. The first swallow of water caused Phil LaChance to panic even more, but no matter how hard he tried to break out of their grip, he couldn't. They were very strong. It only took a minute more before he blacked out. To play it safe, Mary and Seth kept LaChance's body scissored between their legs for five minutes more before they released him.

"Look at those beauties," said one of the agents on the beach, ogling a large-breasted girl who walked by. "D-cupping beautiful!"

The three men appreciatively watched her, then looked down the beach to see what else was coming their way.

"What the fuck," one agent said suddenly. "Where's the director? I don't see him."

Panicked, they looked to the left and to the right, scanning the entire beach. Perhaps LaChance had come out of the water without their noticing him and was down at the other end. They focused their binoculars on that part of the beach, but there was no sign of him.

One of the agents approached Elizabeth's umbrella. "Mrs. LaChance, do you know where the director is?"

"Well, yes, he's over there," she said pointing, "snorkeling in his favorite spot. The place he always goes."

The agent ducked quickly back to the others. "You go that way, all the way to the end," he said. "We'll go to his usual place."

The two men ran to where they had last seen LaChance. As soon as they got there, they saw something floating in the water. With sinking hearts, they knew immediately what it was. They rushed into the water and pulled out the lifeless body of Phil LaChance. Though they knew it was futile, one of them started to give him CPR while the other used his cellular phone to call an ambulance.

Mary saw the agents trying to revive LaChance. Several people gathered around them. She strolled away toward the path that led to the road, suppressing the urge to run or to betray her tension in any way. She had planned everything flawlessly, as she always did, and she knew everything would proceed smoothly. Seth walked at her side. He had done his part perfectly.

Mary had left the rental car in the beach parking lot, and they had plenty of time to catch the boat in Gustavia that would take them to the island of St. Martin. She had chartered a small plane that would fly them on to Puerto Rico. That night they would fly back to the States. As they walked over the rocky path, she knew all the other children were once again leaving their homes and gathering together.

Mary ran her hand down to her belly. Her palm gently circled her stomach. She was only two months' pregnant and it hardly showed yet. She knew she was going to have a boy. Josiah's son. The seed of his loins. The new Josiah! She would lead the group until he was old enough, then he would lead. She had never felt this contented and at one with herself before.

Mary and Seth got into the car and drove away.